Camp Love

ELLIE BELMONT
& LACEY COLE

Developmental editing & proofreading by Kristen with Kristen's Red Pen

Editing by Sara with Telltail Editing

Cover artist: Andra Murarasu with @andra.mdesigns

Map artist: Mary with Books and Moods

AX RANGE
THE BONFIRE
MEDITATION MEADOW
CRAFT CABIN
LAKE STARLIGHT
CAMP STARLIGHT
ZIPLINE
THE MESS HALL
FRONT OFFICE
CAMP STARLIGHT
FOXGLOVE STABLES
WILDWOOD

To all the kids at heart who just wish they could go back to summer camp and make crafts

ONE

Jamie

"REMEMBER that promise you made to me, like, eight months and twenty-three days ago? Well, I figured out how you can make it up to me." Ren leaned against my desk, pouring champagne with focused precision while I closed out the notation for our biggest client yet. Another case closed, and everything was clicking into place.

"Your friendship comes with too many conditions." I took the glass he waved in front of me before he could accidentally spill on the documents we'd painstakingly worked on for the better part of a month.

He parked his ass on the corner of my meticulously clean desk and took a large glug of his fizzing beverage. "Oh, you mean, like, being there for your best friend's birthday party? Your recently divorced best friend who works too much to have time for other friends?"

"You don't want other friends," I joked. "And no more guilt trips. You know I wanted to be there."

"Clients shouldn't be calling late expecting you to have no life."

"That's the job." Sacrifices had to be made. All I had to do was remind Clint and Margaret that I was the obvious choice for senior associate. Only two slots would be offered to me and my colleagues, and that meant two people would be leaving our firm in the coming weeks. I was not going to be one of them.

"James, haven't you heard the phrase 'work hard, play hard'? Where's the play?" Ren tried again.

Begrudgingly, I had to admit that he wasn't wrong. We put in the long hours because our highest-profile client had been running us ragged all month. I wasn't about to turn down their calls, even if they had a knack for calling right when I was in the middle of a REM cycle. Or in the shower. Or when I was eating. All this work would pay off when I was named senior associate.

"I'm listening, and I hear you." I used my best guidance counselor voice. "But can you hand me that file?"

I reached my hand out for a manila folder just inches out of my wingspan. He didn't move. In fact, he sat right on the folder like a four-year-old who didn't understand that there were consequences to his actions. I may have been overworked and went out of my way to get things done, but getting ass-prints out of perfectly flattened paper wasn't part of the job description.

"No. I can't." Ren's face was dead serious as he crossed his arms over his chest.

I tugged at the small bit of yellow I could see, pulling at the file until it was fully out from underneath him, grinning as I dropped it into its folder in my filing cabinet and pushed it shut. I reached for the next case on the docket, but he smacked at me, and it fell to the ground.

"I know the indelible list of goals you've got burned into the back of your skull, James. 'Graduate at the top of your class. Make partner by forty. Lead a life of luxury and stability.'" He mentioned all of this as if it were stupid, even though that deadline would be here before I knew it. "You're even ignoring the champagne, which is incredible, really, but it only illuminates the fact that you have problems. So hear me out. We're locked and loaded on the Bradley case, and the hearing isn't for another month." He put the file back on the shelf haphazardly, as though it wasn't going to fall from its crooked placement.

"Perfect, time to prep. I'll visit the site again—"

Ren turned back to me, his pretty-boy face shifted into a frown. "Or..." His voice was firm. "What if you just enjoyed the moment for, you know, a moment? We could finally take a vacation. You'll be taking on more responsibility when you get back. Which means that *I* need a break before all the madness starts, and *you* need a distraction. Or what most people call a *vacation.*"

Time away on some white-sand beach with a mai tai in my hand sounded fantastic. Of course it did. I'd been working nonstop for as long as I could remember. In high school, the motto was "be the best." In college, it was "be at the top." And with internships, it was "work the hardest." Proving myself over and over didn't allow for vacations. As much as I hated to admit it, Ren was right. Everything was out of my control. This case being closed meant I could finally take a moment for myself. Only, I didn't know what that looked like.

I'd been working so hard for so long that life outside of work was nonexistent. But I didn't mind it. Work was where I fit in, where I could rely on my instincts and drive to do what it took to get our clients the win. There was no need for any personal life outside of the quick hookups I sometimes indulged in through impersonal apps. I'd tried dating a few times and met some interesting people, but when first dates rarely became second dates, whether on my end or theirs, it would be better to pursue dating once I had more time. And I'd have time after I was promoted. Okay, maybe not in the first few years while I proved that I was the obvious choice for partner, but after that happened, I'd make it a priority.

My new plan was to start dating at thirty-five, even if my family gave me a hard time about it. By then, the most suitable prospects who had married naively in their twenties would be divorced and seeking their second marriage anyway, so I might as well wait for round two. Not everyone was meant to find their life partner at twenty years old like my parents and my sister after them.

"You need to make time for yourself." Ren snapped his fingers to get my attention off life planning. The little shit.

"You'll drop it if we take that weekend rafting trip that you've never shut up about?"

"Oh, James, sweet James. That was last year's vacation we didn't take." Oof, he had a point. And he also... Looked devious? "I'll arrange everything, and it'll be unforgettable. Just sign right here." He pointed to a blank sticky note. "In blood—"

"In blood?"

He sighed in annoyance. "Surrender yourself to my will already. What's the worst that could happen?"

☆
☆ ☆

"It's about time," my overenthusiastic sister, Marley, exclaimed, shaking her phone over video chat after my news. She acted like I hadn't come out of my bunker for years when we still had check-ins regularly. But she was right, and the idea had grown on me just a little. I was starting to feel more confident in the decision, seeing how happy it was making her. "So, where are you going?"

"Ren signed us up for some sort of camping adventure, complete with 'life-changing experiences.' Whatever that means."

"Camping? That's so unlike you. Have you even been camping since that trip with the Robertsons freshman year of high school? Didn't you have to sleep in the car after the tent flooded?" It was spring break that year, and it had gone well for the first few days, but yes, we did end up sleeping in a car, and yes, it was my first experience with back pain.

"Yeah, that was terrible, but it's summer, and this time, I have an extensive list of what to pack and how to relax—"

"Only you would have a list for how to relax," she teased. "It's a far cry from the big brother I used to know, who was more concerned with pranking his track coach than making sure he had the right books on him for class."

I took the pen from behind my ear, crossed off bug spray from my packing list, and wrote it on the paper taped securely to the corresponding tote.

"Yeah," I mused. "Coach didn't appreciate it when we gift-wrapped every item in his office. Or when we staked his lawn with pink flamingos."

I moved on to my monthly check-in about our family. "How's everything going with the move? Should I come out and help?"

My sister had moved from a one-story ranch-style home into a two-story with enough bedrooms for her two kids to have their own space.

"There are boxes everywhere, but no, it's under control." She sighed as if she was gearing up for something. "You'll come for Thanksgiving, though?"

I hated that she had to plan that far in advance, but based on my track record, she was making the right call. "I think I can get the time off, but if it would help, I could—"

"You're not using us as an excuse to get out of your 'life-changing experience.'"

"I thought you loved me," I play-whined, but the truth was, I felt relief. After hours of research, I'd started to feel the tickle of anticipation. Hearing the excitement in Ren's voice and seeing it on my sister's face only piqued my interest, and I anticipated the trip more.

"I do love you, and speaking of love or any kind of connection, why don't you tell me about your plans to date? Now, there's a life-changing experience for you."

I nearly spat out my iced tea. Of course, my sister would

think I'd be going on some sort of singles vacation with the idea of finding my soulmate. It didn't work like that for anyone but her.

Marley and Savannah met each other at a concert ten years ago. Their shared interest in music became a conversation about the books and movies they loved, and that turned into enjoying time with each other, which turned into them falling in love.

"We've talked about this. I'll take up dating after I've settled into the new position. When there's more time."

"I don't know what's funnier, the idea that you'll take up dating like it's a hobby or the delusion that you'll have more time when you're a senior associate."

"Why not? I'll have more of a choice in clients. And remember, I took up bowling, and now"—I lifted my phone and gestured at the neatly packed pile of clothing, shoes, and toiletries with a *ta-da* flare—"camping."

She chuckled at me before she went in for the kill, which I appreciated. "Bowling only lasted a month, Jamie."

"Not my fault my teammate moved to Ireland, and 2 Legit 2 Split couldn't stay together."

Marley predictably moved on. "And since when do you do wilderness? You're more crisply ironed shirts and time-blocked schedules. Not really the flannel and hot dogs type." She had me there. Of course, she did.

"I can still schedule my days if I want, and yes, you know me so well, but I'm turning over a new leaf. What do you think this is for?" I held up a dorky-looking floppy fishing hat that was covered in a mesh sort of netting.

Marley just shrugged at me, and I packed it up with the other maybe-I'll-need-these items.

I held up a compass next. "Think I'll need this?"

"How *Man vs. Wild* is this trip anyway?"

I gulped, imagining an episode of *Naked and Afraid*. "I have no idea."

THE NEXT MORNING, I woke up earlier than usual with an anxiousness I hadn't felt since the moment I finished taking the bar exam. Stretched out after my morning workout and fueled by an expired protein bar, I checked emails over coffee.

My foot tapped as I waited for Ren to show up. He'd always been the life of the party since I'd known him. His high energy levels meant he never stopped moving. He reminded me of how I was in high school, though I'd never tell him that.

It felt like I hadn't really stopped and just enjoyed anything in forever. After college, it was directly into law school. After graduating with top marks, I had several options and chose Clint and Margaret's corporate practice because theirs was one of the most reputable firms in Seattle. After years of proving myself, I was ready to take the next step in my career.

Speaking of time, Ren was actually punctual for once. "Are you ready for your worst nightmare?" he asked through the intercom. I almost didn't buzz him in. He could stand in my condo lobby forever for all I cared. "I have donuts."

Dammit. I let him up. Well, at least he could help me cart the totes down.

"Whoa, whoa, whoa." Ren's gaze bounced from tote to tote, then he pulled the checklist from my hand. "What's all this?"

"Brittney loaned us her outdoor stove. She insisted on the tie-downs because you can't rely on the weather. One thing led to another. And oh! Here's the rain fly." I was proud of myself for knowing some of the equipment our law clerk lent me. She had hiked the Pacific Crest Trail last year and had plenty of advice for our trip.

"No, no, no, none of that. They'll have everything we'll need." He took the rain fly out of my hands and jammed it into an already full tote of outdoorsy supplies.

"How is that possible?"

"I take my duty as your paralegal very seriously, but this week, I'm taking on an even more challenging task. My duties as your best friend include making sure you actually cut loose and try to have fun—you know, that thing you literally never do? It's going to be quite the undertaking, but I can be resourceful."

"And your point is?" I asked, already knowing and dreading the answer. Like Marley said last night, he'd argue that I never take time for myself. That I never put myself first or stop to live my own life.

It was somewhat true. I enjoyed what I did, and my clients needed me. The firm needed me. It was important to be dedicated, to give parts of myself with every case. How else would I achieve my goals?

Ren tapped my briefcase with his toe, and it fell over. "You're not taking your laptop."

"What? No." I shook my head, bending over to scoop said laptop up and clutch it like Gollum with the One Ring. Precious thing that I'd be lost without, and yet it drained my will to live simultaneously, depending on the day.

"We'll have our phones, and you can check your email to see *if* there's a dire situation. But I'll reiterate, you need to cut the cord." He pried the laptop away, gentle yet firm. "Disconnect, be present, it's all the rage."

I'd still have my phone. I'd be able to check emails. The thought soothed me.

"And I should probably tell you." He used a gentle tone to soften the blow of whatever bad news he might finish that sentence with. "We're not just going for the weekend." His words were rushed under his breath as he pulled out the handle of my suitcase.

"Hey, get back here." I followed him to the car. "What do you mean, we're not staying for just the weekend?"

He didn't meet my eyes. "We're staying a week."

"No, we're not," I insisted. "We can't do that. We agreed on a long weekend. Long. As in half day Friday and back on Sunday."

"That's called a weekend." His tone was patronizing. "I've been on the waitlist for this place forever and someone dropped! I cleared your schedule, and you need this. *We* need this."

"I only bought one sun shirt."

"As if your collection of sun shirts has ever stopped you before," he said sarcastically. We both strode back inside.

"Wait up while I pack some more clothes, at least." I didn't have it in my heart to argue with Ren, and after I talked with Marley last night, his words hit home. People took weeklong vacations all the time. Just because I hadn't didn't mean I couldn't. And with all the changes at work coming up, I didn't need to obsess myself off a cliff. I'd find out and return to work with a new perspective, ready to tackle a new project and more responsibility. It was time to do it. Time to take a vacation.

TWO

Autumn

IT WAS NEVER easy gearing up for the last camp session of the year.

We were tired. We were filled with a mix of emotions from saying goodbye to a summer's worth of campers. But we were also excited. It was a confusing cocktail of feelings that I both loved and hated. But mostly loved.

At Camp Starlight, there were six of us camp counselors and five daily staff members, as well as the owners, Hazel Matthews and Leo Lovejoy, also known as camp mom and camp dad.

I'd worked as a counselor since its inception five years ago when I was a know-nothing twenty-four-year-old with no idea what to do with her life. Helping build the first ever adults-only camping resort had sounded like a great idea.

My dad and stepmom might have attributed my venture to a quarter-life crisis, but I could see a good idea when I heard it, and haven't looked back since. Somehow, that had turned into a career that the Stanford-bound me would have laughed off back when I was in high school, but it wasn't funny or disappointing. This place was my home.

Hazel had inherited the lake property, formerly known as Snowberry Resort, from her great-uncle. The resort had been known for its proximity to the mountain and used for skiers and snowboarders who frequented the nearby ski recreation sites. Built in the 1970s, the two-man cabins were constantly in use but had fallen into disrepair. She hadn't known that he'd designated her as the beneficiary of the resort but when the opportunity fell in her lap, she didn't let it go to waste. She and her best friend, Leo, hashed out a plan, and together, they'd gotten a bank loan to put work into the space. Most of the original cabins had been close to functional, but some still had to be knocked down because they'd been completely unlivable.

The nine months before we opened for the first session had been some of the best months of my life, even though they were filled with a million pitfalls and every problem you could come up with during a reno project. That first year had been a definite learning experience. In the five years since, we'd developed six pods that consisted of five cabins, plus a counselor cabin for each pod. My best friend and fellow counselor, Jack Hawthorne, was a former construction worker and was currently working on our seventh pod, an expansion we looked forward to utilizing next summer. He was going fast, working weekends in the summer and full time after campers left in the fall. I helped during the offseason, but his tenacity was unparalleled.

I loved the place I lived in—a one-bedroom cabin on Starlight Lake in the beautiful Oregon wilderness. I got to enjoy the seasons beyond summer. Crisp falls, snow-covered fir trees in the winter, and rainy springs. I'd lived all along the West Coast, and people were always surprised that I'd left Palo Alto for Wildwood, Oregon, but it was no contest. Being only a few hours from the Oregon Coast and just minutes from the mountain and the Columbia River Gorge made it the prettiest place I'd ever been, and I never wanted to leave.

For me, this was a year-round gig. Winters were spent promoting, running retreats, and working on growing the camp. I spent spring traveling the West Coast recruiting staff and campers for the busy season. Summers were spent watching over my campers, adults in their twenties and up, many of whom needed a respite from their day-to-day lives and chose running away to summer camp as the best move to spend their hard-earned money and vacation time.

And for the majority of my fall months? Well, they were spent on Autumn time, which might sound confusing, but that was what I called it since my name was—

"Autumn! Lookoverhere," Jack cough-called me. He was practically bouncing.

"I'll take bets in the order they were assigned, Jack." I glared at my best friend. If he thought he could edge out a single person during a serious betting session, he was an idiot.

He'd have to bribe me like every other respectable liar in this place.

Long Barbie-pink fingernails tapped the profile picture next to me. "I'll put twenty on Cherry Lips Cheryl," Nat said, "and Teacher Terry, they're gonna hook up. I swear I'm right this time."

Three months ago, I'd been sure the perfectly coiffed, model-esque brunette wouldn't have been interested in this game, but that was one of the few times I'd been wrong about people.

Light bounced off Nat's diamond halo pendant necklace, causing it to glimmer and reflect, a surprisingly beautiful sight borne from ambient lighting in the mess hall. Even in short shorts and a flannel, she accessorized.

I looked at the two candidates and wrote down their names on my shipping whiteboard, a sight campers could never catch wind of, or they'd have serious questions. We had to have fun ourselves. That was why I'd invented the shipping board. Underground betting rings had nothing on the seediest part of my job. People told me who they shipped or wanted in a relationship together and put money on it. It was a disgusting display of poor character on the staff's part, but it was our way of decompressing from long workdays and the occasional entitled camper. It pitted staff against staff and led to minor skirmishes over trivial pairings that rarely amounted to anything.

"I will stress, yet again, that we should not have a bracket for hookups." Leo mocked being sly as he handed me twenty bucks in the most obvious manner possible. "Nor should we be pushing people together for meet-cutes." He dropped two profiles on top of my sheet and tilted his head toward them, indicating his picks.

His counterpart, Hazel, stopped eating the popcorn she'd been chomping, and looked at him mid-chew as if he were ridiculous, probably because he did this every session. She handed me her money like a normal adult. As if there were such a thing.

Leo and Hazel were in their early thirties—a little older than me—and I considered them family. She was sarcastic and responsible, perfectly balancing her best friend's silly. He played into being the goofball of the group, which he prided himself on, and I always loved his theatrics. I also loved taking ten percent of the winnings, my bookie fee for coordinating these betting sessions all summer long.

"Can we get back to announcements, please?" Leo pushed his black frame glasses up the bridge of his nose, and attempted nonchalance. We knew what he was doing. He got his bet in, so he was more than willing to move on. "The next time someone parks in my space, they'll be towed to a stall at the horse camp. I'm serious about this, people." He wasn't serious. He was respected, but he was mostly screwed with.

The horse stalls he was threatening us with belonged to Foxglove Stables, which shared our western border. He smiled that golden-boy smile we all loved and continued. "Reminder that the construction on the new lot—"

I cupped my mouth with my hands. "Which would be finished if Jack stopped taking his sweet time."

Jack's mouth dropped open in mock shock, his hands clutching his heart.

Leo ignored me. "Please keep campers away from the construction site. They don't need one more place to bang." The group let out a collective laugh. We all had stories. "But more importantly, they do not need a place to injure themselves on cabin scaffolding." His tone was serious. "It's blocked off for a reason, so please inspire them to stay within the confines of the resort. Lord knows we don't need a lawsuit."

Hazel jumped in. "Reminder to gently push all of your campers in the direction of craft hours this week. Autumn is planning to clean out the craft shed, and the more supplies we use, the better."

Hazel and Leo rattled off a few more announcements to signal the start of yet another week.

Half a decade later and I still couldn't believe this was my job.

"I LOVE the cast of characters this week," Nat announced to no one in particular, as if this were a TV show.

We were having drinks as we lackadaisically passed around profiles of our incoming cohort. Photos were attached to a questionnaire each person had filled out. They answered questions like "What is your favorite way to relax and show self-care?" to logistical questions like "What's your preference for sleeping arrangements? A. in the quieter cabins. B. with the night owls. C. I'll roll the dice."

They talked about their dietary restrictions, why they were taking this trip, and whether they wanted to attend activities such as "All Day Book Club" or "Wet and Wild Water Skiing."

It was in-depth, and most campers were willing to answer everything, some going as far as to attach extra pages because we were catering an experience to their needs as best we could. That and the fact that this year's waitlist was miles long, and they may have wanted to edge out the competition. Not that that was the way we worked. We were a first come, first served resort, but many didn't know that.

Camp Starlight was a unique adventure the likes of which didn't exist anywhere else in the country. People loved the idea of going back to their roots while also attending a resort.

"Hey, Leo, do they ever say their fave way to practice self-care is jacking it, or do they all just answer like grownups?" Fellow counselor and resident horndog Felicia was emphatic. "No one is ever immature like I'm hoping."

Leo tipped his beer bottle toward her as he answered. "It has happened once, and it was you." The whole room burst into laughter. "Zel, do you remember anyone answering like that?" he asked seriously. Five years meant a couple of hundred campers and even more profiles.

"Not that I can think of, but I'll keep my eyes peeled for you."

"Go through them again if you have to, Hazel," Leo implored with mock seriousness. "You're the only person we trust to get to the bottom of this."

She didn't look up from her clipboard. "Forget about all the intake I've yet to do. This will be my top priority."

"I'm serious about Cheryl and Terry getting together," Nat interjected, as though she needed validation. "Look, they both have huskies, they both put down 'hiking with my dog' as their favorite pastime, *and* they signed up for sunrise yoga. They're perfect for each other," she said defiantly. "And more importantly, they listed themselves as 'single' and 'bisexual.'"

I looked over their files and perused the forty-three-year-old with a passion for "humbling the fifth graders I dunk on at basketball during my lunch period." The man could have just left it at teacher, but he really painted a picture, and I appreciated that. We were great at attracting the wackiest people. It made this place that much more magical. Cheryl was a geologist with a penchant for drinking wine and reading in her free time.

"Look at that," Nat added. "She even reads. See? Teacher... Books... Teachers use books. This is practically a Hallmark movie."

"Oh my god, she is gorgeous." Nat handed me a packet featuring a stunning blue-eyed bombshell. "She loves crocheting and crafting—yay, Autumn—playing the ukulele, and smashing the patriarchy. Says she's interested in anyone and everyone, looking to meet adults with 'a vocabulary broader than the men I bartend for.'"

I nodded as I looked over another packet, this one for Kelli, an environmental scientist from Portland with a penchant for cats and karaoke.

They continued, and I pondered my options. I hadn't had the time to pick my contenders for this year, but I had every intention of helping them find their way to each other. I had the magic touch and a twelve percent success rate, which was relatively high for shooting fish in a barrel. I liked to wait until day one of camp before even looking at the profiles, which wasn't against the rules. These idiots chose to go in half-cocked by making decisions before meeting people and then walk away losers. I loved them so much.

I looked up to find side conversations all around me as my coworkers learned about the new campers. It was a fun ritual that never got old.

"Check this out." Jack pushed a profile into my hands and pointed at the question. "If you could do anything in this life or the next, what would it be? His answer: sleep."

"It does not say that."

He turned the sheet to me and smiled. "This Ren person sounds perfect for you. I'm going to draft the save-the-dates tonight. Oh, or this guy, James. Not super outdoorsy, but he's open to new things. He's a lawyer. Not really your bag, but he—"

"What about this one?" our adrenaline-junkie counselor Lamar offered. "She loves to eat junk food. Ahem, makes a mean chili. You love chili. And she's traveled to Japan, and you love sushi, so…"

"Naw," Leo interjected, "she hates flying. What she needs is someone who will cuddle her but also give her space. Like this guy—"

"When did this turn into the Autumn dating show?" I snatched the paper away from him. "Remember, we don't set staffers up with campers? Isn't this in the employee handbook?"

"You should know, you wrote the thing," Hazel teased.

There wasn't an official rule against dating campers, but it wasn't encouraged. My friends of course knew about my dry spell, which I was willing to rectify when the time saw fit, but not with the help of a bunch of know-it-alls who chose to discuss it as if our paper profiles were a part of some dating app.

I lived in an unusual community, a mishmash of personalities coming together with one goal in mind: to make people feel welcomed and joyful the moment they strolled through the Camp Starlight archway.

Camp Starlight was part of the ski resort town of Wildwood, which definitely had its own personality, but our camp was a special village within that boasted its own quirks. Several of us lived on property year-round, while the remaining counselors called it home from early May to the end of September. That meant we'd seen each other at our best and worst throughout the summer months, and it also meant that we were always in each other's business. I never knew how, but word traveled faster than you could say "prying busybodies," and I was reluctant to say that I was one of them, but I was. I was absolutely one of them.

Everyone moved on and had conversations about god knew what, which had me happy to be under the radar again. Too bad a serious-looking Jack didn't get the memo.

"You're in need. It's been, what, a year since Chris?" Jack

asked, clearly already knowing the answer. Chris was a local I'd met during ski season, but that was mostly a no-strings-attached hookup that went south when he called me by the wrong name one too many times. "You and I are together all the time. I know you aren't getting away to bone."

"Which means you aren't either, dummy."

"I am in a happy and committed relationship, ma'am. And she's going to be here in less than a day." His eyes lit up as enthusiasm painted his every word.

Jack's girlfriend lived an hour and a half away, so they were doing the long-distance thing with plans to revisit the agreement in soon. He was head over heels in love with her, and I was worried this would be his last season with us. It was a reckoning I was in no way prepared for.

I'd known Jack since my first year of college in Palo Alto. I'd been sharing an apartment with too many of my coworkers while I'd lived the barista life at a coffee shop on campus. He'd come in every morning like clockwork before heading to the construction job site a few blocks away. His trusty Americano with a splash of half-and-half and the sticker-covered gallon water bottle I'd fill up for him in hand. We'd hit it off pretty quickly and started hanging out and getting to know each other, and I'd soon found his friendship was what I'd needed in my lonely academic life. We'd been inseparable ever since.

"Thanks, but I need a camp love affair like I need a kiss with poison oak," I said, repulsed. I didn't fraternize with campers no matter how desperate my lady bits were for some attention. I decided to deflect, turning back to the whiteboard. "What do you think about Kelli and Kelly?"

"Ooh, the Kellies," a delighted Hazel chirped. "One's an introvert and one's an extrovert, but you know how that can go."

I looked back on my short relationship history and remembered the one that got away, and how we'd been on different sides of the personality spectrum. Back then, we complemented each other, and I was sure that could be the case for someone else.

"Stranger things have happened," I said without thinking before glancing at my best friend.

Jack looked at me knowingly, and I glared at him.

I hated that he knew things about me.

THREE

Jamie

THE SCENERY CHANGED the farther from the city we drove. I knew it would, but seeing everything turn from bulky gray concrete to untamed verdant green was more stunning than I'd imagined. Newly orange and yellowing maples scattered throughout the city became interlocked evergreen trees that framed glimpses of Mount Hood as we drove farther into the wilderness. Windows down and elbows out, we soaked in the mountainous fresh air and possibility. Driving a world away from the heart of the city in one bold decision for more adventure.

Seattle was all I'd known since moving back home after college. It wasn't idealistic, but it was bursting with life, industrial buildings, art galleries, and some of the best food anywhere. Downtown was a rich mix of tourists in a hurry or Washingtonians having a relaxing lunch in the grass of parks within view of the Space Needle. City life also had its downsides—traffic, noise, and light pollution. I was fond of Seattle, sure, but the thought of driving four and a half hours to set up in the wilderness was invigorating, especially since this time on a Friday I'd still be working. I'd always thought about driving out past the city but never had much reason to. Now the trees alone were worth the view as they grew larger and darker green. Glimpses of the mountain beckoned us closer to our destination as we listened to the road trip mix Ren had curated for just this occasion.

Driving his car was a new experience. The clutch slipped a little in third gear, and there was a concerning noise I'd hear every now and again that Ren assured me was "just her purring." Control balanced the car-sickness that overwhelmed me when I was in the passenger seat. Being at the wheel helped my mind settle, and I realized I missed driving. Having a destination in mind made me appreciate the journey. Living close to the office had its benefits, so owning a car had never made practical sense.

Ren grabbed his backpack and unzipped it in his lap.

"What's all this?" I glanced inside his bag. There must have been three different types of chips and several other baggies of food.

He opened one and began eating with an unholy amount of enthusiasm. "Road trip food," he spouted around a mouthful of M&M's.

Fine with me. It was his car. "And this?" I gestured to the only water bottle.

"Emergency water."

"There's one bottle."

He shrugged. "In the event of an emergency, I guess we'd have to fight to the death."

"Peachy."

He stuffed the remaining bags into his backpack and dropped it between his feet.

"Tell me more about this summer camp for adults." I flexed my fingers around the steering wheel. It was time for a little more information. We were already in the car. There was no turning back. "How did you find this?"

"Well, first, I was thinking of signing up for a singles safari, but I don't think they'd let you drive the rover, and we both know that would be a problem."

I nodded, before the explanation fully caught up to me. "Wait, what the hell is a singles safari?"

"I don't actually know," Ren admitted honestly. "This was my backup backup plan. Originally, I wanted us to go on *The Amazing Race*, but those producers wouldn't know talent if it tap-danced right in front of them. Plus, this way, we get our own cabins."

Something told me Ren had been rejected from the TV show, but I didn't want to ask. "We don't share a cabin?"

"Hell no." He vehemently shook his bag of M&M's at me. "I'm not hooking up in the same sleeping quarters as my boss."

"Oh, so now I'm your boss?" The man was a world of contradictions.

"You are when you're hearing me go balls-deep—"

"I get it."

"—into a buttered-down piece of man meat."

Buttered down?

"I get it, Ren," I cut him off. Oh, how I wished I'd cut him off sooner. "So what you're saying is we're going singles camping?"

"Not exactly. This isn't just for singles, and there's a lot more to it. Just you wait." Ren pulled out the next surprise from his Mary Poppins bag of wonder, a colorful trifold travel brochure. "Apparently, the owners met at a summer camp when they were kids."

"That's cute."

"Damn right it is. Now listen: located in the heart of the Oregon wilderness on scenic Mount Hood, Camp Starlight has been decades in the making." He paused for dramatic effect. "But this was what sold me on it." Ren got comfortable and began reading testimonials in different voices:

"'I came to Starlight in desperate need of a break from my loudmouthed family.'" He mimicked a southern drawl. "'What I found was dozens of loudmouthed adults and a community I was welcomed into. Camp was the vacation I didn't know I needed. I try to come back every year…' Or listen to this one." Now he spoke in a Valley girl-like voice. "'I thought we were only going to tell ghost stories, little did I know I learned more ghost stories about exes…'" He burst out laughing, thankfully back to his regular voice. "Scary indeed, am I right?"

Ren's excitement was palpable. He needed this trip, and as he'd made clear over a mojito-infused forty-five-minute video message last night, he needed something refreshing after his divorce. I didn't have much in the way of exes to speak of—like I told Marley last night, dating was Future Jamie's problem—but I could see the allure of a fresh start.

"Oh, here's a part I think you'll love. The rules."

He couldn't see my eye roll, but it was there all the same. "Ha ha."

"No, really, check it out. First off, 'This is a vacation. You will not be splitting chores or cooking in the mess. Do this for you.' 'Safety is of the utmost importance.' Blah blah blah. There's an open bar, bonfire, crafts. 'Enjoy time connecting with nature, new friends, and yourself here at Camp Starlight.'"

My lips had curled into a smile at Ren's dramatized reading of the brochure. Now I knew a little more of what to expect. This was so far from my normal, but that wasn't necessarily a bad thing.

"Oh, they have sunrise yoga," he continued. "You love being up before sunrise. So do I, if going to bed after midnight constitutes 'before sunrise.'"

Marley's words echoed through my chest, and I knew she was right. This was going to be good. A real vacation.

The highway opened up the farther we pulled away from the noise of the city and into the solace of Mount Hood. A wave of peace settled over me. Hillsides that had playfully dipped soon became a dramatic cliffside. The road weaved and curved, showing views of valleys below, dotted with clusters of wildflowers. Lupines and trilliums I could pick out, but there were so many others I'd never seen before.

Ren put the brochure back into his backpack and turned up the music. Together we belted out 2000s pop song after song with all the passion we had. Time passed easily on the highway, and my dependence on the GPS allowed me time to converse and goof off. It was only after we exited and drove down country roads that nerves crept back in. Soon, friendly signs guided us as well.

This way to Camp Starlight.

I HAD no idea what I was getting into.

The parking lot was a madhouse. When we finally found a spot, Ren directed me to go check us in, and he would grab the bags.

"Hi. You're James, right?" A cheery-faced brunette in a blue jumpsuit approached me next to a welcome sign, where people were posing for photos. Her hair was in a ponytail, and her mirrored aviator sunglasses were shiny enough to reflect me and everything around me in their glare. She reminded me of a short pilot straight out of a fashionable flight school. "If you're wondering how I know that, I'm psychic." Her eyes were narrowed, and no trace of a smile could be detected.

"That's... Great." I tried to sound enthused.

"She knows you don't mean that." A tall man with square glasses and messy hair sticking up in every direction grinned over his contribution, which was said with false seriousness. Who were these people?

"Because she's psychic?" I asked, omitting as much dryness from my tone as I could manage.

"You are? Since when?" He smiled at her with a slight twinkle in his eye. "She just knows all. There's a difference." He extended his hand, and we shook. "I'm Leo, this is Hazel, and you are... James, right?" How did everyone know my damn name? "We saw your profile packet," he answered without my asking. "You know, the questionnaire you answered to be here? Yours was pretty memorable. You gave us a photo of you mid-crescendo belting into a microphone, if I remember correctly."

Now things were lining up.

Of course he'd picked that damn photo, the only embarrassing image of me that he could have given them. Was I ever going to live down last year's holiday party?

"I didn't actually submit anything. My friend Ren did. He's here now if you want to rip into him about consent forms." I looked for him behind me, but surprise, he was nowhere to be found.

"That's why we have a lake. We'll throw him in first chance we get," Hazel deadpanned. "We should get you to sign your own forms before we take you to your cabin though. Then the lake."

"Come with me." Leo jubilantly offered his elbow. "We'll take care of everything. NDA, DNA, DNR—"

"I swear, if Ren signed another *do not resuscitate* order for me," I joked.

Leo smiled a mile wide. He gave off no signs of annoyance over this issue, though the pessimistic side of me wondered if this discrepancy could lead to me getting kicked out of the camp at the start. Maybe Ren was right if this was where my mind went to at the first sign of trouble. I really did need a vacation.

A three-minute walk had me in the camp office, which turned out to be four desks in a portable building with images of fun times everywhere. I looked at bulletin boards covered in photos of smiling faces, woven friendship bracelets, and what looked like random crafts. I'd never been to summer camp before, but the little kid in me felt like bouncing in my chair. The grown-ass adult, however, kept the bouncing to the absolute minimum.

Leo twiddled his thumbs as he twisted in his desk chair, patiently waiting for me to read over everything. There was a standard liability waiver and photo release, nothing out of left field. I wasn't signing away my kidneys, and it said nothing about giving up my life savings or being forced to participate in any prayer circles or ritual sacrifices.

Ren was a stellar planner when it came to work, but he was a little more impulsive when it came to personal decisions. So when I'd told him it was okay for him to take me to the woods, the slim chance that he was accidentally taking me to join a cult somewhere may have crossed my mind. I didn't do my due diligence like I normally would. That was how desperate I was for some space from the office once it was offered.

"So, you're a lawyer?"

"I am," I answered, not looking up from the liability waiver. "I specialize in corporate law out of Seattle." I glanced at the bulletin board behind him. "Do people come here so much that they develop relationships with your staff?" It was none of my business, but the wall of invitations behind him was slightly confusing given the short duration of a typical camper's stay.

He looked over his shoulder. "I wouldn't say I get *that* much time with campers, but there are some lasting impressions. Some people keep in touch, and many return for a session the next year. The invites are for weddings from campers who... Connected with each other during a session."

"We're here a week." I figured that said more than enough about how crazy that concept was.

"Some utilize their time more effectively than others." Leo grinned yet again. I was beginning to wonder if the guy had frowned even once in his life. I cocked an eyebrow. "Not that that's the purpose of camp. Most of you are here to enjoy yourself in the great outdoors, but there are a fortunate few who have met their person while they were under our starry umbrella. A week can be a long time to some people." He touched the board reverently and smiled. "And I do love weddings."

He genuinely seemed to mean it. I tried to get more of a read on this guy but was coming up empty. He had this unexplainable chaotic yet calming presence that made me want to learn more. He came off as a romantic, maybe a jokester given his interaction with Hazel back at the start. Something about his easy laughter pulled me in, making me appreciate the short reprieve from the noise outside as more and more campers arrived.

"So, James, have you ever been to summer camp before?"

The cynic in me questioned if admitting I hadn't been to camp would be some kind of sin, like maybe I wouldn't belong here if I had never been involved in this world as a kid. But Leo's honest gaze told me that maybe that was all right.

"No, I haven't."

"A camp newbie? That's amazing." His happy demeanor assuaged my fears. "You're going to have so much fun, I promise."

He took the papers I'd finished without looking at them and tossed them on a disorganized desk, clapping once and bouncing up. There was something so sincere about him, and instantly, I wanted to know more while also knowing now wasn't the time.

I hadn't realized how desperate I was for friendship until today.

He walked me outside and I practically ran into Ren, who was smiling from ear to ear. We made our way back to the entrance where people had gathered, taking photos next to the Camp Starlight sign.

"I'm only going to be gone a week," a lanky man promised three children and a woman by an SUV. The kids were crying. The woman shrugged as if she didn't know what had come over them. He picked up his duffel bag and waved them off as the woman pressured them to get back into the car. In any other circumstance, the roles would be reversed, and the kids would be dropped off. It was surreal.

We found Hazel again, talking with another camper with a precariously teetering cast iron skillet on top of his bag next to what looked like a kettle. I was a little grateful that Ren had forced me to downsize, because showing up with a tent would have drawn too much notice. He listened to Hazel with rapt attention.

"So nice to meet you, Leroy. I'm Hazel, and this is my camp." She threw a thumb over her shoulder and pointed at Leo, who was already crouched down talking to a little boy. "That guy over there will say the same thing, but he's really just the co-owner."

"Aren't those the same—"

"They really aren't," she interjected.

Leroy smiled as if he didn't understand the joke. He handed her a waiver, and she took it without looking while checking something off on her clipboard.

Ren extended a hand to Hazel, introducing himself before praising our new home away from home. "This place is so cool. How'd you come up with the concept?"

Her eyes lit up. "That's a great story, actually—"

"Hey, are you Ren and... Janes?" a man said as he approached us. He looked like the quintessential lifeguard from a teen movie, if that character were in his forties.

"James," I corrected.

"My bad. Leo always makes these packets up, and he has shit handwriting." He shook his braids from his face and grinned, flashing his clipboard to me, and I tilted my head to read the chicken scratch. "Looks like you are in Orion pod. I'm Lamar, and I will be your cruise ship director. So if you two are ready, saddle up, and we'll take off."

"That's too many conflicting ideas, Lamar," Hazel teased. She handed us folders with our names on them. "Good luck. Don't let him sell you on motion sickness relief. You won't be sleeping on a boat."

I took my folder and saw a big *Orion* marked at the top. I tucked it under my arm, ready to begin. Maybe I was going to like this camp thing after all.

I WAS RIGHT. I had no clue what I'd gotten myself into.

I followed my camp counselor, a term that made me laugh inwardly because I was thirty-years-old and it sounded like I was twelve.

On the walk, I saw some cabins, a zipline, and a gorgeous lake replete with a dock and a sandy beach. In my info packet was a map containing activities I hadn't had time to go over yet. Lamar was happy to explain when meals were and what activities he led, as well as a silly story about the early days of camp. Apparently, Hazel and Leo had been messing around with a metal detector and found a chained-up ammo box that turned out to be filled with Hot Wheels toys.

I was completely caught off guard as we approached and he pointed us to our mini cabins. I expected tents. I expected tarps... I didn't expect glamping. There was a campfire and outdoor tables at the center, with a larger cabin at the back as well as five tiny cabins surrounding it. I approached my own, suitcase in tow, and opened my welcome packet to find my key code.

"We've got a two-hour window before dinner at the mess hall, so go ahead and unpack and then we'll reconvene at five fifteen."

I went into my cabin, and my jaw dropped. A massive window in the back faced the shimmering lake. The room itself couldn't have been more than seventy-five square feet, containing a floor-level queen-size bed and a small dresser with a mirror, but the first thing I thought as I entered was, *This is perfect.*

I dropped my duffel next to the dresser and sat on the edge of the bed facing the lake. It was magnificent. I could already imagine myself jumping off the dock, feeling the sun wash over me as I swam amidst the rippling water. I was in visual overload as I looked out the window. Blue sky was surrounded by gorgeous fir trees, and wildlife—*there was an actual chipmunk* outside my front door. I couldn't help but feel that this was exactly what I needed.

"Now that's what I'm talking about." Ren's voice carried through my cabin door.

I placed my last pair of pants in the drawer and went to see what the commotion was about. I found him sitting at the long wooden table at the center of our pod.

"What is that?" A purple-haired woman stepped out of the cabin across the way from mine. She reminded me of one of those pinup models from the fifties, with pinned curls and winged eyeliner. Only, she looked like she belonged in the wilderness, wearing a tank top and tied flannel shirt rolled to the elbows, with jeans that hugged ample curves. The chalk-written name on her cabin read *Emerson*.

We both made our way to the table and found out what the fuss was about.

"Never can have enough snacks, right?" The man Ren was in conversation with opened his bag to the rest of us, revealing a ten-year-old's paradise: a plethora of individually wrapped snacks. Chips, candies, fruits, and even chopped-up veggies and packs of hummus. Ren was already snacking on one of them, and his new friend passed them out to the rest.

"I'm Grant," our new pod messiah introduced himself with a shy smile. His blond hair hung over one bright blue eye, his demeanor practically euphoric as Ren parted the contents of the bag as though he'd just dived into Scrooge's money pool. Grant didn't seem perturbed.

"All hail Grant." Emerson waved a piece of hummus-covered celery in the air.

"Oh my god, are those Gushers?" a new voice asked, their eyes electric and haunting. I looked at her cabin. Our one remaining straggler's name was Gia. The redhead had a skip in her step as she rested her knees on the bench seat.

"My ex-wife sent this care package with me," Grant explained.

"She was here last year. She knows the game." He pulled four packs of Gushers out of his magical snack bag and tossed one to each of us. "She promised food was the best way to make friends."

If I were to make an assessment based on looks and attitude alone, Grant was a gentle soul. His polo was buttoned tightly, his glasses shoved up his nose three times since I'd met him. I liked him already, and not just because of the snacks.

"Your ex has been here before?" Gia asked.

"Wait, your *ex*? Packed you *snacks*?" Emerson's dark-red lips were partially open in an unintentional pout.

"She came here last year and loved it so much, we made a pact to take turns with the kids so we could attend." Grant pulled out a well-loved picture of two middle school-age boys and passed it around to us. Both of them sported the same half-smile as their father.

"What about everyone else? Have any of you been to camp before?" I asked.

A warm smile enveloped Emerson's face. "Every year from fifth through twelfth grade. But that was youth camp. My guess is this is going to be different."

"Yeah, this is definitely not that," Gia said.

That garnered chuckles out of all of us.

I loved our group. We talked for the next hour, explaining our reasons for coming here, laughing at Gia's constant jokes, and moving to the beat of a playlist Ren had curated and played through a Bluetooth speaker.

"Looks like we have a great group." Lamar exited the large cabin behind me. He'd changed into a blue T-shirt that showed signs of wear and tear through the small holes at the hemline. His jeans were faded and ripped, and his relaxed posture and demeanor were effortlessly calm. I wondered if a week here could unwind me in the same way.

Ren threw a pack of Gushers at Lamar as he made his way to our table. *Our table.* That had a nice ring to it. We'd all just met, but it was clearly a group mentality, probably out of a need to protect the snacks, but still. We were obviously all new to this, and friendships seemed the way to take the initial leap.

Lamar popped one of the jelly drops of goodness into his mouth and moaned. "This takes me back." His wide grin instantly put me at ease. "So we have Grant and Gia." He high-fived Gia as if he'd done it a million times before. "And Emerson, Ren, and Jamie round us off. Since it looks like we're all present and accounted for, I'm here to answer any questions you might have, but I can start by addressing the camp counselor of it all. I'm your host of sorts. You have a list of activities you signed up for, and you'll be able to participate as planned, but there are gaps in your day, and some people change their minds about what they want to do. That's what I'm here for. I lead some activities, but I like to participate as well. Counselors are here to help you have fun, and any of us are willing to help you with whatever you need. I'm also an incredible cocktail and mocktail maker."

"Speaking of which, when does the bar open up at this place?" Ren asked sweetly. He'd told me on the drive that Starlight was an all-inclusive resort, and he didn't mince words when it came to the important questions.

"We have a mimosa bar at breakfast, as well as beer, wine, and hard seltzers in coolers throughout the premises. In the afternoons, we have a full bar and two mixologists on hand." Lamar gestured behind his shoulder. "You'll soon see that you've walked into an adults-only oasis in the wilderness. We recommend that you pace yourselves, of course. No one wants to go in the camp drunk tank. It's infested with raccoons. But if, for any reason, you aren't feeling well or become injured—I'm talking bug bites and unfortunate run-ins with poison oak—needing a toothbrush, calling family, or whatever else comes up, I can assist in those kinds of issues. If you have any first aid needs, you can alert a staff member, or go to the front office."

That made a ton of sense. I was beginning to realize just how prepared the staff was to meet the needs of its campers.

"I'm sure you're already aware that there's spotty cell service. The whole purpose of camp is to get away from doom-scrolling the news and reading work emails. The one thing we ask, apart from being safe, is that you use your phones as little as possible. You've no doubt seen the disposable cameras in your cabin with your name on them. We'll print them off for you before you leave, but we ask that you leave phones in your cabins and detach from technology if possible. We know it's ingrained, but it can hinder your ability to unwind."

This week would be more challenging than I thought. I wouldn't be able to get calls from clients. I wouldn't be able to answer emails. I was being forced to have a good time.

FOUR

Jamie

FOLLOWING THE CROWD, Ren and I approached what had been lovingly referred to by Lamar as the mess hall. The massive log-framed lodge was idyllic, nestled between the main office and the craft cabin. It was the center of camp activities. There was a wraparound porch with padded high-back chairs and side tables facing the lake. The perfect place to unwind with a drink and a view. I let the wonder sink in. It truly was beautiful in the middle of nowhere.

Nothing about the warmth inside should have surprised me, and yet there was nothing messy about this hall. The first thing that caught my eye was the focal point of the room, a striking river rock stone fireplace. Bucolic wagon wheel chandeliers draped from the open rafters, and a raised stage took up the right side of the room. Sidled in the corner next to the kitchen was a reclaimed wood bar. Six rustic tables offset each other, filling out the middle of the room facing the stage. Each one was set with sage-green placemats, soft lighting, and centerpieces with each pod name atop them.

Directly across from us was a classic buffet. My mouth

watered. Dill-covered salmon cucumber bites, wild mushroom risotto, whipped ricotta crostini, and prime rib were all calling my name. This place pulled out all the stops. The spread looked like it belonged at a food and wine festival, and the drinks were just as sophisticated. I twirled the charred sprig of rosemary into the best whiskey sour I'd ever had. It had been smoked and tasted like a delicious campfire.

Conversation at our table flowed easily as Ren returned from the buffet with heaping plates, eager to get to know our podmates further. Ren took the seat next to Grant. When their elbows bumped, they both turned to each other, then immediately looked away sheepishly. Everyone came from different backgrounds, different financial statuses. It made me wonder how much it cost to go here.

"Well, if it isn't my favorite troublemaker. Lookin' good, red." Hazel made a show of lowering her sunglasses at our new friend.

Gia launched up out of her seat to be wrapped up in a big hug by the camp owner, who was no longer in her flight instructor suit. Now she was wearing black jeans and a simple tank top.

"It feels like it's been ages since we've seen you." She turned toward the rest of our table. "Gia is the foremost veterinarian on the West Coast."

"No, I am not." Gia playfully smacked Hazel's arm.

Gia intrigued me. She hadn't given us much information just yet. It was mostly superficial details about her life. I wanted to ask her more, but she continued talking with Hazel, their rapport cute in its own way.

"How did you become a counselor here?" Emerson asked Lamar upon Hazel's departure. We were all enthralled by this place, and a huge part of the puzzle of Camp Starlight was the people running it.

"Well, before this, I was a skydiving instructor, but I get frequent ear infections, which made the pain from jumping from high altitudes unbearable. So, as much as I loved jumping out of planes, I also like to enjoy the simple things, like hearing, so I did the responsible thing and took a step back." He chuckled. "I found this place through word of mouth, actually. My scuba diving friend went to camp the year prior and hooked me up with the owners. They had an opening, and just like most things in my life, the stars aligned. Get it? Stars? Starlight?"

Gradually, the room got quieter. Most people had a lifted hand with what looked like a shadow puppet-style dog. I put my two middle fingers to my thumb with my pinky and pointer fingers up in the air and raised my hand to do what everyone else did. Everyone caught on to quiet coyote, and suddenly, I was back in elementary school, in Mr. Knudsen's class as Charlie Alcott elbowed me till I was quiet. I'd always been the last one to catch on. Not this time. Ren was still talking beside me, and I elbowed him in the ribs till he got the memo and put his fingers up in the air.

"What's this for?" Ren asked, looking around the room.

"You never did quiet coyote in school?" I asked. Ren shook his head but complied.

Hazel waited for everyone to quiet down another moment before she spoke, effortlessly chill. "Welcome to Camp Starlight!" The group of us cheered, some clapping the tables loudly. She introduced herself as Hazel Matthews, owner. "I'm looking for my assistant, Leo Lovejoy." She lifted her hand to her brow, scoping out the crowd.

Leo joined her on the stage. "I think you mean co-owner and camp dad." He gave a charismatic wink. He exuded an excitement I usually reserved for Ren. He was genuine and had the right levity when meeting her at center stage.

"No one is calling you that. Don't call him that," she said to laughs from the crowd. "All righty, folks, let's get things started. To begin with, we like to introduce you to our staff, who you'll be interacting with all week. Let's give it up to our chefs, Azalea and Bobby, and our culinary student, Sebastian, for this lovely dining experience."

"Thank you for making me gain fifteen pounds this summer," Leo chimed in as the three of them joined him and Hazel on stage. Each took a small bow and gave hearty waves.

We cheered, and Hazel looked toward stage right. "Our bartenders, Luis and Lola, have been creating something special for all of you. Remember, it's an open bar, but if Lola has to carry you back to your cabin—"

Hazel cut in as an image appeared behind them on the projector screen. "You'll be cut off, and your face will be drawn on." Her smile brightened at Leo, while her eyes held pure wickedness. He scoffed, feigning annoyance at the sight of him passed out on a chair with his mouth open and a fake mustache gracing his upper lip.

Luis pointed at Lola. "I told her not to do that."

Lola shrugged. "I also told him he'd had three too many appletinis."

Leo stepped in front of her, speaking quickly before she could continue. "And that's our onsite staff. Before we get to our counselors, we wanted to do a little housekeeping."

The staff exited the stage, and Hazel continued. "The cameras on your tables and in your cabins are yours to create memories with. But be warned, they will be viewed and displayed on our projector screen." She looked to Leo, who cringed. "Parents will be contacted if we find any inappropriate photos," she deadpanned. Our emcee held for laughter yet again.

"We'll have some get-to-know-you games and competitions. You've probably seen the activities list and have noticed that we like to focus on wellness and relaxation, as well as crafts and hobbies. Our schedule is meant for your enjoyment, not your obligation, so feel free to go to activities or spend all day introverting in the Meditation Meadow and knock out that TBR pile. We host sunrise yoga every day and meals and activities will start at the same time each day as well. Every night, we have a campfire, and we do different activities each night of the week. Tonight will be a meet and greet, and tomorrow is karaoke night. All of this is printed in your welcome binders. For now, set your focus on our incredible staff as we kick off our get-to-know-you game.'"

Leo jumped in on cue to applause. "Thanks, emcee Hazel. Now let's welcome our counselors to the stage one at a time to play two truths and a lie." More cheers and some oohs followed. "The counselors will share correct answers before we move on to the bonfire for stories and s'mores."

"First up, they're small but mighty. Our resident yoga guru and popcorn gremlin, camp counselor Sawyer!" Hazel was right. Sawyer had big curls and a small frame. Their animated smile and complimenting wave to the group lit up their entire face as they took center stage. Sawyer didn't take the microphone. Their voice carried out to all of us, even our table in the back.

"Hi, everyone."

"Hi, Sawyer," we responded.

"I'm Sawyer. My pod is Cygnus. I use they/them pronouns. And my truths are... I love deviled eggs, I hate ice cubes in my drinks, and I can juggle knives." They said each statement with no tone to give it away.

We debated each declaration. The knife juggling stood out as outrageous, so it was most likely true. And all I could see was this fierce person juggling with knives reflected in their eyes, laughing maniacally. I gulped back a little trepidation at that image. We talked and decided that they probably hated eggs, deviled eggs to be precise.

Thanks to our deductive prowess, we were one of the only tables to get it right. I noticed Lamar wasn't with us anymore, then there he was, like magic.

We learned that Delphinus pod's counselor Felicia was a

former travel agent who was one of ten children and was allergic to strawberries.

"Next up, Lamar from the Orion pod," Hazel announced.

Lamar took the stage, taking the microphone from her. "I've been on a thousand hikes, I've auditioned for the *Great American Baking Show*, and I had a small role in the soap opera *Days of Our Lives* twice."

"I knew I recognized him." Emerson's eyes were wide with victory as she swore that the last statement was true. Lamar's hiker boots gave him away, so we decided our counselor had probably not auditioned for the *Great American Baking Show*. We were right and so was the table in front of us.

We were on a roll with our guesses, only missing Andromeda pod's counselor, Nat, so far, not realizing that she had over a half million Instagram subscribers and that our camp dad had even been a follower before she joined Camp Starlight.

Jack stepped up next. Leo introduced him as the man who'd built our cabins with his blood, sweat, and tears—Starlight's construction foreman—who was currently working on the newest pod addition, Lynx. And that was when I realized the pods were named after star systems.

Jack had shoulder-length dark blond hair that he pushed out of his face, making him look more like a model than a counselor and construction whiz. The things that gave him away were his tanned skin, broad shoulders, and ripped biceps. I was envious of his closely shaven, full beard, which still didn't hide his sharply defined cheekbones. He had an air of enthusiasm as he took the mic.

"Hi, I'm Jack, my pod is Corvus, and I use he/him pronouns. My truths are that I've seen ghosts my entire life, I've driven a monster truck, and I only get about four hours of sleep a night," Jack said ebulliently, clearly liking being the center of attention.

We submitted our guesses, and he admitted to his lie.

"I have not seen a ghost my entire life," he stage-whispered, "just the last two months since that camper died."

Hazel and Leo both hurried to interrupt him with nervous laughter. "We don't need to talk about that," they said in tandem.

I caught several pairs of eyes with disbelieving looks. Jack waved at us and left the stage as Hazel introduced the next counselor.

"Our next counselor is one of our founding staff who built this place with Leo, Jack, and me five years ago. Our resident lumberjack—"

A laugh rang out, and before I learned her name, I knew exactly who it was.

Autumn Gardner, my first love and the woman who had haunted me for years.

Laughter seemed to come easily to her now, delightfully care-free, unrestrained. My mind tried desperately to connect this freer version of her with the buttoned-up smart-as-a-whip girl that I knew in high school. Just like that, I could see her back then, brushing windblown blonde hair away from her face. My smile mirrored hers. I felt it as I looked up at her. Grinning, getting ready to lie to me and tell me something real. I was desperate for the information as memories of our past whooshed through me.

"You okay?" Ren whispered. He'd always been able to read me, but I went with the lie, anyway.

"Yeah, man." I brushed him off, knowing he'd probably felt my tension as I hyper-focused on Autumn. Her mannerisms and magnetism captivated me. Her hair was still dirty blonde, but the bangs were new, and her golden locks were shorter. It suited her. The happiness in her voice agreed with her most of all.

"Hi, everyone. I'm Autumn. I'm the counselor for pod Phoenix, and my pronouns are she/her." She launched into her two truths and a lie. "I wrote a book of poems, one of which was about a pineapple, I wore a tuxedo to my senior prom, and I've won two ping pong competitions."

I knew the answer immediately, and my heart sank. Then I focused on what I'd just learned. She had written poetry and played ping pong competitively. Interesting. She glowed under the attention, and the room fell even quieter as I whispered the lie to my teammate.

I knew Autumn hadn't worn a tuxedo to her senior prom because I was the reason she didn't go.

FIVE

Autumn

"Good evening, campers!"

A myriad of conversations was broken by the booming voice that always kicked off our first campfire session. Sawyer was the loudest of our staff, which made them the perfect person to grab people's attention.

A barrage of "Woo!"s filled the air, which only got louder as people caught on. The air was electric. Most campers expected something like this at a summer camp but didn't get the general idea until they were able to feel it. It still gave me goosebumps, and I'd done this nearly a hundred times.

"Welcome to your first campfire at Camp Starlight," Sawyer began. "We'll be hosting a campfire every night, with different itineraries—and that's the last time you'll hear the word *itinerary* out of my mouth," they said to laughter. "As many of you already know, drinks are being made at the bar." They pointed, flight attendant style. "As well as s'mores and other fixings down in front. Feel free to grab a blanket and a seat and join us when you're ready."

People started to get cozy, taking Sawyer up on the amenities we offered. We had a great system after five years, and we'd learned what people wanted and what comforted them. The fire was roaring, but blankets were still a must this late in the summer.

Seats surrounded the campfire and the stage in a crescent shape, beside which was an open bar containing every liquor imaginable, tended by our resident mixologists, Lola and Luis, who were arm to arm, each with a cocktail shaker in one hand. I smiled at the couple, who'd been together for five years after Leo set them up in the early days of building Camp Starlight. They'd joined Starlight three years ago, after Lola's daughter graduated from college. Lola owned a bar in town, Fireside, a local favorite that the occasional tourist stumbled into and appreciated for its rustic charm and the massive firepit it was named for, but they loved spending summers here while their daughter ran the bar.

Lola flipped her shaker in the air and poured it into four shot glasses to the pleasure of Luis, who looked at her as though she always surprised him. I'd once asked Lola how they made it work with so many plates in the air, and she'd brushed it off, saying they just loved being together under the stars. They were relationship goals, the happiest couple I'd ever seen, and a reminder that I'd never been with someone I'd want to come home to, let alone someone I would work with. Not in my adult life, anyway.

No drink tickets or wristbands were needed to get a little happy, but we tried our best not to overserve. Campers were in the safety of our wilderness, and thankfully, we kept alcohol-induced injuries to a minimum.

I scanned the crowd of campers to understand the vibe better. As always, a few people looked uncomfortable and tried not to show it, but this was the bounciest group I'd seen all summer, which filled me with joy over the likelihood that we'd have a great session. My pod was clustered together and seemed the quietest. That would soon change. The hesitant ones almost always came around, especially after the next item on the docket.

"Now, it wouldn't be opening night if we didn't participate in a little camp tradition: embarrassing our staff." People cheered as

Sawyer called us to the stage. Hazel, Azalea, Leo, Lamar, and I all took seats. "They're willing to answer almost any question you may have, so we're passing around pens, slips of paper, and our fabulous fedora for you to place questions in. Please, keep things appropriate."

Jack booed jokingly, but he was ignored.

"So, no questions about sex or politics. Anything else goes. If they don't want to answer, they drink." Sawyer looked a little too excited by the prospect.

I loved this game because it showed not only parts of us but parts of the audience and the way their weird minds worked. We always got some interesting questions smattered with the usual suspects: "Most embarrassing moment" and "Have you ever done anything illegal?"

The fedora moved from hand to hand, and they began working fast enough to tell me that this was going to be entertaining. A woman from Nat's cabin whispered something to someone from my cabin, and they looked like little schoolgirls with a secret. This place had its way of taking you back to the good days before obligations, back when we were free to have fun without the constant stress and anxiety of consequences that would affect our lives for the worse. It was also why we asked people not to have phones out.

Each staff member held a red solo cup. Except for Lamar, we all had an alcoholic beverage in hand, prepared to take a drink if we turned down a question. Lamar "My Body Is a Temple" Jones had a sparkling water he chugged instead of liquor. I held my alcoholic Capri Sun, a concoction made from scratch by Lola. It was my go-to beverage after her most famous cocktail, a s'mores-inspired beverage with marshmallow fluff and a graham cracker rim.

"Some of these are sweet," Sawyer exclaimed as they rifled through the fedora. "Let's start with an easy one. What's your favorite part of camp?"

Some "Aww"s were supplied by counselors and campers alike,

but in a mostly snarky manner because most of us were self-proclaimed assholes by the time we hit thirty.

We answered in non-sarcastic tones because the question was more of a kindness to us all. My friends responded with things like bingo night, and the talent show, but Azalea answered with skinny-dipping before I could. I stayed in the safe zone by telling everyone about my love of jet skiing instead.

Sawyer pulled out a new slip of paper. "What's the strangest thing you've done while drunk?" Our emcee chuckled. "First things first: are there any cops in the audience?" After ten seconds of literal cricket sounds, Sawyer clapped their hands once. "Okay, Hazel, you're up."

Hazel gave Leo a knowing look. "One summer, Leo and I broke into a miniature golf course and played moonlight golf."

I imagined the two of them falling over themselves as they tried to get golf balls past a windmill and smiled.

Lamar supplied us with his contribution. "Back in college, I bought five hundred dollars worth of Surge soda." He raised an eyebrow as we all laughed at that admission. "What? It was discontinued."

When it came time for me to give away my secret, I dove right in. "I replaced all the Wildwood city council member photos at city hall with images of Nick Cage."

A shocked Leo gasped. "That was you?"

"Me and Hazel." I shrugged unapologetically. Apparently, there *were* secrets between the two of them. I addressed the crowd. "One of them kicked me out of a town meeting for wearing red on a Wednesday and threatened to have me arrested because of some pointless law. They thought it was hilarious."

Leo beamed at his best friend. "Common denominator: Hazel Matthews."

"You don't know everything about me," she challenged, without explanation.

Sawyer moved on. "Silliest injury you've ever received."

We found a winner in camp darling Azalea, who started by telling us that she would need a minute because she'd done a ton of dumb shit and ended with us learning she'd broken her arm crafting a DeLorean-themed human flying machine meant for Flugtag—a Red Bull tournament where she and her friends built a vehicle to see how far it flew off a platform into the Willamette River. She also took part in said extravaganza anyway and had to get her arm recast. "And I'd do it again," she said to laughter. I had no idea our head chef was so bold and slightly foolish, but you learn something new every day.

"Oooh, this is a great one," Sawyer said, announcing the next topic. "Your secret shame."

Campers were loosened up, and almost in unison came an "Oooooh!" like they were ready to get the tea.

Hazel admitted she had seen *Twilight* in theaters twenty times, Leo cringed as he told us he didn't know how to read analog clocks, and then it came time for me to go.

"I'm deathly afraid of bunnies. And no, I'm not joking." Dozens of jackass laughs resounded. "Have you seen *Monty Python and the Holy Grail*?"

The laughter didn't stop there. This happened every time I revealed this truth to someone, which was, thankfully, not outside the safe space of campfire games.

"Don't even bring up *Donnie Darko*," Leo said through tears.

I blew my bangs out of my face. "Um, you just did," I said, half-joking, half-murderous rage. I wished more than anything that it wasn't true, but that was the whole point of *secret shame*.

"On that note, we're going to change gears," a serious Leo said to a collective groan. We knew these buzzwords were used in workplaces across the country, and we liked to lean into it on the first night. "I'm just kidding, kids. You aren't at work, you're at—"

"Camp!" numerous people shouted.

Leo chuckled. "I meant to say, for the next activity we're going to do a little singing. Can I get everyone to stomp-stomp clap, stomp-stomp clap?"

The crowd stomp-stomp clapped and repeated the sound as the beat to the song and all the counselors shouted the lyrics to Queen's "We Will Rock You" with cupped hands. People started to pick up on it. A collective excitement bounced off the trees as campers joined in.

Our campfire songs were top forty hits from the past fifty years, so it included everything from yacht rock to boyband hits, which the crowd got into. This part always took people by surprise, no matter what song we sang. Many campers had never been to camp and didn't expect to know any songs. We did fast renditions of favorites, while everyone had drinks in hand and ate s'mores. It didn't feel forced at all, which was something I loved.

Jack was missing from the singing. That was pretty strange because this was the part of our first campfire he looked forward to the most, but I found him cuddling behind us with an amazingly gorgeous redhead, recognizing her as his girlfriend, Gia. I knew she'd be coming up here, but I assumed we'd see her later. I waved at her, and she smiled and waved back. I made myself a s'more as we launched into a rendition of Abba's "Dancing Queen" and looked into the faces of our camp group behind the fire.

Camp made me feel everything. Absolute joy, gut-punching laughter, tear-inducing sadness. It was a range of emotions I hadn't experienced during years of growing up in a family where displaying your emotions was frowned upon, and I leaned into my feelings every time. I didn't know how long I'd keep working at Camp Starlight, but I was all about living in the moment, and I wasn't about to squander this one.

SIX

Autumn

SHARPENING axes was a hobby I never expected to love. Could it even be considered a hobby? A chore? Either way, it was therapeutic. There was something rejuvenating in the act. The freshly filed metal and dual grit sharpening stone coming together to make something new again just made me happy.

I made sure to give myself enough time to sharpen the ten axes needed for my first activity. I was in charge of ax throwing, archery, and wood chopping—a surprisingly loved exercise. If you wanted to take out some aggression on wood or a target, I was your girl.

Target sports were on the far edge of the premises. Our space consisted of three massive wooden ax-throwing targets, three archery targets, and a wood chopping station, which supplied some of the wood for our campfires.

One of my favorite parts about working at Camp Starlight was the off-seasons. I got to work on projects around the camp, help with general maintenance, and learn construction skills. I'd had a hand in constructing every pod in this place, as well as the activity zones and the Camp Starlight entry sign. It was an accomplishment I never expected to have in my life and an excellent stress reliever.

My blood, sweat, and tears went into a lot of places in this camp, but this was the first project I'd taken on my own and I was proud of it, despite its simplicity. I'd shown a genuine interest in woodworking, and Jack had been a great teacher, so four years ago, I dove in and built something with my bare hands.

So how did I end up in a field teaching people how to throw sharp-tipped weapons on a Saturday? It was a funny story. We'd been low on wood, and I'd joked that we should have the guests cut it as an activity. Hazel hadn't found the idea as hilarious as I had. She'd seen thirst traps on TikTok and had immediately been all in. I'd expected no one to be interested up the first time I ran this activity, but ten people had shown up, and we hadn't had enough wood to chop.

Now we were prepared. I'd added ax throwing and archery. They were just as popular as chopping these days, which was great because wood was a finite resource and we only had so many fallen trees to chop. This was my life now—thinking about the logistics and cultivation of wood resources.

My first class started at nine, and today was gearing up to be perfect. There was a new pod energy buzzing throughout camp, and cherry on top, my hair was actually cooperating. With the last ax sharper than a model's jawline and in its bin, I stretched my arms high over my head and tilted into the feeling. The skies were a cloudless bright blue, and the sun shone over Lake Starlight, high-lighting carefree ripples. The birds nearby soothed my soul as I soaked in the Oregon summer, which was just a few short months of sheer beauty that I never wanted to take for granted. I always carried sunglasses because my eyes never adjusted to the sun after nine months of rain, overcast weather, and darkness. Today, it was gorgeous.

Most campers were early and bright-eyed, with very few strag-glers. I let them rest on my periphery while our seventy-six-year-old sous-chef, Bobby, introduced himself as my assistant. I placed axes in each of their boxes and gazed upon our area. Everything looked in order. I grabbed a bow and held an arrow along the arrow rest, meeting everyone on the edge of the woods.

I took in my group of eleven, happy to see some from my pod had shown up. Kelly and Kelli, now known as Kell-y and Kell-i, were the only two with the same name this session of camp, and thanks to an oversight, I'd been lucky enough to get both of them in my group. Thankfully, this didn't turn out to be a negative. They were already thick as thieves, goofing off together and whispering whenever they were around each other. They were comfortable with us giving them nicknames, and they even seemed to enjoy it a little bit.

"Welcome, everyone." I smiled brightly. "I'm Autumn, the activities coordinator at Camp Starlight, and I look forward to meeting everyone. Today, Bobby and I are going to be working with you as you aim sharp objects at targets." I pulled an ax from the nearby box with a grin. "I know it goes against your instincts to do that, but we won't tell your parents if you don't." A couple of chuckles were emitted, but I'd have to up my joking game, even if it was early in the morning. "Today, we have ax throwing and wood chopping, and we're also going to shoot arrows at targets, which is not as difficult as it sounds. How many of you have participated in any one of these activities?" Four people raised their hands. "Okay, so most of us are beginners. There's no pressure here, but I guarantee you'll have a fun time."

I scanned the crowd and found the anticipated number of smiles before my heart jumped into my throat. All of a sudden, a high-pitched ringing in my ears drowned out the sounds of trees rustling in the slight breeze. He was blocked by a tall redhead who was fit to bursting, but he was unmistakable. A very handsome and reticent man in a forest-green T-shirt and khakis had caught my eye for the briefest second, and it knocked me on my metaphorical ass.

He always did look good in green.

Leo insisted we learn the list of names before each activity. I ignored it, but now I was kicking myself for this oversight.

Jamie Davis.

I couldn't have predicted this scenario in a million years. I figured we would have seen a celebrity here before I saw my high school ex-boyfriend.

A million memories came flooding back. The first time we met. The first time he weaved his fingers with mine. The night he cried, head in my lap, when his grandfather died. The way he always held me as if he'd never let me go.

But he did let go.

My stomach twisted in on itself as I gasped for breath, feeling like I'd had the wind knocked out of me. The last I'd heard, he was still living in our hometown of Seattle, which was not a world away or anything, but it was still hours away from camp. Either way, this was crazy. His family didn't do the outdoors. They flew to historical sites across the country or the occasional theme park. He wasn't an outdoorsy type. But there was a lot I didn't know about him.

Maybe I was drawing conclusions off a cursory glance, but this man in his buttoned-up polo and khaki shorts screamed composed adult. Reserved, well-dressed, and nothing like the cocky comedian and party-loving goofball I'd stupidly fallen in love with back then. This guy used to wear athletic training pants and high school track T-shirts, not anything with buttons. He did still wear his go-to Adidas Sambas, though, which filled me with a sense of nostalgia.

He topped off his look with wayfarer sunglasses, almost hiding behind them like a shield. I knew exactly what those eyes looked like. And they were trained on me.

Shouldn't there be a rule against hot exes? I found myself glad I'd showered today, but I wondered if I'd worn my best sports bra. The one that made my boobs lift instead of smush.

It was definitely the one that smushed.

The logical side of me knew Jamie had obviously grown in the decade since I'd seen him, but this man looked different. He had a freshly trimmed crew cut, far removed from the longer textured style from his teens.

He lifted his sunglasses as though he needed a better look at me before his gaze darted away. In the brief look I allowed myself, he looked regretful at worst and apologetic at best.

I thought back to my late teen years and sighed. We had dated for three years, and it'd taken me just as many to get over him. Too long for a relationship from my formative years that had crashed and burned. And that still made me angry.

"You know what? To change things up, we're going to start with ax throwing. What do you think?" I looked at Bobby. Confusion marred his face, but I didn't care. The urge to get rid of some aggression rose up in me, and I needed more than a bow and arrow to release it. I didn't want to finesse anything. I needed to use blunt force.

We walked the thirty feet to the ax-throwing targets, and they lined up beside Bobby in the safe zone.

I tossed the bow to the ground unceremoniously and bent back down to pick up two axes. "For those of you with an ax to grind"—I held for the guaranteed forced laughter—"you'll have to wait just a moment while we go over the ground rules. I know it's obvious, but safety is the most important thing when using sharp objects."

I threw an ax and it hit the bull's-eye to everyone's surprise. They clapped and whooped. It was probably my coolest introduction ever, but I wasn't focused on that.

"Oh my god, I think I'm having a sexual awakening," a girl with raven-black hair whispered. I almost laughed, but I was trying to keep my shit together.

I held up my second ax and touched the tip, just hard enough not to break the skin. "You can throw two-handed or one-handed. Remember, these are sharp, so when someone else is throwing, everyone is required to stay back and away from the throwee, cool?

As you can see, we have several solid targets for you to get out a little bit of aggression." I smiled, moving to another target away from the campers. "So, just imagine the anger you've felt over work problems, friend drama, or that shitty breakup that took you years to get over—"

I usually recommended taking your time, taking a breath, and focusing on the release because it didn't take too much force, but not today. Using a two-handed hold and throwing every ounce of my weight behind the action, I grunted like a tennis player, hitting the target hard enough that it would have knocked it down if not for the stellar craftsmanship.

"And take it out on the board."

Genuine claps and gasps emitted over the second bull's-eye I'd landed, as well as some semi-terrified gazes, specifically from men in the group. The one person whose reaction I didn't see I avoided on purpose, even though I wanted to look at him. I hated wanting to look at him. This too-good-looking man had no business here.

I made my way to the targets and pulled both axes. I walked back then put them in their designated boxes. I went over the remaining activities, going through the motions and running through my usual spiel. I might have blacked out because as soon as I started, it was over and Bobby looked none the wiser.

Twenty minutes later, I was calmer, and everyone was in full swing. There was laughter over failed throws and whoops over objects that just hit the boards, none of which were close to bull's-eyes yet. I'd been there before, and I was cheering for them all the same.

I was able to avoid Jamie as he practiced archery, but he came over to my zone seemingly without realizing until it was too late. He looked like he wanted to turn tail and run the other direction, but his friend didn't notice.

A freckled man offered his hand to me. "Hi, I'm Ren."

I nodded as I returned his handshake with the same level of

intensity. He looked slightly mortified at his formality, but I brushed it off and turned to the true offender.

"And this is James."

I stood there with my lips half open. *James.* How did he sound both timid and pretentious at the same time? Ren was practically bouncing while *James* looked like he'd seen a ghost.

That was somewhat accurate.

"You're really skilled at this," Ren said, unaware of the drama unfolding.

"I'm just having a good day." Would seeing someone you never thought you'd see again constitute a good day? I wasn't sure. I put on my camp counselor smile. "Thank you though. If you two would like to take the open targets..."

They both did as they were told and picked up an ax.

"So this isn't so much about strength as it is about focus and form. A little bit of advice: I like to take a breath before I throw because it calms me and helps me focus, but to each their own. Ren, if you'd like to go first." I pointed at his target.

He threw his ax, and it made it to the target, but the handle made contact, and it fell to the ground.

"Great job. You were barely off. Maybe try releasing the handle a little higher in the arc next time." I went through the motion without an ax, and Ren followed me through the action. "There's a lot of trial and error involved."

He threw again and it caught wood right outside of the target. "I hit it."

He jumped up and down as Jamie clapped. Ren looked to me for a response, and I gave him a thumbs-up.

"Hey, Autumn," Kell-i asked from behind me. "Can you show me the form again?"

"Be right back," I told them, relieved to be pulled away so I could catch my breath. "You might want to use two hands, Kell-i," I told her as she demonstrated her original form. "It has nothing to do with power but helps you straighten your body correctly."

"Are you gonna go?" I heard Ren ask Jamie. He was probably worried about needing my go-ahead, but I didn't turn around.

I heard him skim the target, and it landed on the ground. Kell-i threw her ax and hit the farthest circle of the target. I gave her a high five before turning back to the men. "Try it with two hands, James. You saw how close I got to the target."

Jamie placed both hands on the ax and pulled back, aiming and practicing a swing. I turned, waiting for him to throw, but he seemed to notice me out of the corner of his eye, because not only did he miss the target by a mile but he threw it so hard that it left the vicinity of the ax range and landed farther away than I'd ever seen.

Right into the lake.

Ren burst into laughter, garnering the attention of several campers who missed what had happened, but without explanation, their curiosity abated, and they went back to what they were doing.

"Shit." Jamie waited to walk behind Kell-i and Kell-y once their throws were complete.

I passed my role off to Bobby and started the trek toward the water, ensuring the girls' area was also clear. He powerwalked his way to the lake, dodging trees as I jogged to catch up.

"This is so embarrassing." His hands were clenched into fists.

I wanted to laugh because he looked like a toddler not getting his way, but it wasn't the time. "What are you doing here?"

He did a double take. "What am *I* doing here? What are *you* doing here?"

It wasn't a crazy question. The last time I saw him, I'd planned to become a doctor, but now that sounded as optimistic as a kid saying they would be an astronaut. Ten years had passed since our surprising breakup via an impersonal phone call, and it seemed like a lifetime ago.

"Well, I'm not throwing axes into lakes, that's for sure." I didn't care if I sounded like a petulant child. Did I see the hint of a smile?

We found our way to the ax's resting place near the rocks.

"I didn't throw it into the lake. That's... Lake adjacent." The level of arrogance in that sentence would be astounding if I hadn't known the man in our formative years. It'd been charming back then, but now I knew he meant it.

It was amazing how cocky he could sound after *that* throw, but that was Jamie. He had confidence and swagger. He was the homecoming king, the guy everyone looked to for ideas for the next fun thing to do, and he wore it well. He was playful, the class clown who also turned out to be the most challenging person to debate. And the most stubborn. That part, at least, was proving to be true.

I shook the thing so he could see. "It's wet."

He placed his hands on his hips. "Aren't you supposed to be at Stanford?"

"I'm almost thirty. Are *you* still in college?" Ha! Point, Autumn.

His shoulders fell as if he felt even more embarrassed. If he was going to get information out of me, he'd have to do better than that.

I wasn't about to make things easier on him. "So, Jamie, how's your life been since you kicked me to the curb?" Oops.

"I prefer not to have this conversation when you're holding a weapon." His captivating smile came out.

My knees weakened just a little bit. Goddamn that handsome bastard. "You're right. Why don't I just throw it into the lake?"

"Autumn."

"Jamie."

Just say it. "*What are you doing* here *when you have a degree from Stanford?*" He didn't know I didn't finish. He didn't know anything about me. Not anymore.

"I didn't realize you would be here. I didn't expect—"

I analyzed the words he didn't say. If he'd known I was here, he probably wouldn't have come. And that hurt.

I cleared my throat. "Things have changed."

"And I'd like to hear about them," he started. "And I guess I'd like to apologize for..."

You guess?

"It's been ten years. You don't need to apologize, and we don't have to get past anything. I'm over it." I smiled my best *I'm over it* smile. I avoided his gaze, which meant I had nowhere else to look but his biceps. He had much more muscle than before. And damn, did the ten years difference look good on him.

His eyes, however, were on my thigh tattoo, a wildflower piece about ten inches long that started at the low part of my hip. I tugged at my jean shorts, but they didn't cover the thing entirely, so I gave up.

"It's really, really nice to see you."

Did he think I didn't pick up on that extra really? Because I really, really did.

I rolled the ax handle between my fingers, and he stared at my hand, slightly scared. I rolled it again and extended the handle to him. He didn't take it. Smart.

"So you... What I mean is... How are you?" The recovery on this kid.

"I'm doing great, just great. How about you?"

"I'm great," he said, though he didn't sound like he believed it. "I'm here with my friend. He signed me up."

"That's great."

Great tally: four.

"I work here," I stated the obvious, like an idiot. He didn't say "got that" like the teenager I'd known would have. "I'm a counselor. But that's not all I do." Why couldn't I think of what else I did here? And since when was I embarrassed to call myself a camp counselor? "I do other things. And I live here year-round with Hazel, Leo, and Jack... Have you met Jack?"

He stiffened slightly. "No, I haven't. My counselor is Lamar."

"Oh, he's great. I love Lamar. And Jack is... Well, he's awesome, as I'm sure you'll find out." This was beginning to feel like the longest conversation ever.

He smiled at me, and I tried to hide my mortification.

"You look good."

I laughed at the clichéd response. "You too."

I wasn't going to lie to the man. He looked so much better than good. He rubbed his neck, which drew my attention to the spot I'd loved to kiss and breathe in back when we were together. He leaned in closer, and I caught a whiff of his amber and spice scent. So much better than the Axe body spray he'd worn like all the boys in our high school.

I glanced down and took in the rest of him. He had filled out. He was more muscular, as if the man spent all his free time at the gym. And could he have gained height? There was no way, right?

I actively avoided looking at his muscles, no matter how hard I wanted to gaze at them. Maybe run my finger down each line and ridge or fully investigate with my tongue.

I changed the subject because we were on shaky ground. "Are you still living in the Pacific Northwest?"

I needed to keep him talking. Otherwise, he'd ask me something senseless, like whether I had downtime to *talk*.

"Yeah, Seattle," he confirmed. Looked like my sources were correct.

"So, you're a lawyer then?"

"I've been practicing for a while now. I live and work downtown." He didn't ask about my work, but that was probably because my career spoke for itself. For the most part. "What about Nancy and Robert? Are they still in their old place?"

I nodded. We'd lived in a small suburb just outside the city. My dad still lived there with my stepmom in a five-bedroom house fit for a larger family. It'd been a lot for us even back then. My biological mom, however, was... Wherever moms who left their kids went. Probably Florida. Ever since I was ten, I liked to think it was in some hick-ass town in Florida. Somewhere she had spotty cell reception and no friends. It was what she deserved.

Maybe I was slightly vindictive over her. Back then, I hadn't gotten that way about Jamie. All I got when I thought about our breakup was sad. Even now. God, seeing him had me feeling like I was seventeen again.

Thankfully, we made it to the field, and things were literally in full swing again. I walked to a target that wasn't being used. He pursed his lips as I picked up an ax from the box on the ground.

"Hey, James, you can borrow one of my axes if you want. Yours might be too... Slippery." Ren dropped his ax into its designated location and watched his friend.

"Go away, Ren." Jamie held back his laugh.

Ren looked from him to me and back again, putting up his hands, his eyes penitent.

I piled on. "Whoa there, turbo. I think you may want to start with something easy. Let me see if we have a beginner's ax." We didn't have one. There was no such thing. "It's bright orange and made of plastic so you don't injure yourself or others."

Ren snorted and looked away quickly, making another attempt at the target.

"Beginner's ax? You know I don't have that bad of a swing, right?" Jamie took a dry ax from the box.

I shrugged. "Can I teach you something? Okay, so you hold it like this." I mirrored my typical stance, my feet the right distance apart. "You don't pull back as far as last time, and you hit the board. The trick is more aim, less fear."

Jamie mimicked me, throwing his ax again and hitting wood.

"Look at that."

He waited for the people throwing around him to pause before retrieving his own. Then he threw for a second time and hit the middle ring. I'd seen this happen hundreds of times, but goddamn if this one didn't turn me on.

Don't fall back into old habits.

He was only here for a week. Why was I even thinking about that? That was irrelevant. Nothing could happen. Nothing *would* happen, not if I wanted to keep my heart intact. Because the last time I saw him, I hadn't thought it was going to be the last time. He hadn't given me a choice.

SEVEN

Jamie

COME TO CAMP, they said. It'll be relaxing, they said.

I stretched my fingers along the back of my neck as I paced the adorable cabin that didn't match my insufferable mood. I wanted a distraction. I wanted my cell phone. But Ren had taken it when he caught me going over emails behind the mess hall after dinner last night.

Was it breaking and entering if I knew the code to his cabin?

"You okay?" Ren caught me outside his door and invited me inside. His cabin resembled mine but had a view of the campfire across the lake.

"Yeah, fine." I sighed, sounding closer to *there's a thorn piercing my side* than the *I'm calm, cool, and collected* I was going for.

"You look like you're still shook after, you know." He made a wild throwing gesture, imitating my first throw.

You'd throw like shit too if you just saw your high school ex, the one you never could forget.

Autumn had stayed away after my ax-in-the-lake incident. Professional and cool, she'd walked back and forth, offering tips, and we'd continued taking turns throwing at the targets. It'd seemed like she imagined my head at the center. I'd kept looking, trying to catch her eye for the rest of the session, but she'd clearly had no intention of continuing our conversation.

"Nah, it's not that." I should have known better than to give him anything.

"Is it the ax-wielding Valkyrie then? Don't worry, she scares me too." He noticed me tense up and jumped to conclusions like he always did. "Or is it that you have history with said Valkyrie?"

Usually, when he jumped to conclusions, he was right.

I let out a puff of air and decided to get right to the point. "We dated in high school."

"You and the lumberjack went to school together? In suburban Seattle?"

"The romance capital of the world."

"What was high school James like? Don't worry if you were the weird kid who preferred to hang out with the teacher and the quiet kids playing *The Oregon Trail* game during lunch. Wait, don't answer that." He ran his hand through his auburn hair. "It doesn't matter who you were in high school. Now you're this super-ambitious lawyer with a huge promotion in the bag. You're handsome, objectively speaking. You mostly have a sense of humor."

I shoved him good-naturedly and grinned.

"You looked like you still have chemistry." Ren gave me a knowing grin. "Does that mean James Davis is going to relive his glory days? Maybe hook up?"

I cringed at the thought. We meant more than that. She meant more than that. "No, it's not like that. You saw how she almost decapitated me at the lake."

"Ah, I feel that," he commiserated. Glad he'd understood and asked. It felt good to talk about the tsunami I was in after seeing her all these years later.

Autumn looked amazing. I'd caught a glimpse of her last night, but up close, she was truly beautiful. I wanted to explore every part of her, from blonde bangs to her sun-kissed skin. She had these wildflower tattoos I'd never seen before. They playfully climbed her thigh, leading to... I didn't know what, but I wanted to find out.

And those were thoughts I shouldn't be having. My sex-starved brain went directly to undressing her, and I tried to feel bad about it, but I just didn't. I wanted to see where else she had tattoos, if maybe she had a sunflower somewhere. I wanted to memorize them, preferably with my tongue.

Not the point.

I had to get my mind off her. Her stunning smile, the sound of her laughter for everyone but me. The haunted look in her eyes when we'd talked, her voice filled with indignation. On the surface, she was a wronged woman, but underneath, there was this added layer: hurt.

I'd hurt her back then. The memory of our phone call was still etched in my mind. But witnessing it in person was a whole new experience. Seeing her in her element, the way she carried herself, it was like looking at a different person. The sight of her stirred up a mix of emotions within me. Should I act cool? Should I address it? I'd never anticipated seeing her again, especially not here as a camp counselor. It was all so unexpected, a shock in its own right.

Last night, as I tossed and turned, I'd had the luxury of time to come to terms with our impending reunion. But she had only found out that I was here an hour ago, leaving her no time to process. Naturally, her initial reaction was a blend of shock and anger, and I couldn't blame her for that. I'd had time to think. She hadn't. And I deserved her anger.

The image of her last night on the stage in the mess hall and playing two truths and a lie around the campfire, sharing her secret shame, brought a smile to my lips. The memory of her fear of bunnies was amusing. Who was afraid of bunnies, anyway? And who would have the courage to admit that in front of a room of strangers?

Here, she seemed so much more liberated than I had ever seen her before. In high school, she'd been the intense bookworm, the one who only emerged once you pulled her out of her shell, and boy, had that taken time. She'd always been striving for the highest peak, leaving little room for personal enjoyment, especially before we started dating. She'd constantly tried to please her Ivy-educated parents, an impossible task. But now, confidently throwing axes, she was a different person entirely. She looked carefree and adventurous. It was evident I didn't know her anymore, and a part of me questioned if I ever truly did.

I pushed those thoughts away, but they kept circling like vultures overhead. For Autumn, for our past, for the chance I never took.

THE SUN BEAMED MERCILESSLY, evaporating all moisture from the typically cool morning air. The sound of laughter and the thud of the volleyball hitting the sand provided a welcome distraction. I had been carrying so much restlessness and uncertainty since seeing Autumn last night, and I needed physical exertion after facing all those memories.

"Ready to do this?" I looked at Lamar. He wore a fitted long-sleeve top, long brightly flowered board shorts, and a bright smile.

"You two, up here." Lamar waved Ren and me over to the opposing side.

Emerson was already on Lamar's side of the court. She wore a bright blue one-piece bathing suit with polka dots and sunglasses that covered half of her face. Her bright purple hair was pinned up in fifties glam, as Emerson as ever.

"Hey, Em, did you bring any of those Gushers?" I asked, spying the floppy beach tote she'd set down by the table.

"Just because we're in the same pod, doesn't make us friends right now, James." Her tone was completely serious, but the gleam in those mischievous eyes told me she didn't mean it.

"Bonding over Grant's snack stash does," I argued, and she cracked, her face lighting up.

"I still don't get that man," Ren declared, an almost-smile over his lips. Ren was still processing his recent decision to divorce, and I had to admit I also wanted to chat up Grant about this whole friends-with-exes thing. What if Autumn and I could become friends again? What would that even look like?

"Leave Grant's snacks out of this." Emerson playfully narrowed her eyes. "This is war."

Lamar and Emerson began stretching in tandem as if they were preparing for some kind of battle. This was supposed to be a casual game of volleyball. Neither the years of sitting in bed poring over legal briefs nor the occasional weekend game of golf with the partners had prepared me for the spectacle they were gearing up for.

I looked over at the woman on our side. She was maybe a few years younger than us, tall, and confident if her deep red lips and power stance had anything to say about it.

She introduced herself. "Hi, I'm Cheryl."

"Hi, Cheryl. I'm James. This is Ren." I reached my hand out to shake, and she took it.

"Hey, nice to meet you. So, did you get stuck with this one as your counselor?" Cheryl tilted her head playfully toward Lamar.

"Yup, he's ours," Ren said. "Who do you have?"

"I'm in Andromeda—Nat's pod."

I'd yet to meet her in person, but from last night's game, I'd learned that her social media status was celebrity-level intimidating, she'd danced with Dolly Parton, and her favorite movie wasn't *The Goonies*, because she'd never seen it thanks to the sad fact that she grew up on the East Coast and it wasn't a rite of passage like it was for a kid in the Pacific Northwest.

"There she is, goddess of sustenance, and our third, Azalea." Lamar introduced the gray-eyed chef, spinning her in a hug, both of them laughing before he put her down. Her tightly curled hair whipped around wildly in the lake breeze.

We lavished her with compliments, and she basked in the attention. The cherubic-faced woman was all of five feet tall and squeezed the ball tight enough that I wondered if it would explode. It was no wonder that Lamar referred to Azalea as a goddess, considering her amazing food. I was still infatuated with this morning's spread. From bacon-wrapped dates to chicken cordon bleu, everything we'd eaten so far had been nothing short of decadent.

Quickly, I learned my volleyball skills weren't nearly as impressive as I'd hoped they would be. Emerson, Azalea, and Lamar worked together like a well-oiled machine. Ready for anything. Which, unfortunately, included demolishing us.

Strangely, Lamar suggested conversations between Cheryl and me. First about school, then about her fur baby, a husky named Poppy. After the third icebreaker about whether we both liked walks on the beach, I started to get suspicious. Ren cocked his head at Lamar. Was he some sort of matchmaker or was he trying to distract us? The scoreboard proved that subterfuge was unnecessary. I wondered what that was all about.

Soon, we accumulated an audience. A woman I recognized as one of the campers in Autumn's pod introduced herself as Kell-i to Terry, who was cheering on both teams with so much enthusiasm, I wondered if he was a sports coach or maybe even a life coach. Either way, I felt coached. Ren, Cheryl, and I tried to recover enough to make him proud. Cheryl blushed when he complimented a particularly graceful return serve.

"Mine," Azalea called out, and Emerson was there, lined up for the pass with precision under the volleyball Azalea had popped up high.

"Got it." She set the ball with a flourish, this time to Lamar, who meant to decimate us with another calculated strike. Cohesion like that made it look like the three of them had been working as a team for years.

Diving into the sand for what must have been the fourth time,

I laughed as I finally scrambled fast enough to pop the ball up toward anyone on our side. Ren seemed surprised we'd finally made a play on one of their brutal bump, set, spike combos.

"Gloves are off now." Ren whooped as he chased, desperate to get under the ball. With his back to the net, he let out a loud grunt as he bumped the ball with no finesse.

Luckily, Cheryl was there to give it the redirection we needed, landing a perfect tip over the net and sealing our first and only point of the game. We may have lost nearly every point, but we'd started to return volleyballs with fervor, so I counted it as a win.

Kell-i and Terry stormed the court, clapping us on the backs. Lamar, Emerson, and Azalea all came to our side to hug and high-five us as well. Goofy reenactments of *Top Gun*, complete with frozen high fives, had me laughing harder than I'd had in years. The next twenty minutes were an ensemble of more dives and taunts stitched together with wild laughter.

We wiped the sweat off our brows and put our hands on our knees to catch our breaths with matching goofy grins.

"You weren't kidding when you said give it one hundred and ten percent." I loved teasing Ren about his overuse of workplace mottos.

He shoved me back, laughing. "About time you had a little fun."

Covered in sand and sweat, we made our way toward the communal showers full of individual locking stalls. Only one thing could have improved our beautiful cabins—private toilets. I scrubbed off the sand and felt the heat of my skin under the sun's attention with a contented sigh. Ren was singing a surprisingly exceptional rendition of Beyoncé's "Love on Top" in the stall next to mine, and I found myself singing my friend's go-to karaoke song because I'd heard it so many times. That was, until we heard several ladies giggling at us outside of our stalls.

I couldn't help but laugh along with them. I was having a great time. Seeing him in this environment was nice, and his unabashed glee today warmed my heart. Sure, we worked a lot. Some might say too much. But amidst our busy work lives, we'd remained friends. Being here on this adventure only reinforced our ability to thrive together in any situation.

"Are we doing Paint and Sip tonight?" I shouted over my stall. I'd looked at my itinerary this morning and found an art class led by Nat. Ren loved painting.

"Painting tonight, yeah. But, uh, you might be a bit more on your own for that," Ren informed me.

I emerged from the shower, wrapped a towel around myself, made my way toward the spacious dressing room, which was divided into individual sections that were locked, and started getting dressed. "Oh, yeah?"

"Well, Grant is painting tonight too." A towel-wrapped Ren wiped the condensation from the mirror.

"Ahh, got it." I smirked. "You and Grant then?"

"What? He's cute."

"I can stand by the sidelines while you get your flirt on." I was genuinely happy for him. Ren had always been open about how he was into blonds, and now that he was single, it didn't surprise me that Grant had caught his eye.

Autumn's face briefly flashed through my mind. Would she be there? If so, it would be an opportunity for me to apologize and possibly rekindle our friendship. That was how it had all started... Well, maybe not *friends*.

We hadn't started as friends, but maybe, by the end of the week, we could end that way.

EIGHT

Autumn

JACK AND GIA extended an invitation to hang out at his cabin before our pod dinners, but I turned them down so they could have some time alone. I adored my best friend's girlfriend. She possessed a witty sense of humor and a loving, free spirit. Allocating the time to get out here to visit was difficult ever since she found a job as a full-time veterinarian in Portland, and Jack was always busy with camp. Jack was a romantic. His mantra regarding love was to put yourself out there and trust it'll work out, but that had me wondering if that meant he was ready to take their relationship to the next level. If he'd truly leave, for good.

One crisis at a time.

Memories of Jamie's carefree gaze and lackadaisical smile took over as I paced my cabin like an anxious performer.

If I had more time, I'd have burned off this restless energy in the lake, but that would have to wait until after campfire. This week would go off like all the others. Just because he was here didn't have to mean anything would be different. And I didn't want to take away from his experience. Camp would be good for him. Camp was good for everyone. I was a firm believer that no matter your career or your hobbies, you could find something to fall in love with here.

Steam filled the cottage-style bathroom as I stepped into the hot shower. Ax throwing rarely got me this hot and bothered, but seeing Jamie? I grinned at myself, remembering his face as we retrieved his ax from the lake. He may have been more off-kilter than I was. And that was saying something.

Was I ready to let this man back into my life, even for a week? It seemed like a risk being in the same state as the person who'd destroyed my heart. And my traitorous body still lusting after him was a definite no-no.

The truth, which was hard to admit, was I'd enjoyed flirting with him earlier today. No one had interested me in a long time, and even if it was someone I had history with, I wanted to do it more. It wasn't like we were going to date or anything. I also wanted to get to know this new Jamie. We were so different from who we were back then. Not to mention it had been a decade since he broke my heart. I'd moved on. For the most part.

At least I'd be prepared next time I saw him.

Towel-clad and lotioned up, I smelled more confident than I felt. I needed something else. Rooting around through my DIY teal vanity drawers, I successfully located the shoebox brimming with hair accessories and makeup. Questionable expiration dates of cute bottles of half-used pinks and purples lined the countertop. Separated lotions that just required a shake or two, random concealers in different shades, and something glittery with the hint of a strawberry scent. I used it. All of it. It was strange applying makeup when my usual routine consisted of sunblock and lip balm. Sometimes, if I felt fancy, a swipe of waterproof mascara. I found the trusty mascara and applied my pink lip gloss last. I felt pumped and ready to take on whatever tonight offered.

I dug through all my cherished flannels and cozy sweatshirts until, nestled between bandanas and T-shirts, I spotted it. As I held the top against myself in the mirror, my heart thudded. I'd need to wear a real bra instead of a sports bra. I didn't know if my boobs knew how to mold into that shape anymore, but the alternative was a sports bra with guaranteed sweat at the hem after five minutes of wearing it.

Am I actually gross?

Laughter echoed all around me. As beautiful and serene as they were, our cabins weren't soundproof. One laugh in particular caught my attention.

I scurried over to my kitchen window, where I had the best view of the guests milling about. If I craned my neck daringly enough, I could make out the walkway to the craft cabin where Nat was hosting her paint and wine night. Jamie's laugh carried like my own personal siren's call. Palms pressed firmly onto the kitchen counter, I watched the campers as they walked through the sliver of trees like a creep. Walking and chatting with his friend, he effortlessly blended in. He looked like he belonged here, too, a vision that both captivated and unsettled me.

Without taking the time to analyze it, I slid on the skirt and sandals combination that made my legs look longer than they were.

A moment later, mind made up, I strode into Nat's Paint and Sip class.

I walked through the doors and found that Jamie's table was already full. Of course it was. His friend sat at a different table in the back. Cheryl, Terry, Kell-y, and Jamie were just getting familiar with the paint colors already squeezed out on the individual pallets for them. There were brushes out and well-loved mason jars half full of water. Blotches of different paint showcased all their use.

There was an open spot up front next to Janna. Perfect. I knew both Janna and Kell-y, and they were one of the couples I'd bet on ending up together because they had so much in common. After all, how many people listed writing fanfic on one of our forms? Yes, this would work.

I strode up to Kell-y and made my move. "Kell-y, hey, did you see Janna up front, over there? I was thinking the two of you could hang out a little more, since you're pod mates and all."

Kell-y didn't hesitate. She looked up at me with no suspicion and smiled brightly. "Yeah, good idea."

She hopped up eagerly, waving goodbye to her table. Sunshine followed her as she moved to take a spot next to Janna, and the two of them immediately hit it off, just like I knew they would. Jamie looked stunned but not at all fooled by my blatant move.

"Permission to approach the bench?" I asked. He rolled his eyes, but it didn't hide the tug of his lips into a smile.

I took my seat with self-satisfaction radiating from me. The old me never would have orchestrated moving people around to get what she wanted. No, she would have stayed back, quiet, and waited her turn like a good girl.

Nat tilted her chin toward me. No doubt she'd heard. Taking the recently evacuated chair, I felt her curious eyes on me. I gave her a look that I hoped conveyed "I dress up every time I come to this class." I tried not to look down at my beloved first date blouse, wondering how I could avoid getting paint splatter on it by the end of this. After painting countless cabins, I'd accepted that I was a messy painter.

Jamie seemed to give me the same sort of look, all too aware. Then his eyebrow went up, and charming Jamie came out to play.

"You don't want to sit next to me," he said, his grin as self-assured as I remembered.

"Really?" I put my chin in my hand and my elbow on the table. "Why's that?"

"I don't want to make you feel bad." He leaned down to speak with his chest puffed out. "Next to my canvas, you'll be sporting hot garbage."

"Sure, Monet, let's see what you've got," I said, knowing he'd rise to the challenge.

"All right, everyone, have some wine, check out the display picture, and let's get started," Nat instructed.

She gave step-by-step directions as we began painting a hillside with grass first.

"Confession time," I said conspiratorially. "I still haven't read *The Hobbit*."

"But you've seen the movie?"

"Of course, why do you think I've been able to create such a flawless hobbit hole?" I tapped my brush against the circle I'd just created for what was supposed to be a perfectly round door. The finished picture would be a hobbit house tucked into a flower-covered hillside. It was colorful and serene. Now, if only I could get this hole to look like a circle.

I looked over at Jamie's canvas as if I were cheating on a test. He caught my eyes and smiled brightly. God, it still warmed me up seeing him smile at me like that. I bumped his paint arm, and he tried to hold back a laugh as his brush dipped a little extra green onto his hillside. He continued his line, ignoring the smudge.

"You're not going to fix it?"

"It's basically impeccable. Yours, however..." He pushed my elbow, causing my paintbrush to jolt against my canvas. My beautiful blue sky had a slash of a lighter blue through it now, and one of my hillside flowers became a harsh smudge. I couldn't hold back my snorting laughter.

"I can't with you," I teased, and he playfully jostled my shoulder again, taking me back to us in his converted den playing video games when we couldn't study anymore. I wondered what his life was like now. "How's your family doing? Is Patricia still volunteering at the Seattle Humane Society?"

"No, she's working at the one in Portland. She and my dad moved to be closer to my sister and her kids a couple of years ago."

"So, Marley had kids?"

"They're incredible." He whipped out his phone like the good uncle he was and showed me their pictures.

The Jamie I'd known had taken a lot for granted, but this

recognition that he was making enough of an effort with his family showed that things might be different.

"I'm jealous. I've always wanted to be an aunt."

"And you still don't want kids of your own?" he asked.

"You can blame that on the abandonment issues," I said, pasting on a grin after realizing the conversation had taken a turn for the serious. "Things have gotten better with my mom. I get calls on my birthday *and* Christmas now. That's an upgrade."

Jamie paused what he was doing and looked me dead in the eye. "You know, you don't have to make light of it. I know how things can get with your mom."

I almost shut him down. Almost. But he'd known more than anyone how tough my childhood had been and everything I kept bottled up when it came to the subject of the woman who'd given birth to me.

As if he'd sensed that it'd been too much, he tapped a red paintbrush onto my painting and created a small patch of flowers. "So, how are Yasmine and Liz?"

I nearly dropped my paintbrush, my mouth open wide. "I didn't even know you knew their names."

Jamie nodded somberly. "I guess I wasn't great with them."

The sincerity in his eyes nearly had me melting, and it was confusing as hell. Back when we dated, I'd used to hang out with his friends all the time, but he hadn't made an effort with mine. Back then, I'd brushed it off, but now, I felt like he had under-valued my friendships.

"They're good. Yasmine just adopted her foster daughter, and Liz just won second runner-up in the Seattle Film Festival."

"Wow. Well, if you must know, Ezra is probably stoned right now, Thomas is selling fake IDs, and Gabe absconded to Barcelona with a Spanish flight attendant." Straight-faced, Jamie didn't appear upset by this.

"Wait, really?"

"No. Your friends are just more interesting. They have normal lives and are still living near the old alma mater. You know what? I lied. Ezra probably is stoned right now, but to each their own."

I laughed loud enough to catch Nat's attention, and she met my eyes and pinned me with a look. Lips pursed, she spoke to me without words. I didn't know her well. She was our newest counselor, and we'd been ships passing in the night. Rumor had it, she might not be returning next year. Her big brown eyes told me, "Mess around with my class, I'll mess around with yours." I gulped. Something in her look told me she'd be backing it up.

I looked over at Jamie's canvas. We might be a few steps behind, but we could still pull this off.

A charming little hobbit door and welcoming walkway later and Jamie grinned at me.

"There. What did I say?" He turned his picture toward me, presenting it.

"Well, it's certainly not hot garbage."

"Thanks. And your painting skills are on point as well, counselor." He eyed my bright color-bomb of a hobbit hole. The streak he'd made in my sky was now joined by a couple of more intentional ones, making the sky look like it was full of shooting stars.

"Why, thank you, counselor." Both of us busted up laughing again. Resting my hand on his shoulder, I gasped to catch my breath. I shouldn't be touching him, laughing with him like this, but Jamie had always had this hold on me. A way of making any situation more fun and drawing out my silly side. Cheeks sore, I worked to recover.

"Do I need to kick you two out?" Nat's sculpted eyebrow arched up threateningly.

"Just her," he said at the same time I called out, "Just him."

Our laughter rang out with renewed vigor at the jinx. Now we had our entire table laughing. Even Nat couldn't fight it anymore, letting out a chuffed laugh before she shook her head and aggressively plunged her paintbrush into the water. I'd have to make it up to her later.

"I mean, I'd live there." I gestured toward his lopsided door in the hillside.

"You're living in the woods now, so that's not a surprise." He winked.

I immediately remembered the first time I met Jamie, day one of freshman year on the speech and debate team.

He'd flashed his eyes and said, "Show me what you got."

It had been an exercise in impromptu speaking, and I hadn't prepared, but as a seasoned sophomore, he'd goaded me into annihilating him. He'd complimented my delivery and wanted to bounce ideas off each other, which spurred me on to do even better. He'd distract me relentlessly when we were up against each other in debate but had been my biggest fan.

This man next to me had changed since I'd known him. And yet, his teasing and competitive nature all reminded me that some things never change, including the way he made me smile. The way he looked way too kissable, too sexy, too everything I didn't need this week.

Janna and Kell-y were having a great time deep in conversation comparing their favorite OTPs, whatever that meant. The class was conversing and painting, clearly enjoying themselves, and my cheeks were starting to hurt.

I needed to get a hold of myself. Laughing together like this was a strange, wonderful whiplash into memory lane. Back in school, he'd been the first to crack a joke that would have the whole class roaring, the first to show me there was more to school than just studying, that we could study and make out, that we could push each other to do even better, the first to... This man was even sexier than I remembered. And even entertaining thoughts like that was dangerous.

"So you're not living in a hobbit hole, obviously, but you've got to get out of the office sometimes, right?"

"Well, I haven't been camping or to any place like this before," he admitted, then his eyes filled with wonder. "I just mean, it's nice here, peaceful. I've been living the dream, working all the time, getting closer to partner every day. I'm thriving at work, but it has its costs, too, you know? And some of that is not seeing my family as much as I'd like."

The memory of his family trying to get more face time with him lingered in the back of my mind. Marley begging him to take her to the movies, his mom pushing for more family dinners. But Jamie had always had other plans that took precedence.

"You didn't hang out with them much when we were kids," I blurted without thinking.

A sobering look passed over his face. "Yeah, I sort of took that all for granted. But now that we're miles apart, I can really feel that, you know?" He dipped his paintbrush into the cloudy water, and a ripple of blue expanded in the concoction. "When it comes to friends, family… I've been taking a look at the decisions I've made, and I think I may have put some important things on the back burner when they should have been a priority, you know? Sometimes, my goals make it difficult to see the bigger picture. I can get a little hyper-focused and lose myself in the day-to-day of it all."

That was a surprising thing to hear from his lips.

"That's the good thing about being here. It's easy to forget your responsibilities. There's something about being out in nature to help rejuvenate and reprioritize. Or so I'm told." I wiped my paintbrush dry on a paper towel, blowing away the lock of hair that fell in front of my face.

Jamie blinked slowly for reasons I didn't understand before he nodded, lips tipped up in that too-kissable way—another reason this might be a terrible idea. I wasn't sure how I felt, but I wasn't ready for it to end.

NINE

Jamie

I'D ALWAYS BEEN a morning person.

I'd been like this since I was a kid. I did sports that required morning practices, took early classes in college, and usually made it to the office by eight after a workout at six in the morning. So waking up at five-thirty for yoga on a Sunday wasn't a problem.

There was sunrise yoga every morning, which I'd looked forward to since Ren told me about it in an attempt to sell me on our vacation. When I asked him if he'd like to join, he'd told me that he'd rather be eaten by a black bear. So it was just me for the time being.

The camp was gloriously quiet as everyone slept. I didn't see a soul around, and I wouldn't have been surprised to believe that I was completely alone if not for the birds dancing on the branches above me and the breeze blowing through the trees. The Meditation Meadow was at the far end of the camp, and I wondered if I'd be able to make it there on time. But it wasn't in me to rush before yoga. It'd screw up my chance at relaxation and a clear mind.

So I moseyed. That's right, *moseyed*. Before this, I only knew how to power walk and run.

The air was damp, and condensation gathered on the leaves

and trees around me. It reminded me of the one time I'd gone camping as a kid with a friend and his family at Lake Chelan. I remembered waking up and shivering in my too-constricting sleeping bag as beads of water dripped along the perimeter of my tent. As much as I'd loved that trip, I couldn't lie: waking up in a cabin was so much better than waking up in a sweating tent.

I glanced at the oranges and pinks coming from over the trees and felt happy to be alive. There was no comparison to seeing the sun come over Mount Hood. These days, I only knew the city. The sounds of traffic, people yelling outside of bars, footsteps moving above my apartment from neighbors I'd never met.

So this place was... Different.

The meadow was gorgeous. It was set on a hill overlooking the lake, surrounded by trees whose leaves let in rays of sunlight.

I wasn't the last to arrive, but most people were yawning and rubbing their eyes. It was nothing like the first yoga session, however. There had been some hard partying on our first night, and most people had looked ready to fall asleep or vomit that morning. I was honestly surprised anyone had shown after gorging on s'mores and cocktails, and had been grateful that I'd fought the urge to overindulge, even though my first inclination was to lean into the impulse to get shitfaced after seeing my somehow-more-gorgeous-than-I'd-remembered ex-girlfriend.

Luckily (or unluckily) for me, Autumn had been constantly busy that night, having side conversations until finally leaving with Leo halfway through, so even when I'd gotten up the nerve to say something to her, she was gone.

But Paint and Sip gave me a spark of hope for something different from our ax-throwing meeting. She'd been fun—even more than I'd remembered. And although my painting looked like a three-year-old had taken a brush to it in certain areas, I'd felt a sense of accomplishment. Autumn and I were on the precipice of something new.

She seemed happy to learn about my life, and when we nearly

got in trouble, she'd leaned into it, a far cry from the way she used to be. Seeing her less regimented gave her a new kind of appeal.

I went to the back of the class, unrolled my yoga mat, and sat next to a dental hygienist from the Andromeda pod I'd met in yoga the morning before.

Just like yesterday, our leader for the morning was Sawyer, with help from a counselor named Jack. Yesterday, Sawyer had explained that they had been on numerous yoga retreats and used to teach at a studio in their hometown before coming to Camp Starlight. The yoga classes I'd been to before had all been inside a gym or a studio, so it was a nice change of pace to be in the outdoors, and you could read it on my classmates' faces.

Sawyer was getting people set up and finding out about injuries or areas of the body to avoid stretching while Jack welcomed people.

"If it isn't the most beautiful girl in the universe," he choked out.

Something in his tone sounded sarcastic, but where was the lie? The way her yoga pants hugged her curves had me wishing I could touch her in all the ways I used to. We hadn't been huge into public displays of affection when we were kids, but I'd usually had my hand on her in some way, whether on the small of her back, across her shoulders, or around her in an embrace. I was finding it harder to ignore how my body gravitated toward hers. Hell, I'd take a lingering hug if I could get it.

Jack scruffed his fingers through her messy hair, making my stomach muscles clench. What was that? Jealousy? There was no way. It'd been ten years. Even if he wasn't her partner, I had no idea about her relationship status. She could be with someone else at the camp or maybe in town. She could be in a long-distance relationship (not that it had worked out so well the first time), and I wouldn't have a clue.

Jack raised his hands dramatically and stepped back from the basket of yoga mats as Autumn grabbed one, shoved it under her arm, and turned, smacking him with it slapstick style. It was clearly on purpose, especially with her enthusiasm. I had no idea what was going on with her and Jack, but they were close.

Her eyes lit up when she saw me, a smile warming her features. She walked to the back of the group and dropped her mat right next to me. "Hey," she said, her voice slightly raspy.

Everything she did was sluggish, especially the way she took me in. I'd thrown on a pair of joggers and a white T-shirt, and if I wasn't mistaken, it was doing exactly what I'd want it to do in her presence, if I cared about that sort of thing.

Jack looked to Sawyer, who gave him the go-ahead to start class. "Hello, early birds." He waved before looking right in our direction. "And Autumn."

She gave her fakest fake smile before glaring daggers at him. She looked like she was calculating how far she'd have to throw him before he hit the lake.

Jack paid her no further attention. "We're going to start in a minute, but while Sawyer finishes, let's all do some arm stretches."

We did so collectively, moving into leg stretches before Sawyer walked to the front of the class.

"Welcome again, everyone." They stepped their bare feet onto their yoga mat.

I squished my feet into the ground, enjoying the sensation of a barely level earth surface with the cushy foam of my mat. Sawyer sat down and the rest of the class did as well, so I followed suit.

"Is this your first yoga session?" I asked Autumn quietly.

"No, I tried it once and thought it was stupid because my brain wouldn't shut up."

There was the Autumn I knew.

I wanted to ask her why she was here today, but I thought better of it. Who was I to look a gift horse in the mouth?

"I like to express my gratitude by giving thanks for this opportunity to be in this calming environment with such amazing people." Sawyer's tone calmed me, and I felt myself warm as they held their hand to their heart and smiled at all of us. "Let's shift into child's pose."

Autumn nodded as if she was happy to do the simple pose. She bent over and rested her shins on the mat, emitting a relaxing sigh as she curved her back and put her arms beneath herself. A breeze blew her scent toward me, and I winced. God, even her sweat smelled like strawberries. Strawberries and sunblock.

Deep breaths sounded from all around me before Autumn broke the silence near us, groaning. "It's far too early in the morning for tight yoga pants. I should be back in bed wearing just..."

"Just what?"

"Huh?" She acted as though she hadn't given herself away. "Nothing."

God, she meant her underwear. Or maybe tiny sleep shorts. Nothing at all? Fuck, I was picturing all of those things.

Autumn yawned. "I'm wondering about the likelihood that my arms would fall asleep if I did this all day."

"Hmm..." I rested my chin on my hand and pondered. "What are the conditions?"

"Sixty-five degrees, overcast, and I'm covered in a blanket."

"How heavy is the blanket?" I asked.

"It's one of those fuzzy alpaca ones."

Sawyer didn't seem to notice our inability to remain silent, but I promised myself we wouldn't find ourselves in a similar situation to the one at Paint and Sip. I didn't want to annoy all the counselors and get kicked out of this *relaxing* retreat.

"Now we're going to transition into warrior pose."

I stood up and rolled my shoulders back. "I think the likelihood is high. Now if you had said it was a lightweight *quilt*..."

"I forgot you were a blanket expert."

"Really? That's literally how I introduce myself to people."

Sawyer switched into tree pose, and everyone mimicked them. Autumn tried to finagle her way into putting one foot on her opposite knee, huffing as she failed to do so three times. Man, she was cute. But it was when she tried to raise her hands that it truly went to hell.

"Timber," Jack whispered, loud enough for all of us to hear.

I had to do a double take as she snarled at him. I burst into the quietest fit of laughter I could, but we had definitely distracted the class. Sawyer was shaking their head at him, Autumn was glaring daggers at him, and I had both feet planted on the ground because there was no way I could keep the same pose when I was holding my sides.

I prepared to walk over to her mat, but Jack beat me to it.

"Here." He offered his forearm for her to use to balance herself.

I moved back into the pose and looked away, but it was hard not to notice in my peripheral vision. She took a frustrated breath but went into the pose, adjusting her feet.

"Just like that, Gardner." Jack nodded, last naming her.

I tried not to think about the fact that he had this rapport, and it gave me... Feelings. I couldn't help it. My brain went right to him saying "just like that" in a completely different way that made me cringe. Yet again, I told myself that there was no reason to have feelings of jealousy.

She had always been a bit of a klutz when we were younger. Once, we'd been in our speech and debate classroom, and she'd tripped on a metal desk leg, falling until I caught her, right on my lap. It'd been the first genuine smile she'd given me, and I'd felt privileged to have captured something so special. Feeling her on my legs hadn't hurt matters either.

"There you go." He left Autumn like that.

I released a breath in the least meditative way possible. God, did I envy him. And I wanted to know more about this guy, like do a deep dive or maybe a background check. Learn about whether he'd paid all his taxes. Or had a criminal record. I had to steal my phone back from Ren.

Wait. No. I wasn't going to do that.

Autumn clenched her jaw in concentration as she maintained her position.

"Don't forget to breathe," I whispered.

She looked at me and smiled, letting out a slow exhale and inhaling again until we were breathing in tandem.

We continued without incident for twenty more minutes. For the most part, Autumn did well. She even appeared to be enjoying it. But it had me wondering why she was here in the first place. I hoped it was because she knew I would be here. But that was ridiculous. She was probably trying new things. She clearly had been doing that since I'd last seen her.

So many new things.

So far, I'd noticed her love of wood sports, her penchant for tattoos, the loose way she moved, almost as if the stress she'd been carrying in her shoulders back when we were together had completely dissipated. She was no longer a perfectionist—at least when it came to painting last night. She was always joking with someone, and she seemed more open. She used to just be like that with me.

Yeah, it was jealousy I was feeling.

I was also proud of her. I had told her for years that she should have more fun, but she'd been so focused on grades and extracurriculars with the goal of getting into a reputable school that she'd seemed drained most days. Clearly, this had been deep inside her all along.

We changed positions again, and her side and back came into view. I could see her sports bra underneath her loose-fitting tank top and forced myself to look away before it had a real effect on me. The last thing I needed was for her to see me with a hard-on in sweats that would leave nothing to the imagination once they grew tighter.

Jack pursed his lips as Autumn struggled through yet another difficult move, but she nailed it and threw her hands up in victory.

And that was when I knew. Watching her have fun with this dude all week was going to be awful as hell.

TEN

Jamie

THE NEXT COUPLE of hours went by in a daze. I attempted to meditate after yoga but images of Autumn in tight spandex destroyed my ability to clear my mind. During pottery, I had to resculpt the vase for my sister three times because I kept thinking about all the things I wanted to learn about this new version of her.

She'd always been strong, witty, and cutthroat in debate, which had humbled me. Autumn had been a leader before, but outside of our small debate club, her confidence had always been lacking, no matter how well she did in school. It was a remarkable feat seeing her perform in front of a rapt audience with an air of assurance, as if she was comfortable in her skin.

How did she come to live here, of all places? Dreams we'd once whispered were mostly about status and money. How we'd conquer the world. Back then, just an imagined life that once upon a time we might have had together.

While I'd followed the same boring dream, she was living a vibrant new one. And even if my first impulse was that she was wasting her potential, I could also see the appeal of jumping off the conveyor belt and taking a risk.

My infatuation only grew in the downtime I had in my cabin between pottery and cooking class. I'd been staring at the knots in the wood on my ceiling for a disturbingly long time before Ren pulled me from my thoughts.

"James, hey." I must have looked like a startled deer because he backed up and then started laughing. Ren stretched his arms and yawned.

"Let me guess, you needed a power nap after a long day of pining after Grant."

"You're one to talk. How's Autumn?" He smirked.

"You mean pumpkin spice latte season? It's not for another month."

"Don't play that way with me. Everyone at camp, from the zipline to the craft cabin, could feel the tension between you two at paint night." Ren took a seat on the edge of my bed, kicking his feet like a child waiting for a story. "Tell me something happened right now."

His face dropped when I turned toward him. Feeling the cool wood floor under my bare feet steadied me as I said what I didn't want to say.

"I think she's in a relationship with someone. Which reminds me, I need my phone back."

"You're not going to do a background check on anyone," he said knowingly.

Well, there went that idea.

SIX COOKING STATIONS were set up at tables in the mess hall, loaded with ingredients for the southern dish we'd be making for brunch. I'd joined cooking class today because I'd bypassed breakfast, and I was starving.

Utensils were set next to hot plates for each cooking team, and laughter bounced back and forth between the six students who'd already arrived. Everyone except me was partnered up. Ren and Grant, the newly inseparable pair, sat at a table across from Gia and Emerson who were both inspecting ingredients.

I took my place at an empty station.

"Hi, there. Can I join you?"

"James, of course." A ring-clad woman named Irene stood up to shake my hand, and next to her sat Leroy, who I remembered from my arrival. He seemed more at ease than he had on the first day. "You can pair up with my cabin leader. She'll be here in a sec."

A moment later, Autumn arrived, looking like sheer perfection. Could I get any luckier in one day? Her golden hair shone softly. It almost distracted from her tattoo peeking out, daring me to stare. Big hazel eyes searched mine for a long moment, and I wondered if she was just as stunned to see me.

If she was thrown off, however, she didn't look it. I held my breath and tried to keep my cool as she headed in my direction and sat right next to me.

"Hey," she said.

"Hey." Why did my voice sound deeper than usual?

Subtly, I glanced at my ex-girlfriend, engrossed as she stared at our instructor, determination in her eyes. This should be interesting.

I used to be in my element when I was cooking, and back when I'd had more time, I'd loved it. A renewed sense of urgency thrived under my skin. Maybe I'd be able to impress her.

Things may have been different, but the Autumn I knew didn't cook. Seventeen-year-old Autumn had looked at me like I was a god the day I'd made her a pesto grilled ham and cheese sandwich. Now, she rolled up her flannel sleeves and gave me a challenging look, as if daring me to say something.

Everyone was rapt with attention as Azalea started her cooking lesson for the chicken fried steak dish. She told us she'd be by in a bit to check on each table's progress and then she let us go.

Once in a while, two people find a rhythm and flow in working together toward a common and delicious-smelling goal. This wasn't one of those times.

Autumn and I jostled for control of the same pair of tongs, bumping into each other. We ended up in each other's spaces more often than not, slowing the process down. There was no rhythm. And the fact that we weren't taking it seriously didn't help.

Azalea's voice carried from the front of the room as she joked with everyone not to mess around with the knives because "I'm hungry, and I don't want to deal with any severed fingers in my food."

"Do you always eat this well?" I asked my cooking partner. Everything we'd eaten so far had been stellar and I couldn't imagine dining like this all the time.

"Only during the camp season. In the off-season, the four of us make some family meals, which is nice. And we're lucky enough to be less than a mile from the main part of town, so we have options." She smiled as we measured the flour. "Which reminds me, are you still obsessed with fried ravioli?"

"Obsessed is such a strong word." Images of breaded pasta dipped in marinara flooded my senses. I could almost taste the dusting of oregano.

"Well, there's a place in town you'd love."

Maybe I'd convince her to show me when we went into town tomorrow.

"So, what's it like living here anyway?" I'd take any tidbits I could get.

"It was definitely an adjustment to go from being one in a million to everybody knowing your name. The other day, the general store owner reminded me to buy tampons."

I couldn't tell if she was joking or not.

She added salt and pepper to our flour mixture and asked casually, "But what about you? What's it like living downtown instead of in suburbia? I know you always wanted to live in the city."

I remembered the first day in my condo, and the silence that followed when the movers were gone. Loneliness was not something I'd prepared for. But at some point, being alone felt more like a choice.

"Sometimes I like feeling like one in a million. Other times..."

"Other times?"

"It makes it easier to lean into the anonymity." I didn't mean to get this personal with her, but she'd always found a way to get me to reveal more than I'd intended, whether I liked it or not.

She furrowed her brows. "You used to be so social."

"I've definitely gotten more reserved, if that's the right word." I hadn't noticed the contrast between past me and current me before, but it was the truth. When had I allowed things to change? And was I even happy with that?

"I'm having a hard time imagining that. Back in school, all I did was study and hang out with you and your friends. Sometimes I felt like I couldn't keep up." She avoided looking at me and popped the lid back on its container. Autumn's admission had me questioning my perception back then. She may have been on the quiet side, but I always thought she was having a good time.

I stared off in the distance as I stirred the roux. "I'm the same person. My social battery just drains a little faster than it used to. I think the bigger revelation is how much more outgoing you've become." I was happy to redirect the conversation back to her. I didn't like being on this side of a cross-examination, however innocent it may have been.

Autumn removed the steak from the bowl. "I wasn't that bad back then. Okay, maybe you're right. I guess you brought me out of my shell. Until you left."

And there it was. The elephant in the room. It was practically stomping all over our beef... Which she was now hammering with a meat tenderizer.

I placed a hand over hers. "Listen, Autumn, I..."

Her eyebrows tilted inward, as if she'd regretted her statement. She looked at the other students, who were already at their stoves in various stages of cooking. "Not here, Jamie."

I wanted to press, but she was right. This wasn't the place for it. I knew I'd have to address it soon enough.

Azalea interrupted my train of thought. "Now if you've finished beating that meat—"

Autumn let out a puff of air, and it was as if she'd forgotten about our sobering moment.

I elbowed her gently, my lips quirked as I whispered under my breath. "Be serious."

That only egged her on. "I don't know. Would you rather we tenderly stroked it? Or we could wank it. You would know better than I would." She rolled her lips inward and her body shook, as if she was bursting at the seams.

"This isn't jerk chicken. You need to have some finesse."

Autumn snorted at my bad joke and leaned across me again. I tensed as she brushed against my side. Hell, did this woman even know what she could still do to me? I took a centering breath, trying to push my ill-timed lust aside and focus on the meal. But there she was at every turn.

The scent of strawberries overwhelmed my senses with familiarity, but now there was an overlay of sunblock and the outdoors. Sucking my bottom lip into my mouth was the only way to keep my wandering lips and needy tongue off the only path they wanted to trailblaze: Autumn's neck. I could still remember the taste, even ten years later. I longed to learn more about her earthly sweetness, which had my head spinning.

Get it together. You only have a few more days.

"I'll take that." She grabbed the tongs right out of my daydreaming hands. I hadn't turned my steak like I'd meant to, but her hand brushed over mine and the meat no longer existed. Our eyes locked, and the tongs slipped from her fingers, both of us aggressively diving for the fallen utensil before it hit the ground. The tongs clattered, and in the madness, Autumn's elbow banged hard against the saucepan where our gravy was beginning to thicken.

"Shit!" She cried out at the contact, and the pan was in slow motion.

I tried to recover, grabbing the side of the pan with gazelle-like reflexes, just missing the handle. "Fuck, that's hot!" I yanked my hand back and the pot tipped, spilling the concoction across my shirt.

I pulled the material away with a startled noise, almost embarrassed by the sound that came out of me. Quickly I removed the sauce-covered shirt before it could burn me. I regained my composure and found Autumn's eyes were on my stomach the moment I looked up. Her gaze felt hotter than the sauce ever could.

"Like what you see?" I smirked, my eyebrows tilted toward her. Daring her. Autumn's cheeks flamed pink. I cocked my "I know you still want me" smile at her.

She huffed and grabbed my hand, careful not to touch the burn. "Don't be stupid. We're going to get this looked at."

Azalea had rushed over during the commotion, and was cleaning the gravy from the floor. She waved us off.

"I'm fine." I was still grinning, glad to know I wasn't the only one affected by this thing between us. "Unless this is a ploy to get me alone?" I teased.

But Autumn remained undeterred. Keeping hold of my hand, she led me out of the cooking class toward the front office. "Be warned, Jamie, I know every inch of these woods. It wouldn't be difficult to hide your body." The menacing threat forced a laugh from me, and a twinkling annoyance in her.

Leaves crunched under our feet as we walked side by side down the path. At some point she'd let go of my hand and I already missed it.

"So you've learned about my job, but I know nothing about yours," I said. The pain in my hand was already fading, and I was grateful for the slow pace we'd adopted so that we could continue our conversation.

"What do you want to know?"

"Are you lumberjacking a hundred percent of the time, or…"

She chuckled. "Lumberjacking's part of it. I also manage all the activities, promote, recruit staff, and help with the building of the camp," she offered, much more articulate than she was in our first conversation about her role here.

"That sounds like a big job."

Autumn shrugged. "It's not quite surgery or saving lives, but in its way, I think it helps."

Being here two days was already helping me sleep better. But I didn't think she was looking for a compliment in the moment, and I didn't want her to shut down. Instead, I focused on the breeze, which felt wonderful on my skin, up until I brushed her hand, wanting to reach out and grab it.

"Don't put yourself down. You don't have to be a doctor to have a worthwhile career." She let the compliment roll off her shoulders.

"Well, if you want to see me in action, I'm in charge of craft time later today, it's my last activity. And if you'd like, some of my friends and I will be having dinner after. You should come."

"That sounds great. I'll be there for both."

We walked toward the front office. "You know, before we see to this burn"—she nodded to my injured hand—"maybe we should find you a shirt."

I saw the thing clutched into a ball in her hand and wondered if I'd get that back.

"You'd want to hide all this?" I laughed and gestured toward myself.

She tried to hold back her smile, trying even harder not to look at my bare chest now that we were alone. "You really need to spend some time with Jack. You two would be perfect for each other."

Her smile was wide and teasing, but just like that, the spell was broken. Shit, I'd almost forgotten about the man she'd been laughing with during yoga just a few hours ago. Jack, the luckiest man in the world.

ELEVEN

Autumn

IT WAS JUST like a call from my dad and stepmom to remind me I was exceedingly happy for the two hundred and thirty miles of distance between us. During our conversation, they asked me the same old questions.

"When are you planning to get an actual job?"

"How long do you think this summer camp is actually going to be in business?"

"What kind of retirement program does a place that survives off predominantly middle-class liberal-arts-degree-holding attendees offer?"

I mentally cringed, squeezing my fists together as I tidied up the workspaces where campers would soon make fresh messes.

My biggest wish at the moment was that I'd get through to them. The more responsibility I took on, the less inclined they'd be to hope that I'd give up this dream of mine and *get my life together.* Instead, I was twenty-nine, reminding myself that my parents just didn't understand.

I'd told myself years ago that I was done hiding things that mattered about myself from them, but the conversation left me wondering if I was doing that again. No. I hadn't mentioned Jamie in our conversation, but I hadn't done that on purpose. So why did that make him feel like a dirty secret?

Maybe I'd subconsciously left him out of the conversation because I didn't want to remind them of a particularly embarrassing time in my life when I cried for months on end. I didn't need to hear about the days I'd holed up in my room to do homework, only leaving for extracurriculars and school until my miraculous turnaround after homecoming when I got my emotional shit together. Or I stuffed the sadness down. That was unimportant. I'd long ago learned that believing in forever was a pipe dream. That sweet words like "I love you" and "I'd do anything for you" didn't mean shit. People looked out for their own interests, and I reminded myself that over and over again.

In the beginning, my family had been big fans of my and Jamie's relationship. They'd loved him, which was easy, and they'd loved that we were in speech and debate together, which meant I had someone to help me navigate my new extracurricular activity. I was so anxious about my new surroundings the first few months of freshman year, I'd barely gotten out of the house, let alone gone to things like football games and dances. They'd been worried that I hadn't made any friends yet. Jamie, however, had been established at school. He'd been popular. And he'd had goals. These were all qualities they'd liked about him.

But things got more serious with time, and they couldn't handle that with my senior year fast approaching. Suddenly, my parents weren't big fans of our three-year-long relationship. They were also unhappy with the fact that he'd found a college in Southern California, six hours away from my dream school. We weren't banking on me getting into Stanford, but I'd applied to other prestigious colleges as well, and they were afraid that if I didn't get in and got into another school farther away, I'd turn it down. Putting UCLA on my backup list did me no favors with them either.

But it'd all worked out the way they wanted anyway. And now

I was working in a place I loved that didn't even require a degree, and they were beyond disappointed.

There was also the chance that telling them about Jamie's life would have resulted in them jumping down my throat even further, especially after learning he'd followed through with his plan. That he was a lawyer with a condo with actual amenities instead of a free-rent cabin in a forest with little more than a kitchenette.

It was pointless to debate with myself. He was only here for a week. This was temporary. *Temporary.*

"Hey." Nat looked over her shoulder, pausing as she unloaded some acrylic paints I planned to use for squeegee painting—a new method of madness that involved using drops of paint and a literal squeegee to spread the colors down a canvas. She'd loved my idea and jumped at helping me bring it to fruition.

I wondered if this was what Jamie would want to do when he showed up tonight. I was looking forward to it and tried not to read into things. "You doing okay?"

I recovered. "What? Yeah."

"I'm ready to craft the living daylights out of this place," came a voice I recognized. Jamie's friend Ren stood in the doorway like he'd entered a saloon, sunlight blazing behind his spread-armed form. He walked in with another man I assumed was from their pod, since I'd seen him and Lamar together multiple times. I explained the options to them: candle making, string art, projects that involved wine corks (of which we had plenty, what a surprise), and jewelry crafting. Ren pulled out a ring and flipped it between his fingers. There were always people who saw the option in the craft activity description and came prepared for one of my favorite activities: repurpose your old wedding band.

I pointed toward the jewelry soldering supplies and headed his way. This was one of my original ideas, back when I'd had more angst about my relationship with my birth mother. My ten-year-old self had realized she hadn't packed all of her things when she'd left, and I'd been working through my issues by repurposing that shit ever since.

Maybe I was being unfair. Or maybe she should have picked up her phone and talked to her daughter more than twice a year.

I shook out of my anger haze and focused on the people walking through the doors. This was more of a drop-in class. People came and went as they pleased, usually staying for longer than the time allotted. No two sessions were the same, and I enjoyed listening to conversations and seeing the wacky things campers came up with.

"How's your day been, Janna?" I asked the always chill blonde from my pod as she worked on a succulent cross-stitch. She was quieter, but bits of her personality had shone through in the day that I'd known her.

"Swell. I just came from baking. Kell-i was there too." Her eyes filled with something dark, her voice going deadpan. "I think I found my nemesis."

My eyes opened wide as her face didn't change. I'd never had nemeses in my pod before, let alone foes in the science of baking. I was fascinated.

"That's... Great," I said awkwardly as one of my pod members, Diego, came in through the building doors. Yet again, no Jamie. "Hi." I sounded altogether too cheery, trying to mask the little bit of fear she'd inspired. "The room is divided into sections, and the options are on the whiteboard. But if nothing appeals to you, a list of all available crafts is up front, and I can get stuff out for any project you're interested in."

Sitting next to a glass of white wine was Nat, who started pouring essential oils into a soap mold as Ren and the man I learned was Grant grabbed beers from the cooler I'd filled a few hours prior. I walked the room and stopped as Felicia explained soldering to a woman with a diamond ring.

Things were going well, but I wasn't nervous about that at all.

Turned out, adults liked to craft, especially when there was alcohol involved.

Ren plopped down at the jewelry table near the back, just where I happened to be grazing.

I decided to take my chance. "Hey, is Jamie meeting you here tonight?"

"He didn't say anything about coming." Ren shrugged. At the table next to him, Grant waved a bag of Gushers, beckoning him over. Ren abandoned his ring in favor of the fruit snack and joined Grant. "I still can't believe your ex sent you here to have some time to yourself."

I moved about the room, trying not to look like I was eavesdropping, but I couldn't help it. It was impossible not to find yourself absorbed in one of the many engrossing subjects campers spoke about, and this was a conversation I was particularly interested in.

Grant twisted a piece of cream rope to start a macrame plant pot holder. "She loved her time here."

Ren twisted one of Grant's ropes absentmindedly. "But, like... How does that relationship work? You two go out of your way to help each other vacation? What else do you do for each other? Swap watching the kids when you're going on dates?"

"How'd you know?" Grant ran his fingers over the terracotta container, measuring it against the string. "Though she's with someone new now, and she's a homebody, so she stays in more than anything. It makes her open to watching them when I go out myself. Her new boyfriend is great with our kids. I really like him."

"I just didn't realize you could have a relationship with your ex after..." Ren shifted in his seat. "My divorce has been contentious, I guess."

My ears perked up at that.

"Why do you think that is?" Grant had stopped what he was doing and gave him his full attention.

Ren blushed at the eye contact and looked as if he was thinking about it for the first time. "He and I are just..." He sighed. "There are a lot of problems we couldn't work through. And it's only gotten harder with lawyers involved."

Grant nodded as though he'd heard it before, his pot set aside as he faced Ren and put his hand over Ren's fidgeting one to reassure him. "Is it about things? Pets? Friends?"

Ren nodded. "Things and friends, I guess." He shrugged. "I wish it didn't sound that petty. What happened with you two?"

Grant turned toward Ren. "Our tastes and feelings evolved. We did couples counseling when we started to feel the changes, but after ten years, we realized we weren't happy together... Like that."

Images of hand holding and stolen kisses flashed in my head, and I shoved them down. The situations couldn't be more different. Jamie and I had only dated three years, and then we'd been separated for ten, not the other way around. There weren't feelings anymore, no matter how weird I felt around him. It wasn't justifiable for me to feel things after all this time.

"I think I'm having a hard time wrapping my head around you choosing to be friends with someone you used to be intimate with, especially after having painful memories together."

"I get that a lot. Actually, I get 'how can you be around her when she's happy with someone else?' a lot more. The fact of the matter is, I want her to be happy. I want us both to be happy, especially for the benefit of our kids. There's just nothing romantic there anymore. I love her, but I love her more like a best friend."

"Becoming friends with your ex..." Ren concluded. "What a novel concept."

I looked down at the yarn I'd been rolling and realized I had tangled it into a bunch of knots instead. I tossed the yarn onto the table with dead mismatched crafts. Was it possible for Jamie and me to be friends? After all this time?

The mean voice in my head told me no and that he'd bail on dinner, too, because he obviously didn't care about meeting my friends, or about me, or about anything but himself.

TWELVE

Jamie

"It's okay to have big feelings, Adam," I told my nephew, talking him down from a crying outburst of epic proportions. "You can tell me about them any time."

Ren gave my phone back when he'd seen my family was calling. He'd made me promise not to sink into my workaholic tendencies, and I was making an effort to comply. The emails could wait.

"But I want to *see* you, Uncle Jamie."

That sent a dagger straight to my heart. But I'd resolved to do better. "It's all right, little guy. You're going to see me in four weeks, remember? How many is that?"

He held out his fingers, showing me four.

"Exactly. That's really soon." It was amazing how much time and space didn't matter when it came to my nephew's love. We spoke every month by video chat, but it didn't go unnoticed that I needed to put more of an effort in. Monthly calls might not be sufficient now that Adam was older and asking for me.

"And your mom said if you got dressed and went to dinner, you'd get to have a popsicle when you got home," I tried.

That brought out a smile. "A blue one?"

I nodded, hoping I wasn't lying. "Yep. A blue one." What if they were creamsicles?

"Okay, I gotta go." He dropped the phone on the ground.

"Thank you," Marley's voice said from above, and I got a great view of her double chin. I fought the brotherly urge to point that out. "I know you're on vacation, but he's been having a rough time this week."

"I meant what I said. You can call me anytime."

"But you're supposed to be taking a break from obligations, not—"

"You and the kids are not an obligation."

But did it feel like that to them? Was I giving off that vibe? The dagger dug its way deeper.

"Love you, Jamie." Marley probably sensed the depth of my silence. A crash sounded on the other end of the line, and she looked away. "Shit, I gotta go."

Between the sounds of Adam's fit and the yelping of their chihuahua, now wasn't the time to bring up my ex-girlfriend's reappearance. Maybe next time.

"Love you too—"

And she was gone.

☆ ☆ ☆

AUTUMN'S HAPPINESS was irrefutable when she was in her domain. I watched on my walk across the mess hall as she and Jack laughed together. They were clearly comfortable with each other, and I wondered how long they'd been together.

Ren and I took seats across from them, and it felt so *high school cafeteria*. It transported me to a time when I'd sat as close as a sardine nestled next to her.

A lot of things were different now, but some things had never changed, and I wondered again about her life. How had the last decade played out for her?

Autumn's laugh brought me back to the present. She was happy in this new life and, if I was being honest, happier than I'd ever seen her.

Sometimes, I imagined how different our lives would have been if I'd made the selfish choice. If I had agreed with her back then, just said *okay*. But what did I know at nineteen? Probably not enough to keep her. I could do this, though, keep her now, be a friend to her like I should have been all those years ago.

Jack was the luckiest guy in the universe, and he seemed good to her. His carefree, playful shove told me he knew it.

"Hey, sorry for missing craft night. I—"

"It's fine." Her abruptness put me on edge, but Autumn moved on and introduced us. "So this curmudgeon is Jack." She gestured to the imposing, long-haired blond man next to her. It made me wonder how the two of us measured up if we stood side by side. And who would win at arm wrestling.

"I think I saw you at yoga this morning," he said, with a bright smile and cool confidence. "Some of us were awake," Jack teased Autumn again, and I shook his hand, wanting to make a good impression.

"Why do I put up with you again?" Autumn's words were tinged with mock exasperation.

Jack elbowed her. "Maybe since I brought you here in the first place?"

"You're just going to lord that over me forever."

He nodded, as if to say, "duh."

Autumn turned her focus back to me. "Jack, this is Jamie. We knew each other in high school."

She didn't say we were together, just that we *knew* each other.

Ren looked between Autumn and me with sudden interest. "Wait, you get to call him Jamie?" He whipped his head around, eyes like saucers, waiting for me to explain.

She looked perplexed. "What do you call him?"

"James?"

Autumn's face contorted. "That makes you sound like a lawyer who hasn't touched grass in years because he's cooped up in his office."

"I am a lawyer... *Hey.*"

Jack was also looking between Autumn and me, and something passed when he met Autumn's eyes. He quirked his eyebrows. "This is Jamie?"

"Yeah. The one and only." I did my best not to sound smug.

Jack's eyes focused on me for a moment, as if he wanted to ask something but seemed to change his mind. "I would have paid good money to see a teenage Autumn stumbling over her words on the debate team."

"Stumbling? More like ripping people to shreds and taking no prisoners."

Autumn blushed, and Jack gave her a look, but I couldn't decipher it.

"Like that time at the Hollygrove Debate?" I asked.

"You mean at districts? When we argued that the infrastructure of Seattle could withstand a zombie apocalypse?"

I explained to our clueless counterparts. "Our argument was that we could take the monorail to the Space Needle, and the zombies wouldn't be able to operate the elevator to the top."

At the time, I couldn't believe how passionate she got about something so silly, but her energy and hard facts had won us the debate. That day, no one had been prepared for our level of dedication or our zombie apocalypse knowledge. That was also when I'd learned Autumn had never been to the top of the Space Needle, and so I'd rectified that immediately as a reward for our win.

Ren looked from her to me and back. "So you'd trap yourselves in the Space Needle?"

We both laughed, as if we were the only ones in on the joke.

"There's enough food and drink and a view of the entire city to see where to go next." Autumn chuckled. "Plus, we'd know how to fortify shit, obviously."

I brought up another classic. "My other favorite debate was about two songs by the same indie artist spanning decades and which had the bigger social impact and why."

We'd debated the lyrics, bars, and overall genius. Both songs were incredible. I tried not to look as Autumn's hand found itself on my forearm for the briefest moment before she cradled her chin.

"Later, I'll play the songs for you. Their haunting melodies remind me of that new tune you were working on the other night." Autumn mimed playing a guitar.

Great. And he played guitar.

Jack, to his credit, immediately tried to change the subject. "That's really Leo's thing. You know, Mr. One-man Band," he explained to Ren and me. "He always jokes that all he needs to complete the ensemble is a tambourine. He was so high that night." Autumn started laughing at Jack's mention of a tambourine. She was about to explain, to clue us in on the inside joke, when Ren spoke up.

"Stop already. I'm not used to this. I'm never on the outside of an inside joke," Ren griped before waving his fork between Autumn and Jack. "Tell us instead, how did you two meet?"

I didn't know if I wanted to hear the details. At least Autumn was with someone like him. He made her happy, clearly, but did she need to brag about him this whole damn dinner?

"Freshman year, the coffee shop on 5th?" Autumn looked at Jack, who shrugged in agreement, his mouth full.

"Hey. Sorry I'm late." Gia approached our table in a flurry as she pushed the tangle of red curls from her face. Dramatic eyeliner highlighted her jade-green eyes that lit up as she sidled up next to Jack, who adjusted himself toward her, welcoming her closer. Gia kissed Jack, and I knew I'd been way off.

"We met there, but the inflatable screen showing the double

feature of *Raiders of the Lost Ark* and *The Mummy* was our first friendship date," Jack corrected, pulling Gia into his side where she tucked nicely. "And what, we're going on two years since you stumbled into camp after taking care of those animal deathtraps all day, right?" he asked Gia with a smirk.

She leaned away from him, affronted. "They're called horses," Gia admonished, unable to hold back her smile. "Sometimes, I wished I was still an intern in Wildwood. Homemade s'mores by my new crush after work was the best perk."

Gia meeting Jack here at the campfire, to check out what Camp Starlight was all about made sense.

Jack hugged her side. "It's like you were always supposed to find me here."

"Hard having to find you over and over again, since we're apart months at a time." Gia's tone lost its playfulness. His face fell, but he recovered quickly as she kissed his cheek. "Sorry, I just miss you, babe." She gave him a smile, and the tension lines in Jack's forehead relaxed once again.

"Miss you too." He pulled her in even closer.

Ren jumped in to lighten the mood. "When was our first friendship date?" he asked, as if I could ever forget.

"Easy. Your first day. I think you told me you had access to my schedule and that I couldn't get out of taking you out for a drink to celebrate."

Ren had that way about him. He always knew I needed a little bit of a push to socialize and take care of myself, and he was happy being the one to tug me in the right direction. Case in point: camp.

"A scandalous office affair, I'd imagine," Autumn teased, and we all laughed.

"Songs will be written about this bromance," he told her with all seriousness. "You know, Jamie's a big deal back at the office. About to become senior associate and everything."

Autumn raised an eyebrow. Did everyone else notice that he was directly addressing her?

"I'm not surprised," she said sincerely. "I'm sure he'll be running the place soon enough."

It suddenly felt a hundred degrees in here. I resisted the urge to fan myself. "I don't know about that..."

Autumn focused her attention on me and the world fell away, making the lull in the otherwise boisterous mess hall obvious.

"It's too quiet here. Maybe we should see if the one-man band takes requests?" I asked.

We all looked for Leo, but he was nowhere to be found. Autumn and Gia began chatting about Gia's week, different animals and places she'd gone to help. Turned out, Gia had found a new job doing house calls and equestrian center visits in the Greater Portland area.

The knot in my gut eased. Any tension lines I'd been carrying had probably also left the building. Jack and Autumn were friends, best friends, and based on their interactions, they had an easy camaraderie that I had only come close to experiencing, and that person sat right next to me. How had I never seen it with Ren? I knew then that I needed to do more work to make our friendship thrive.

I'd promised Ren we'd play bingo for the night's activity. We took our plates to the correct bins and headed out, but I couldn't stop thinking of my luck tonight after learning about Jack and Gia's relationship. It was wrong, but it didn't stop me from feeling high as a kite.

"B-10," Felicia called out.

We were playing a bougie twist on bingo, with prizes like

bottles of wine and expensive chocolates, the grand prize being a stay at a winery on the other side of the mountain.

Too bad Ren and I weren't paying attention. I hadn't played bingo before and was having a great time until Ren started delving into my past life, but it was time to open up.

"So, *Jamie*. Can I call you that too?"

"Don't give me that look. It was high school. Of course the pretty girl got to call me whatever she liked."

"The pretty girl you *dated*."

"She was an all-star athlete, on student council, and the most challenging person I ever went head to head with. I didn't stand a chance."

"Bet you still wouldn't." He snickered as he marked another spot on his bingo sheet. I didn't know how he was paying attention.

"I wouldn't take that bet," I agreed, realizing I'd admitted too much thanks to whiskeys number three and four.

"What were you like in high school, anyway? Let me guess, you had that same *all-work, no-play* ambition that I love so much about you?"

A smile tugged at my lips. I'd worked a lot in high school, sure, maintained top grades, but back then... "More like the do-anything-for-a-laugh type."

He gasped. "Really? Tell me more."

Regaling Ren was easy. He was a great listener and would pipe in with his own stories. My favorite was how he'd organized the senior prank at his high school—setting off confetti and glitter bombs in the teacher's lounge and cafeteria. "Teachers still talk about it to this day."

"They do not."

"Well, my brother's a teacher there, and he still does. Blames me for the glitter he gets on his shoes."

"That's the brother that windsurfs?"

"Yeah. He's the cool one. Even lets me call him by his nickname, Pooh Bear, like my mom calls him. That's why he's my favorite." He looked me dead in the eyes.

"You manipulative bastard." I knew exactly what he was on about.

"Are you telling me that sexy lumberjack is the only one who gets to call you Jamie?"

Oh my god, he did not call Autumn "sexy lumberjack."

"Sexy lumberjack has a name and doesn't pester me about whether I do briefs while in my briefs when I go home."

Ren's entire body shook with laughter over our inside joke, referencing a past client who had hit on me every chance she got.

"Well, Jamie sounds like a person who would do briefs in their briefs, and I want to be friends with him... James, however..."

"Fine. Call me Jamie," I conceded.

His head dipped nervously. "I know we're joking about it, but you have experience now. Do you think you can be friends with an ex? Grant has had me thinking, and I realized I kind of wish things weren't completely over with Zachary. We used to be best friends."

"I don't know if you would call what I'm going through 'experience,' but yeah, I think it can work. I hope it can work." I shrugged. Ren stared at me as if he could see right through me, and it made me want to sink back inside my shell, but I fought it anyway. "Autumn and I were close back then, and seeing her now... It's just a lot. But I realized today that I'll take whatever I can get."

"You sound like you loved her," Ren noted, in a moment of seriousness I wasn't used to from him.

The word *love* sounded so wrong in the past tense, but it was the truth, so I nodded.

THIRTEEN

Autumn

"HOLY SHIT," I whisper-shouted as I reemerged from the icy lake.

I never got used to the feeling of the first drop into Lake Starlight, whose dark blue waters beckoned me. It was a windy night, and it was an adjustment to get used to the temperature, but if anyone were to ask me what my favorite spot at camp was, I'd tell them it was right here, hands down. I loved to swim, but I loved the feeling of cleansing myself from the day and the world around me. It was far colder at night, but that was always the moment I chose to take a dip and clear my head.

When it came to Jamie, I figured the best thing I could do was literally cool off.

Normally, I'd have a swimsuit, but I'd foregone it after doing my nightly check at the construction site to make sure no one was messing around or damaging the work we'd done. It was a rarity to find someone there after warnings and wishes from Leo and Hazel, but if there were interlopers, they were usually doing something harmless, like having a drink on half-formed structures or looking at the stars. Hell, even I'd done it myself a couple of dozen times.

The walk back was always quiet and allowed me time to clear

my head. We didn't use the dock I liked to swim off for activities, and it was far from the pods, which was great because it gave me the peace I was looking for at the end of the night.

With each stroke I made, the cool waters enveloped me, soothing my mind. The familiarity of our camp nestled against the expansive lake brought me solace. It was a sanctuary where I could swim and immerse myself in tranquility, far removed from the crowded lanes at the college gym I used to frequent. As I looked up at the clear sky, a sense of wonder brought me peace. I continued the rest of my swim in backstroke, letting my restless thoughts settle.

As I observed the graceful flock of birds above me, all traces of stress melted away, but it only lasted so long. It wasn't a few seconds after I did a twenty-five-yard lap and somersault underwater that questions flooded my mind. Questions I had little time to get answers to. How did he fill his spare time? Did he like his job, his home, his life? Had he enjoyed college after we broke up? That one stung a little to think about, but the grown-up side of me hoped he had. The less mature side wished he'd wondered about me now and then. And maybe pined just a little.

I floated on my back, my fingers dangling as I pondered this, until I heard muffled laughter and righted myself immediately.

"You know you want to," someone said.

Shit. I moved quickly, trying not to splash too much as I made my way to the pylons.

"I am not going to ask him if he wants to Netflix and chill in the middle of the forest. Besides, no one uses that phrase anymore. Which goes to show how long it's been for you since you've tried dating, you recluse."

"Okay, then, hear me out: you do the yawning arm around shoulders thing—"

Oh god.

"No wonder you don't have a girlfriend."

It was Ren and Jamie.

I didn't know how I'd missed them. They must have been at the ax range. The axes and bows were put away, but it was an open, isolated field. *Fuck*.

"It's a classic. Or you could—" Jamie stopped talking.

I tried to see him, but I had no view.

"Or I could what?" Ren said. "Jamie? Hello?"

"You could just ask him out. He lives in Tacoma—that's so close to us. But you can't miss your opportunity now, especially when he's living ten feet from you."

Their voices drifted off, and I sighed in relief, swimming around for another five minutes before two feet stood above me on the dock.

"Breaking the rules? I see I had a good influence on you."

I looked up and sighed. "Hi, Jamie," I said guiltily. I hoped the dark water provided enough cover for me, but it wasn't like he hadn't seen the goods before.

"Autumn, Autumn, Autumn." His shit-eating grin practically lit up the lake. "You know the rules. No swimming without a buddy."

"That's without a lifeguard, idiot. So, if you're not trained, you should probably just..." I waved my hand in a *move along* gesture.

"Yeah, well, there's safety in numbers."

"And there's annoyance in clichés," I joked, pushing my damp hair behind my ear. He was in gym shorts and a hoodie. It took me back to when he'd worn a similar outfit on game days. That was what you got to see when your boyfriend was always on the go and constantly playing sports. When I was younger, I'd wondered why sophomore him had decided to date a quiet freshman like me. He'd had so much going for him, and I hadn't fit the mold of a popular guy's girlfriend. "How'd you even find me?"

"Maybe don't leave a pile of clothes out in the open."

"So you're saying you saw clothes and said, 'Let's see who's naked?' Wow, creeper."

"First off, I'm not trying to spy on some random skinny-dipper. I knew it was you. I recognized your shoes." *Shit.* That was what I got for having neon pink running shoes. "And second off, I've already seen you naked."

A burning sensation ran through me as blood rushed to my cheeks. We'd avoided talking about this part of our past his entire stay, but now he'd thrown it out there, and it filled me with images of a younger us tangled together in the backs of cars and spare bedrooms at parties, desperate for any moment we could find. He'd brought me out of my shell in more ways than one.

Jamie took off his shoes. Then his shorts.

My eyes opened wide with surprise. "What are you doing?"

"Contemplating our place in this vast universe." His shit-eating grin told me he wasn't doing that.

I ignored the ludicrousness of that sentence. "You don't need to be in your *boxers* to do that, Jamie."

"I can go if you really want me to—" He faked like he'd stop removing his shirt before looking to his right. Whatever he saw had him yanking the fabric over his head and grabbing both our clothes and shoes, discarding them on the rocks out of view before rushing to the ladder and dropping down.

"What?" I whispered quickly.

"I heard something." He cringed as he felt the cool water and lifted his finger to his mouth. No words passed between us as we listened intently. Then I heard hooves. I lifted my head to confirm.

"It's a deer, you dork." I splashed him, laughing loudly.

He splashed me back before diving down and swimming away from me. Thank god, because I'd forgotten my sense of propriety and quickly remembered I didn't need him seeing my naked extremities. It was going to be difficult. Doing that while treading water wasn't easy.

I watched this handsome thirty-year-old enjoying himself like he was a teenager again, this time bathed in moonlight. Suddenly, an image of one of my favorite moments with him popped into my head. Six of us had broken into the pool one winter night when I was sixteen.

The risk factor of being caught had been high back then, and even though it was my stomping ground, if we'd been found out, I would have gotten detentions at best, a suspension at worst. But it'd been worth it. He'd brought out the more adventurous side of me. That night, we'd swam together in our own little world, ignoring our friends and holding each other close as we drifted in chlorinated water.

I remember wishing we'd had it to ourselves, and here we were again.

He swam back. "What are you doing out here alone?"

"I do this most nights." By myself. "There isn't exactly a lap pool."

"So you still swim?" He referred to my time on the swim team. Jamie looked down into deep waters, his breathing drowned out by the small breeze around us.

"Yeah, I still swim." I nodded slowly. Every time he realized something about me that he remembered from back then, he went silent, as if he was going inside himself. It filled me with the same anxious need to make him feel better. It was a strange urge. I hadn't expected to feel that way for him again. He wasn't mine to worry about anymore. "You have to stop doing this to yourself." *To us.*

"I can't help it. Every memory feels like it wasn't—"

"That long ago, I know." I shivered at the thought. When these feelings washed over me, they made it hard to remember that enough time had passed that I was over it. Over him.

Jamie nodded, biting his lip as he stared at the stars above us and then looked at me heartbreakingly. "I want to know more." He didn't raise his voice above a whisper.

"More?"

"About what you've been up to. I love goofing off, but it doesn't negate the fact that there's still so much I don't know. A lot has changed over the last ten years."

"Oh." *That.* Of course, he was interested, and admittedly, I was just as intrigued by what he'd been up to since leaving me. "How about you go first?"

He didn't press. He didn't know how hard this would be for me to bare myself to him, give him a bit more of myself after years of dead air.

"Me? Well, I stuck with UCLA for undergrad. Moved back to Seattle for law school.

Then I was immediately hired by the company I'm at now."

"Wow." It was impressive, really. I'd had plans, too, and I'd deviated from every single one of them, but he'd followed through like I was supposed to. "You did the thing."

"I did the thing." He nodded, but his expression didn't demonstrate pride in his accomplishments. I couldn't figure out what he was thinking, and I wanted to know so much more. "You already know I'm an uncle now. And I'm still living in Washington."

There was a twinge of sadness there, as though he wondered if he'd made the wrong decision. It felt so unlike him. He was always the guy with his eye on the prize, much like I'd been back then, but now that his goal was within reach, it seemed like he was unhappy. Like he was missing something.

"And now you're about to be promoted."

"Now I *might* be promoted, yeah."

"You'll get it." It may not have been my place to say, but I had this gut sensation. I'd been fighting this persistent feeling that I still understood him, yet I couldn't possibly. I had to remind myself that we'd had just a few interactions, and no matter how familiar things were, that meant nothing.

"What about you?"

"Well, I did the Stanford thing for long enough to rack up the down payment on a house..."

"And how long is that?"

"A little under three years. I dropped out, and it was the best decision I've ever made. I worked random jobs for a few years, and then this came up."

It made me uncomfortable to be talking about myself this way. To show him I'd made the right choice, to demonstrate my success.

He beamed at me, a twinkle in his eye. "I'm happy for you."

He looked at me with an intensity that had me sinking into myself, and I immediately blabbered on to take away its power because I straight up couldn't handle it. "I just didn't fit there, you know? I was getting good grades and all, but despite making friends, I still felt so alone. Coupled with the fact that I just didn't know what I wanted to do with my life and it was a recipe for disaster." Not that being in school blew up in my face or anything. That came later, after I told my parents. "I think I knew that the doctor path wasn't for me by the end of freshman year. But I kept on going to the point that I—"

"Burned out."

"Yeah, exactly."

He nodded slowly, almost as if he were putting a puzzle together, and I wanted to pick his brain so badly. Was he happy? I kept getting a mixed read on him. He was on his way to achieve his goal, but it sounded like, apart from Ren, he was living in Seattle alone. Back in school, he'd thrived when he was surrounded by other people. It was like it powered him. Now his energy felt... Off.

I stared deep into his eyes, and he opened his mouth to say something, but there was yet another commotion. We both jerked our heads toward the noise. I wanted so badly to know what he was about to ask, but I knew what those sounds meant. I couldn't make out what they were saying, but they were absolutely coming in our direction. Several of them, if I heard right.

"Goddammit." I sighed in frustration. "Do none of you go to your cabins when you're supposed to be in bed?" I sounded like I was talking about a group of wild youths.

Jamie swam under the dock, holding his hand out to pull me closer so that I could grab the ladder next to him.

Please don't let them come here.

"I think most of us are used to being allowed to be up as late as we want," he whispered as my wish was dashed.

"Dammit."

He moved his hand down the ladder, grabbing the one rung below the water. There was a high likelihood they would see our hands if they came to the edge. I moved closer to him and overlapped his hand by accident, disentangling them as if I'd been burned. There was space a few inches away, and it'd have to be enough.

He avoided looking down, as though seeing my lower half would turn him to stone, and I would have laughed if not for our potential audience. His gaze went up as the campers sat on the dock, beer bottles clinking together, placed on hard-worn wood. That was when I realized we were going to be stuck for a while. I imagined the spirited group of them diving into the water, joining us unknowingly, and cringed. Them jumping in wasn't even my worst worry. The paranoid part of me worried that the wood from above might collapse on us, but I kept focusing on the fact that our pinkies were touching on the rectangular wooden pegs.

"Okay," one said, I assumed gulping beer. "Favorite counselor. Go."

Jamie's legs drifted into mine, our thumbs barely touching.

"Nat's the hottest," another voice chimed in. Several voices grunted in agreement. There had to be at least six of them based on the feet hanging over the edges of the dock. "Did you know Nat's last name is Breckenridge? Like, one of *those* Breckenridges."

"What? I thought she was just insta-famous. You know I followed her before I got here?"

"We're getting off-topic here. I asked who everyone's *favorite* counselor was." Another voice joined in. "But in response to that ignorant statement, I say *hell no*, it's no contest. Autumn is the hottest by far."

"Fuck, she is gorgeous," another voice—this time a woman—lauded.

It was weird hearing people pointing out my attractiveness, but if it was going to happen, I wasn't complaining that it was right in front of my ex-boyfriend. In fact, I preferred it to go down that way.

"Did you see those biceps? She looks like she can bench press me, and I can only imagine her stamina—"

My heart rate picked up in anticipation of what else they might say. Jamie looked like he was ready to climb out of the water and shut down the conversation, but I squeezed his hand to stop him. It wasn't getting obscene yet, but I really hoped it stopped there.

"So wait, you want a woman to bench press you?" A fresh bottle was opened. "That's what you're looking for in a love interest?"

"Not necessarily. Now, if you'd asked me if I wanted her to be able to suffocate me with her thighs—"

Laughter broke out. I couldn't help it. I joined them. Jamie rolled his eyes and smiled.

"I want to explore more of this place. Did you hear there's a make out tree?"

There was a clinking of bottles and some side chatter. Jamie mouthed, "Make out tree?" to me, and I nodded and shrugged. The things he didn't know about this camp.

"Yeah, didn't Monica and Marisol already christen it?"

My eyebrows went up, and Jamie watched me with rapt eyes as I mentally tracked what they were saying. I didn't care about being intrusive. Hell, they'd stood over me for god's sake. Finding good gossip was an art form, and my allegiance was to the shipping board and its veracity, not to these unsuspecting campers. Also, I needed information to win this game. Monica and Marisol had been my sleeper couple—one I had added on at the final due date, so I was very pleased.

"I heard it was Tara and Crispin."

"I didn't know they were hooking up."

"I thought Tara was with Leroy."

"No, Leroy is with Priscilla."

"Who's Leroy?"

Jamie snorted quietly, and I nearly lost it. This gossip would be harder to decipher, but I'd wade my way through it. The takeaway was that even with all my distractions, I knew who all these people were. I was proud.

That pride dissipated as wind-touched waves started picking up, pushing me closer to him. I instantly covered my chest and peaked nipples, right before pushing into his body. I swear I could feel the hem of his underwear up against my thigh, our feet bumping into each other. His eyebrows went up, and his free hand shot to my hip, helping to hold me back. Except I didn't think he remembered how little clothing I was wearing. The waves didn't let up, however, so he kept his hand there, staring deep into my eyes while I bit my lip. A million questions went unsaid. Did I want him to touch me like this? Did he like it? If I moved just a little bit closer, would I be able to tell how much he liked it?

His hand flexed beneath mine as he gripped the ladder tighter. The water rippled around us and pushed me a smidge closer to him. One more wave and we'd be chest to chest, and the wind definitely wasn't letting up anytime soon.

"Fuck, it's windy," one voice said, their feet raising off the ledge. The rest of the feet followed, and soon they were walking away from us.

One set of footsteps stopped. "Hey, look—"

Another set. "What?"

We both held our breath and waited as someone presumably saw our clothing. We were about to be outed.

"Nothing," the voice responded, feet carrying on as before.

And then they left us, as if they hadn't just created tension between two unsuspecting people who were relearning how to be around each other after a decade of nothingness. Jamie and I didn't move for a full minute after they'd gone, until we knew the coast was clear.

"That was close," he whispered, his hand still on my side.

"Yeah," I breathed out, but my failure to speak at a normal volume had nothing to do with almost being caught and everything to do with his skin touching mine. A little lower and he'd be touching me right where I wanted him. "Are you okay?"

"Okay?" Nothing had happened to him to warrant the question. "I'm good. Are you?"

"Yeah," I blurted. "I'm good." I didn't know how I got the words out because his thumb was caressing circles into my side. He must not have noticed he was doing it.

"Did you recognize the voices?" he asked.

"No." Thank goodness they weren't from my pod.

"That's too bad. Sounds like there's a man desperate to have his head squeezed—"

I stopped covering my chest to splash him as we separated. He burst into laughter. I pressed my hand to his pectoral and shoved him back, but he barely moved thanks to the rung he still held. He didn't stop laughing. The wind breezed around us, and I winced as it weaved through my loose hair. Jamie pushed it behind my ear and smiled. Could you melt in a body of water? Because I was about to find out.

FOURTEEN

Jamie

FUCK. Why did I do that?

I was only hurting myself. And I'd been doing it the whole night. She'd admitted that our memories still felt fresh, and if it was anything like I felt, they were right there, ready to steal my attention at any moment. Reminders of happy times mixed with past mistakes. I couldn't believe I almost asked her the question I'd been avoiding the entire time I'd been in her presence: does that mean you still feel the pain I caused when I broke your heart?

She didn't have feelings for me anymore, but I still wanted to ask her if it hurt her when she looked at me, because as much as it sucked to admit, it fucking hurt when I looked at her. The idea couldn't be tamped down. It spread through me like a drop of watercolor on paper, expanding wider and wider until it reached every edge and corner. Apparently, I'd become a masochist, probably because it was what I deserved.

Autumn's shallow breaths were killing me and filling me with more pernicious thoughts like, *What would happen if I ran my thumb across her bottom lip?* and *What if I learned the locations of all of her tattoos?* She'd run away, that was for sure. And remembering that made things so much worse. I'd been sporting a heart hard-on since seeing her throw those axes.

Autumn's hair almost looked brown when it was wet like this in the dark of night. She was so beautiful with her tresses in damp plaits grazing her shoulders, small drips slowly cascading down the sides of her face. I nearly forgot that she was naked under the dark water, but I was fairly sure *she* was well aware. She took on this timid-like quality as she stared at me after touching her below the pylons. My fingers seared from the contact.

"We should—" we said in unison, breaking the moment before things got too serious. We chuckled, yet again in unison, and I realized what I needed to do. I needed to get out of here, and I had to be the one to make the first move.

"Yeah, just give me a minute," I responded without thinking.

What she might have thought I required a minute for, I wasn't sure. But I needed to redistribute the blood from my lower half, which, despite the coolness of the water, had been a problem since we'd moved under this dock.

She dipped her shoulders underneath the water and popped back up, absentmindedly drifting closer, but I touched her shoulder to hold her back.

"No, I, like, can't physically swim right now. Matter of fact, get away from me." It sounded like a joke.

Recognition spanned her face before Autumn burst into laughter, and more drops fell, this time creating ripples in the water between us. She didn't stop laughing, speaking through failed breaths. "At least the effect you had on me doesn't mean I'll sink to the bottom of the lake."

Hilarious.

Wait, did she just admit I was affecting her too?

"You always did have a shitty sense of humor." Lies.

Her laughter didn't abate. "Okay, horndog. I'm going now, so look away. Think like a noodle."

I placed my head in my hands, sinking into the water without thinking. Think like a noodle? Who the fuck was this girl?

She didn't stop laughing, and it echoed off the water. She was going to wake up the entire camp and expose me, which would add another layer of mortification. Then she went silent.

"Close your eyes." Her tone brooked no argument.

I didn't even think. I just did as she asked. Then I heard her climb out of the water. Oh, yeah. She wanted me to close my eyes so I didn't see her naked. Thank fuck, because if I had looked, I would never be getting out of here.

We walked on the well-worn path just far enough away from each other that our arms didn't touch, both of us in clothes that grew damper the more they soaked up the water from our wet bodies. The camp wasn't exactly quiet. It sounded like other people were enjoying themselves around pod campfires, which crackled from the heat on mostly dry logs.

The night air was blissfully rejuvenating as we strolled. Peaceful sounds emanated from crickets and frogs along the way as Lake Starlight danced in its bowl. I took a deep breath in. This was what magic felt like.

But Autumn was so quiet it was starting to get to me.

"I didn't mean to jump in like that earlier," I tried just above a whisper.

"I know," she deadpanned. "You heard a deer."

Her face was completely neutral, reminding me of my funny girlfriend of the past. I was probably reading into it, but I didn't know that it affected me back then like it did now.

"I don't like it when animals see me in my underwear, Autumn. You know that."

There was no point in whispering when she laughed as loud as she did.

"I forgot how funny you are." Her rueful smile had me wondering what was going on behind those glassy eyes.

I didn't have a response to that. A long-lost feeling tightened my chest, as though I'd been missing something for more than was reasonably acceptable. I used to be a lot more lighthearted. Maybe it just came with being older. Maybe it was for another reason.

I made my strides slower, and she met me without saying anything. It felt as if I was living under a ticking clock. Who knew how many more minutes until we'd be to her cabin, one pod over from mine?

"How did this place come to be, anyway?" I asked, genuinely curious.

"It's kind of a long story."

"And we have kind of a long walk."

Autumn nodded as her foot broke a branch, but she took a beat before continuing, almost as if she was resigned to giving me what I wanted. "After Stanford, I worked some odd jobs. I waited tables for a bit, did the barista thing—as you now know, that's how I met Jack. He came in frequently. He's addicted to caffeine. He was a contractor and did a bunch of odd jobs around Palo Alto and Stanford and was on a site nearby. We hit it off quickly and were friends for a couple of years before Hazel and Leo reached out." She twirled a piece of her hair between her fingers and continued. "He knew Hazel from his hometown, so they were already friends. They told me about their vision, and I couldn't sleep the next few nights thinking about it. It was such an amazing idea, building something like this. Constructing some-thing that would bring joy to people's lives. I mean, I might not have dreamed that big back then, but I've been told so many times over the years about the magic of this camp that I have to believe it."

I imagined what it'd be like, me working through my first years as a lawyer, her creating something like this and coming away as she was now: happy. It hurt hearing about these things I had no part in —because I *would* have been involved, cheering her on from the sidelines and showing up to support her as she built this wonderful thing. I could picture everything as if I were staring through a department store window, watching them decorate for Christmas and knowing I'd never be able to afford to go inside.

"The camp was Hazel and Leo's baby, but they couldn't have done this without me and Jack. And they've recognized that a million times over."

This was new. Autumn had always been overly humble, never taking credit for what she deserved, never admitting she was crucial to anything. Back on the debate team, she'd acted like she was just a part of a group, but she'd been the one winning at meets over and over. I loved that this part of her had changed.

"Is it weird to say that I'm proud of you for what you built here?" I cleared my rapidly closing throat. "The more time I spend in this place, the more I'm amazed by it. You did a remarkable thing."

Even in the dark, I could see the slight blush on her cheeks. She didn't respond right away, as though she was trying to fight downplaying it, but she chose not to.

"Thank you. It wasn't easy."

"And you like being here? Like, that's your plan?"

She looked at me, a wistfulness to her stare. She was feeling me out. I had to fix whatever negative thoughts permeated her consciousness.

"Not that you need a plan, but if it is, it seems like a good one." Still nothing. "This camp is obviously successful."

"Tell that to my parents." The words were a whisper on her lips that she corrected quickly, almost as if she hoped I hadn't heard. The Autumn I knew had been desperate for her dad and stepmom's approval, so I could only imagine how things had gone over after she'd dropped out. But she'd made this decision anyway. Yet another way in which she'd changed. "It is successful. In our first year, we sold out. Now we have a waiting list a mile long."

"Ren told me. He was surprised he got us in." He'd used it as a reason I couldn't back out "But Nancy and Robert must be impressed with how this place is doing, right?"

"They haven't visited, actually." She turned her head away, as if the dark trees were more interesting than the conversation we were having.

"I'm sorry, Autumn. That must hurt," I said dumbly. That was shocking. They'd been wrapped up in everything she did, whether it was seeing her debate or going to her swim meets. Was this a message they were trying to send?

"I don't think it's so much about being disappointed as being too busy to prioritize it. But regardless, I've drilled the point home that I'm happy."

"Well, they're missing out," I said, wanting to hug her but knowing that she'd never loved drawing more attention to herself after opening up. "What matters is you are proud of what you've accomplished. They have to see that. Anyone would."

We'd been walking slower since we started talking, almost as if we couldn't do two things at once, and I was worried she'd start walking faster, so I brought up the first thing that came into my head.

"Can I ask..."

She slowed her steps. "Ask what?"

"For those of you who are here all summer, it must be hard to —" I rubbed the back of my neck.

"You mean how does one get a partner when they're traipsing through the woods all year?"

We had always been in sync with each other, but I wondered how transparent I'd been for her to draw that conclusion that quickly.

Autumn nodded slowly and sucked in a breath. "It's really, really hard."

"But Jack and Gia..."

"Are the exception. We joke about how the man who's afraid of horses ended up with the horse girl." She chuckled. "He says it was fate and that he was lucky Gia stopped by at all. She had a week left of her internship, and they got together," she said, as if it made the most sense in the world.

"*A week?*"

"A lot can happen in a week." I'd heard that once before.

I wondered if there wasn't a hidden meaning to her words. And I couldn't say I wasn't wishing for this week to change things. How I wanted them to change was a question I wasn't willing to ask myself.

She dove in quickly. "So they had a whirlwind romance. And they've been doing long-distance ever since."

"And you don't agree with that?" I could sense it in the way she said "long-distance" as if it was a burden more than anything.

"I think that can only last so long." She sighed. "And I don't love the idea of my best friend running away."

Those words held extra weight.

"You think he'd be running away?"

"Maybe 'running away' is the wrong phrasing. I think... He was lonely. He wants to settle down. Wants kids. Hazel and Leo have been clear that even though we're in an atypical situation, if we wanted to bring our real lives into this camp, they'd make accommodations so we can stay. As much as Gia loves visiting, I don't think she's interested in living here."

"It takes a special person to want to live in a commune," I jabbed.

She tilted her head in my direction and rolled her eyes. "It's not a commune."

It was exactly the reaction I'd been looking for. "I'm just kidding. There's a lot to be said about a group of people who can create a family and be able to rely on each other."

"It really is." There was a warmth in her tone that made me glad she'd found what she'd been looking for. I just hoped everyone else realized how lucky they were to have her.

She paused in front of a small cabin, standing on a single-step porch under a flickering light bulb. It was bigger than the pod cabins that surrounded it. It was taller than the others, with a bright blue door and a chimney, so there had to be a fireplace.

"So this is where you live." The cabin just made sense. It was the right size for someone who lived here year-round. I wanted to get inside and see more, learn everything I could about her life.

"This is where I live."

Nervousness filled me, taking me back to a different time, the first time I'd been on her front steps as she dangled her keys between her fingers as if she were about to go inside. She hadn't gone inside then, and I wished she'd do the same now.

"I like it. From the outside, at least." The words fell from my mouth without thought. It didn't appear to bother her.

She just laughed. "Oh, you're not seeing the inside."

My cocky smile came out of hiding. "Why's that?"

"Because you've already been in my naked presence once tonight, and I'm not going for two times. You're not that lucky."

Shit, she went right for it.

"Who says I was expecting to get naked?" I asked, and the blush returned to her cheeks. I decided to bring it out even more. "There are a lot of things you can do with clothes on. You are well-versed in this."

Then she did something that used to spin butterflies in my stomach. She tugged her lip between her teeth.

I raised an eyebrow. "You're telling me you've never invited a camper to see the inside?"

She gave me the hint of a smile. "No, I... That wouldn't be appropriate."

"It's not like there's a power imbalance, Autumn. You'd probably make a camper's dream come true." I stepped closer, touching her icy hand.

She squeezed my fingers as if it were a reflex, a need. "I don't know about that."

"I do." I closed the rest of the gap between us, reaching my other hand to the spot on her neck that I remembered her loving, massaging her with my fingers. She leaned into it, her wet hair brushing against my knuckles.

"You were always really good at that," she breathed, and I felt like the luckiest man in the world for being the one to touch her. How did I go from being worried she'd ax my favorite appendage to having my fingers against her skin in a little over a day? If I had my way, I'd be holding her close, kissing her neck, making her moan my name.

"I'm good at a lot of things."

She didn't look surprised. She licked her lips, her eyes fluttering closed. I tilted my forehead against hers, and she moved hers against mine.

"Jamie," she breathed. A moth flew up between us, hovering at her porch light. Neither of us moved, unable to be taken out of the moment.

"What is it, beautiful?"

She pulled her head away from me and stared into my eyes. "I..." Her pained expression filled me with dread. "I can't."

"I know. I'm sorry—" I tried, failing to recover.

That lit a fire in her, and instantly, I knew it was a mistake. "Sorry? You're sorry."

I backpedaled. "I didn't mean it, Autumn. It's that whole situation, and the night and..."

"Please give me more excuses for why you don't want to kiss me."

"Can we take a step back?" I asked. She nodded and backed away from me. "No, Autumn, wait—"

"Let's just act like it didn't happen, Jamie."

There was a double meaning to her words, and our almost-kiss tonight wasn't the reason they were laced with venom. She sniffed, rubbing the back of her hand over her mouth, and shook her head. Then she turned and walked away, typing a code into her door and closing it behind her.

I stared at it, as if that could change my circumstances, wishing

I could do something, wondering if I should just take that step and knock. To fix this. But I didn't. I didn't even know how.

Shit, it was official. I was being thoughtless, and it was affecting another person. Someone I didn't want to hurt again. And I had the whole walk back to my pod to ruminate on this.

The fire was out, but some campers were still away from the vicinity. All the lights were out except for Lamar's, and it felt especially quiet, probably a cosmic sign that I needed to sit in the mess I made. Thoughts of my failure were interrupted when I heard a small giggle next to my cabin.

I stopped in my tracks, tilting my head to see where it came from.

It looked like someone had the same idea I'd had in mind before being kicked to the curb. Maybe this place was rubbing off on me, but I couldn't help it. It was dark as hell, but I still had to see.

That was when I recognized camp counselor Nat's long French braids, her perfectly manicured pink fingernails running through my fellow podmate's distinct short red hair.

I did a double take. It couldn't be true.

Clear as day, there was Jack's girlfriend with her tongue down Nat's throat.

To call tonight a clusterfuck would be an understatement.

FIFTEEN

Jamie

"SHE REMEMBERED!" Excitement danced in Ren's eyes as we eagerly rifled through the care package Lamar had dropped off for us from the Monday mail haul. My mom had truly thought of everything. The box overflowed with an abundance of our favorite candies: Swedish Fish for her surrogate son, sour Warheads for me.

"I can't believe you got my mom to do this."

"Patricia's her own person."

I caught a whiff of chai as Ren opened a box of assorted tea bags, then something chocolatey. He waved a bag of salted caramel hot chocolate at me with a grin. Alongside the treats were some practical items. Bug spray, sunblock, lip balm, citronella candles that promised relief from pesky mosquitoes, and the newest mystery novel she'd recently finished that would provide hours of thrilling entertainment. Completing the box of thoughtful gifts were walkie-talkies. I imagined him using them to communicate in the office if I took too long to respond to his emails once we got back to work and considered hiding them before he saw them.

I snatched a homemade oatmeal raisin cookie from his hand. "That doesn't negate the fact that she knew about this trip before I did."

"Snail mail takes time."

Ren zeroed in on the walkies while I carefully unfolded her handwritten letter. Mom's words held the sort of love you could feel, tight as a hug. A pang of guilt shot through me, reminding me of all the time that had slipped away since I'd last been home. Living three and a half hours away wasn't much of an excuse, even though my family supported my career aspirations.

I enjoyed working for Clint and Margaret. I'd learned a lot over the past six years about case management and reading between the lines. How to seek out clients and create contracts that served their best interest. A surge of excitement went through me as I recalled our discussion about my accomplishments and why I'd be a good fit for senior associate last week. It went well, but I knew better than to get my hopes up. My fellow colleagues each had proven themselves in various degrees as well.

The firm's promise of better work life balance after I hit this milestone seemed like a pipe dream. If it was real, I wondered if I'd actually follow through and spend time with my family like I'd promised for years, or if I would continue working this much. Maybe I did need to rethink how I prioritized my life. Not that they'd ever asked me to.

We didn't have enough time for me to write a return letter. I'm sure she wasn't expecting one, but I resolved to write back before leaving camp. Ren and I left Mom's box at my cabin and gathered with the other pods, ready to board the yellow school bus to take us into Wildwood proper. Leo had on some sort of tour guide getup with a floppy hat that paired perfectly with the ever-present goofy smile that was just part of him. Hazel sported overall shorts with a bright white tee, and her standard aviators sat on top of her head. Her outfit was more subtle than Leo's, and yet the red bandana she tied her hair off with clearly matched his.

A quick buzz against my leg stunned me. Ren pulled out his phone, looked at it, and shoved it back into his pocket as if it had burned him.

"Zachary?" I asked.

Ren's mood shifted, and he gave me a terse nod before looking back out the window. "He's having a hard time with a clogged disposal, but he can get his new partner to help him figure it out," he grumbled, then immediately backtracked. "I'd meant to show him. It can be finicky, you know?"

Ren huffed as he settled farther into his seat. My best friend wore a rare sad smile, which I hated seeing on him. As he worked through his recent divorce, this vacation was something he'd needed just as much as I did. They'd been friends since they were teens, and this was an adjustment for both of them.

"I don't know how to talk to him anymore." Ren's shoulders slumped.

"It might be more than a wonky disposal. Maybe he wants you in his life, you know? I mean, you've known each other—"

I'd tried for months to give my friend the pep talk he needed, but he hadn't been ready.

This time, however, my chance to shine as a friend was interrupted by the dazzling voice of camp owner and *Top Gun* tour guide herself, Hazel. "Let's go, campers. Pick a seat, any seat. We're all friends here."

Ren faced the window, and the moment passed.

Bumping and bouncing on the bus, I felt like a kid on a field trip. Hazel faced backward in her seat, holding the intercom up as Leo drove. Before Hazel got everyone's attention, I sought out Autumn. She was easy to spot. We hadn't talked since that almost-kiss ruined everything.

What had I been thinking? Autumn's eyes had been filled with indecision. Telling me yes, then telling me never again. The warmth of our bodies, close but not close enough. I'd watched as her tongue moistened her lips and her hand rested on the door-knob before leaving me in the cold.

I blinked away last night's foolish hope. She didn't want me like that, not after how things ended before.

Today, she was as gorgeous as I'd ever seen. Her hair showed more blonde, catching the sunlight as it swayed behind her, tied back in a way that had half of the locks in her face. The other half was secured tightly, as if she'd given up on pulling it all back but hadn't wanted to lose her *don't fuck with me* look.

I kept stealing glances, hoping to draw her gaze back to me, but it didn't work. She was bubblier than I'd seen her the entire trip, possibly to distract from the fact that she was uncomfortable being within ten feet of me. Or maybe I was being ridiculous, and it was just a blip of her strange week.

Icing me out, she gave Hazel her full attention. Guess I needed to as well.

A vibrant stack of bright yellow papers suddenly dropped into my lap. I took one for Ren and me and passed the rest down to Emerson, who sat behind me, before scanning the scavenger hunt checklist. The list would take us through Wildwood's Main Street. We were tasked with gathering items and pictures from various locations in town to complete the list.

"This isn't the honor system, people," Sawyer exclaimed, distributing Polaroid cameras to each pair on the bus. "The first place *prize* is far too valuable to award without photographic evidence."

Ren checked ours, ensuring the film was loaded and the viewfinder was clear, while I continued to peruse the list.

"Wait, what's the prize this time?" Leo asked.

"Well, I'm glad you asked." Hazel waved a stack of gift cards. "The winners will receive gift cards to Wildwood Books, and"— she tapped her hands on the top of a bus seat like a drumroll—"a nifty keychain that says, 'I'm the best.'" She pulled a blue and white plastic key ring from her fanny pack and dangled it from her finger as people oohed and ahhed.

She explained the rules, most of which were predictable. Except the one prohibiting us from discussing fishing with the mayor if we encountered her in town, and under no circumstances were we to mention the Santa Run—an annual costume holiday race that came to blows each year. We were also warned not to speak with the owner of the diner, unless we wanted to delve into the three different ways to prepare a tuna melt sandwich, then be goaded into trying all three variations.

Autumn's voice rang out, interrupting Hazel's explanation. "Not sampling each sandwich because you 'dislike tuna' is an insult to Wildwood and Wanda's Diner," she playfully shouted.

Jack practically giggled next to her. Tearing my eyes away from them, I returned my attention to Hazel.

"We're not going to talk about that."

Autumn's laughter at Hazel's mock outrage was contagious as the bus started laughing and commenting. Across the aisle, four seats ahead, the sound of her delight drew me in, and I feared she would disappear like she had last night.

The counselors weren't taking part in the scavenger hunt. Something about how it wouldn't be fair since they knew every nook and cranny in this adorable town. Jack passed out pens to our group, and I shied away. The idea of talking with him about what I saw last night gnawed at me again. I was between a rock and a hard place. On the one hand, his relationship wasn't my business, and it'd been dark that night. Who knew what I actually saw? On the other hand, he was important to Autumn and an altogether decent guy. He knew the new Autumn, this sarcastic, gorgeous goddess of a camp counselor. I knew the past version of her, and she'd always been an excellent judge of character. She'd chosen Jack as a best friend, and I liked the idea of maybe having him as a friend, too, as presumptuous as it sounded.

"Don't forget to get a stamp at each place you visit. Except for the post office. Mabel's ferret was the last to see it," Hazel pointed out.

"Which reminds me, if you see a snake-like rodent carrying

around a handstamp proudly, please get it out of his clutches. Bribe him with anything he wants," Leo implored. "Bonus points will be awarded."

Next to me, my bouncing best friend was delighted to take part in this ridiculous hunt. He offered me a piece of his favorite candy, which of course my mother somehow knew he favored.

"Think I'm her favorite son yet?" he ribbed me.

"Just stop." I grinned wide. "You're not *my* mom's favorite kid... Not yet, anyway."

Ren busted up laughing. He was the goofiest, most random friend I could ask for, and I loved that he and my family got along so well. The package Mom had put together solidified what we already knew. Ren was already part of our family. His parents hadn't been around. He had an amazing younger brother, and he'd been close to his in-laws, but with the divorce this year, things would be different. I was grateful my mom remembered his favorite candy. The thought settled nicely as he popped another bright red fish into his mouth. His sour mood had completely evaporated.

Briefly, I let my mind wander to Autumn as if it were my new default setting. Would her parents send her a care package for a weeklong trip or maybe for her first week on the job? I doubted it from what I remembered of Nancy and Robert, not that they were cold, but I couldn't imagine they'd be thrilled with Autumn's dropping out of Stanford and her current career choice. Even if it was the happiest I'd ever seen her.

Before that thought could take root, the bus parked with a thud, and campers stood up, stretching and moving about as if we'd been on the bus for the past three hours and not fifteen minutes.

"And that's why we don't mess with the half-done puzzle at the salon." Hazel's cheeks were bright as she finished the rules with a laugh.

My eyes moved unconsciously to Autumn again, and this time, she turned away so quickly, her lips in a firm *I'm not talking to you right now* line. The message was received, and yet my lips tipped up. She'd been looking for me too. I was right here.

SIXTEEN

Jamie

To say Main Street was idyllic would be an understatement. Colorful-looking buildings with cedar shake shingled rooftops made bright blue skies more brilliant. Black metal lantern-style lights covered tall wooden lamp posts lining the streets, their hanging wicker baskets holding pink and purple trailing petunias.

Outside of movies and TV, I had never seen anything like it, and the same could be said for the dozens of eyes staring out of the school bus windows, like children watching their first snow of the school year.

With a flourishing bow, Leo opened the door. Once we poured out of the bus and gathered around, he reiterated the time and location to meet back up before he made sure we all had our Polaroid cameras for picture proof.

Main Street had small streets that branched out, housing small shops and restaurants ready to be explored. On this street alone, there were two restaurants, a salon, a post office, a recreational gear shop, and, no joke, a general store. It felt like something frozen in time, like it belonged in a Hallmark movie.

Wildwood was its own little world, next to a fast-moving highway leading up the mountain. Across the highway was a ski resort and an adventure park with what looked like summer rides, though we'd passed by it so quickly, I didn't get a good look.

Our scavenger hunt list was rather long, and I wondered how we could do everything in the time allotted, but this excursion had presumably been tested a dozen times over.

Everyone split into teams and scattered in different directions. Our three-person team of Emerson, Ren, and I chose to start at the post office, a two-room building about the size of my downtown apartment back home. I thought of my mother's care package coming through this little building, which made me smile.

Our first clue was easily solvable. We had to "get a kiss from Peanut Butter"—a clue that had Ren's eyebrow raised and would have been confusing if not for the four-legged postal worker who greeted us, a corgi by the same name. We took a photo of Emerson, who full-on giggled when our new furry friend pressed his tongue to her cheek, though all of us received kisses.

By the time we had completed nearly half of our twenty-five items, we found ourselves outside of a community posting board with announcements and advertisements ranging from a need for more volunteer firefighters to trail guide offerings to the local taxi service, a one-man operation with a direct phone line to a guy named Todd. Part of me wanted to pull out my ridesharing app just to see how limited it was out here, but Todd was probably the best option for a lift should the need arise.

"Oh my god, look at this." Emerson was giggling again as she read a colorful posting with pictures of hand-drawn dogs and trees. "'Hi, I'm Vivian,'" she read. "'I'm seven years old. I'm opening a dog walking business. I am grate'—that's g-r-a-t-e—'with animals. I love dogs. I have two dogs and am not afraid to get my hands dirty.'"

Ren covered his mouth as he let out a small, happy burst of air.

"'I can walk small to medium dogs. If your dog has high energy, that is okay because most dogs have high energy. I will charge seven dollars an hour. I will be available mostly after school.'" It listed her contact information and ended with "'Thank you for supporting a small business.'"

I was dying of cuteness overload.

Grant came up from behind us. "That is so adorable my head is going to explode."

He was one of the two-person teams, and when he'd partnered up with Ian, Ren had obviously been a little bummed, but he lit up the second he heard his voice.

"Who has a dog? We need to hire this little girl," Ian mused. I'd only met him today, but he worked in an aquarium and thought it was funny that he was in Delphinus pod.

"It'll only be a four-hour drive to watch my dog. I'll compensate for gas," Ren offered to no one. "Give me that phone number," he joked, pulling off one of the phone number slips cut into fringe for the taking.

Ren had an amazing black lab named Goldie—because why wouldn't he name her that?—but he hadn't had her for long, just in the past few months since he and Zachary split. Over drinks one night, he'd mentioned feeling lonely, not that you need a reason for a fluff ball, and I could relate. I'd wanted a dog for years, but four-legged friends weren't conducive to seventy-hour work weeks, and it was looking like I'd never get the opportunity. Occasionally, I wondered if I'd be happier living a different lifestyle, open to new possibilities like taking care of a living, breathing puppy, but I was a long way off from that kind of thing.

"You have a dog?"

Ren's eyes sparkled as Grant asked his question. Not at all probing or deep, and yet...

Ren yanked his phone out of his pocket so fast I wouldn't have been surprised if it flew across the street. Instead, the five of us hovered around his puppy picture-filled phone and aww'd until we couldn't take it anymore.

Our group that wasn't supposed to be a group wandered up the street.

"It says, 'Hug Sasquatch,'" Ian said. "Hell no. You know Sasquatch is native to the Pacific Northwest. They're obviously fucking with us because we can't find one just like that." He snapped his fingers. "Not gonna happen." The rest of us turned disbelieving eyes on him. "Don't look at me like that. Sasquatch is real."

The group burst into laughter.

Grant pointed to the side of us. "Sasquatch."

"Ha ha, Grant. How about you go and—" Ian turned to see a nine-foot-tall statue of the mysterious creature in a cloth bucket hat and laughed. "Okay, now it makes sense."

The five of us gathered around as I took an under-the-chin selfie to get him in the picture. Several oofs were made at the result, and we tried again. The fourth time was the charm because Lamar laughingly took over when he saw us on the street. I glanced at the photo as others shook their heads in agreement and noticed how much we all looked... Happy. It was one more reminder of the fact that Ren had made the right call, though I wasn't going to tell him that. He was one gloaty pain in my ass, and it was impossible to pull him down from his high horse.

We had several hours to explore, so I figured we had time to have a quick break for lunch at the nearby Mexican restaurant. Emerson and Ian were the more serious members of our crew and continued their quest to scavenge no matter how many times we tried to convince them. There were some real competitors in this camp.

We made the right choice. The Mexican restaurant, Beans and Beans, was actually a café/restaurant, with a line out the door for coffee. Grant walked to the glass door to peer through to see what was up and was met with a near swing to the face by an apologetic server on their way to the patio. The host seated us on the other side of the room away from the espresso and cappuccino machines.

The place was unlike anything I'd seen. There was just a beam as a room divider, painted white, with snowboarding stickers covering each other up the ten-foot pole. Nestled between stickers saying, "Don't flurry, be happy," and "Ski ya later," was, no surprise, one that read "Bigfoot is real." In stark contrast, the rest of the room was painted lemon yellow, with rainbow string lights donning the roof. Mexican pottery was attached to the walls, and a bright green wall was behind the full bar.

I couldn't get over this entrepreneurial enterprise. The café had a constant swinging door of customers, and the restaurant was at about seventy-five percent capacity. We perused the menu and found more than we'd bargained for.

"I can't believe this," Ren started. "So I can order a white chocolate mocha *and* a margarita in the same sitting? Are you kidding me?" He ran his finger down the long list of appetizers and entrées, pointing out the coffee menu to Grant.

"You can order a white chocolate mocha and *chips and guac.*" Grant was practically salivating.

"That's even better." Ren was bouncing on the blue pleather-covered booth. The entire seat shook below us.

"We also have espresso martinis," our server offered from behind me.

"This place is magical." Grant's eyes were glazed over like a stoner in the chip aisle at a grocery store.

We ordered drinks and too much food, waiting giddily for our plates.

"You think the other teams are eating?" Grant asked.

"Well, we know Emerson and Ian aren't." Ren took a big gulp of his water, glancing at Grant to see if he was looking back at him.

"They really wanted those keychains," Grant observed, a glint in his eye.

That was the embarrassing moment when I realized I'd become the third wheel on their impromptu date.

I pushed my plate forward after I finished my tacos, leaving the beans and rice. "Well, I'm stuffed. I think I'm gonna go."

"What about the scavenger hunt?" Grant asked. Oops.

Ren's eyebrows went up and down, telling me to proceed as planned and leave him some time with his crush.

"I just need to stretch my legs. I'll go ahead and scope things out. Why don't you meet me at the thrift store when you're done?"

"Ten minutes?" Grant asked.

Ren clearly would have blown the whole thing off if he could, but Grant was too kind to abandon me. Was Grant a better friend than my best friend? I smiled at the thought.

"Sounds great."

I didn't know what to do with my ten minutes and briefly wondered if I was codependent. I walked down the short side street next to the restaurant and found a bench in front of some empty office space. It faced the forest as if someone had purposely sat it there with the express purpose of spending lunch breaks staring at the wilderness. I thought back to the last time I'd taken a real lunch break and realized it had been months ago. It made me wonder if I'd *ever* slowed down since graduating from undergrad.

Being away from work this long felt strange at times, and though I had enough distance to see I needed a vacation, some part of taking time to myself still felt a little wrong.

I chose not to look too deeply into that. Instead, I distracted myself by looking at our scavenger hunt list.

Kiss from Peanut Butter: check.

Find Sasquatch: check.

Find a banana: check.

We'd figured the latter would be at the general store and had not been disappointed. Apparently, the shop owner loved banana-themed objects, and we'd found stuffed plushies, banana candy, and banana milk, which I'd never realized was a thing. We'd bought one and passed it around. It was disgusting.

Buy the weirdest thing you can afford in town: still looking. Especially since we hadn't exhausted our options yet.

Find something that makes you smile.

I wondered where Autumn was and realized I was a lovestruck cheeseball.

I walked over to the town map, a four-foot-by-four-foot painted map that showed Wildwood and the ski-turned-summer park across the street. We'd covered a lot, but there was surprisingly still more in this small town. It was hard to move fast when each proprietor stopped you to talk, but they never asked us what brought us out to their town. The owners must have been used to this excursion from Camp Starlight.

I realized I'd been standing in front of this map for too long but was given a reprieve as Grant and Ren came up from behind me, weaving their arms in mine as Ren ecstatically said, "Get in, loser. We're going shopping!"

THE HUNT for meet-cutes was on. Tradition called for the takedown of Leo at all costs. Too-big-for-his-britches Leo had been kicking our ass with the most successfully shipped couples this entire summer, and all of the staff had banded together to keep him from winning this last session. We were still competing against each other, but Leo couldn't win.

Counselors were catching cute moments all over town in our group chat. I just received a message from Felicia with a photo of two of her campers in funky seventies-looking ties, none of them tied correctly, all of them sporting ridiculous smiles.

We were doing well in the standings, just barely trailing after Leo, and we thought we had the cutest moment in the bag when Diego and Breanna proved they were the real deal after sharing a s'more last night at the campfire. Leo made a compelling argument after he swore he saw Jeremy and Steven have a book-sharing moment at the Meditation Meadow so we considered it a tie... For now.

"Did you hear about Terry and Cheryl?" Jack asked me.

"Nat has been trying to convince me this whole time, but they're never together. You're not getting me with this again."

"Get your hopes up, because one of us is taking Leo down, and it might not be you."

I scoffed. We were each involved in our activities most of the day, so the opportunities to covertly set up meet-cutes were rare. Still, we'd intended to take full advantage on Town Day, playfully suggesting people hang out together. Fake love stories were sometimes created and exaggerated, but occasionally they were real. Leo's impressive display of wedding invitations was proof of that.

"Parkour!" Jack shouted as he leaped over the blue antique-painted bike rack. It was bolted down and secured between the thrift shop and the general store.

I shook my head at the fool as he cleared an easy bike rack and threw his arms up, sticking the landing like an Olympic gymnast. I stepped back to get a running start and followed his jump over the bike rack, clearing the neighboring bench with much more finesse.

He shook his hair from his eyes, slinging his arm around my shoulder as we steered each other toward the general store. *This is what I need more of.* I thought, clutching my side as we laughed. *Not distractions from ex-boyfriends*

"Don't look now, but you're about to be proven wrong." I scooched forward to get a better look at the couple that Nat had favored, like a wildlife explorer on safari. "Shh, don't spook them."

"You're kidding me," Jack whisper-yelled.

Terry turned slightly, and we both ducked behind the bench, evading discovery.

"Nat called it."

Cheryl's hand rested on Terry's hip as they took advantage of a mostly private wraparound balcony. I looked away once Terry's hand pressed against the wall, and Cheryl leaned into him with enthusiasm, her fingers finding his hair as she pulled him into her.

Just like that, my almost-kiss played as if it were burned into my eyelids. I recounted the moment as if every other minute lying in bed attempting to sleep hadn't been enough time already. His brown eyes focusing on me as if there was nothing else in this big, wild world. His gorgeous lips parting, our breaths braided with tension I didn't need in my life.

This was Jamie. There was nothing fun or casual about the look he gave me. Nope, that look promised soul-altering destruction.

It didn't matter how handsome he was, or how he charmed me every time he spoke. I'd learned my lesson. I was done thinking about him. Now all I had to do was *stop* thinking about him.

"Still hung up on your high school heartbreaker?" His raised eyebrows said he already knew I was obsessing about the man. So much for not thinking about him. Thanks for that, Jack.

I held the door for Jack as we headed into the oldest building in town, remodeled into the general store, a wonder-filled emporium and grocery. The bell chimed, and Simon gave us a quick nod in greeting as his black lab, Ashland, welcomed us with tail wags.

"What's Gia up to today?" I asked Jack, steering the conversation away from my tall, gorgeous high school sweetheart. He let me get away with the change. He knew better than to push when I had my hair pulled back.

"She had a migraine and a video call with a client. I tried taking care of her this morning, but she insisted that I go. I'm starting to think that maybe I should have stayed."

I imagined what I would want in this exact scenario. "Bring her back those Pop Rocks she loves."

Jack waved the packets he already held at me. He was such a good boyfriend.

"And..." I dragged out the word as I held up a miniature Nerf gun. "This. You two will love this."

"Nerf guns are for ten-year-olds."

"Exactly." I tossed a gun at him with a grin, and his face lightened at the idea. I'd always liked Gia. In a way, this could be her giving us time before they'd inevitably have the talk and decide to move in together. Before Jack would be... Nope, not having any of that thought today. It got shoved away with all the other can't-think-about-that-now thoughts.

But maybe there was a way. I weighed the pros and cons before deciding to go for it.

"So she can provide consultations without seeing the animal in person? That's cool. Is there a plan for you two, you know, after this session?" I chewed my lip, not sure I wanted the answer.

"No decisions have been made, but you and I will stay friends no matter what, Autumn." He squeezed my shoulder, which turned into one of his famous hugs. Was I so easy to read today?

Good to know he wasn't abandoning me, yet. Still, just the thought made my gut twist. Gia and Jack should get their own place. The distance was hard on them. He deserved the kind of relationship that was long term, special, and heart-wrenchingly amazing. The pang of it hit again deep in my chest as my best friend smiled, warm as sunshine at me. If they moved, would he come back here?

"Jack, got a minute?" Simon, ambled to the register. He'd just finished helping some campers find the sunscreen when he noticed me too. "Autumn, perfect. Wait just a moment."

Simon was in his late thirties and hadn't quite had the realization that he was slightly more breakable than he used to be. That wasn't to say that thirty-six-year-olds shouldn't skateboard, but they should at least keep up on their calcium supplements. Or drink a damn glass of milk a day. Although from what I understood, people in their thirties were all turning to lactase and oat milk these days.

Something to look forward to.

"Hi, Simon, how's business today?" I asked when he'd finished the transaction.

"Inventory just arrived, and this has been acting up." He pointed his temporary cane down at his ankle boot. He'd fractured it when he'd attempted to do a trick on a halfpipe. "Autumn, would you mind watching the front while Jack helps me back here?"

"You betcha." I walked behind the register as Jack and Simon made their way toward the storage room.

Jack turned to me with a huge grin, reached his arms straight up, and hit the Employees Only sign hanging above the entrance to the storage room. Teasing me. He knew I couldn't reach it. Him and his stupid long legs.

"Show off," I called after them just as the bell alerted us to new customers. I didn't know what Simon and Jack were up to, but I had moved on, focusing on Leo's second-choice couple, Leroy and Tara, who were hovering near each other down the aisle from me. The two of them didn't seem to have any chemistry—yet. I looked over my shoulder like a villain to make sure I wasn't being watched.

"Hey, Tara, I heard Sariah was looking for you." I tilted my head away from Leroy. This was about as devious as I got.

Tara dropped the banana-flavored KitKats back on the shelf. "Oh, really? Thanks, Autumn." She left to go down the frozen foods aisle. Hopefully, that wouldn't bite me in the ass.

Leroy took a selfie holding a bottle of banana Nesquik that they'd be regretting soon enough.

I looked down at Simon's open book of expert Sudoku puzzles and started filling in the blanks. I loved it here.

Most worked at a leisurely pace, but you could see who the real contenders were. Tara returned, and meticulously crossed off an item on the yellow scavenger hunt sheet before grabbing the camera from Leroy and tugging him toward the exit. I cringed at the display, knowing full well that I hadn't thwarted anything and Leo was still on track to have a winning couple.

"Thanks, Autumn, I got it from here." Simon relieved me, taking back his place behind the register before spotting a couple searching his store. He tilted his head toward the banana corner, and they nodded with understanding. No one could question his dedication to our scavenger hunt.

Jack gathered his items and shoved them into a bag, heading for the door.

Simon gasped as he scanned his Sudoku puzzle. "Did you just finish the puzzle I've been working on for two days?"

"What, like it's hard?" I gave my best Elle Woods impersonation.

Simon adjusted the emerald green beanie he always wore, smiling warmly at me as he flipped the page.

I started for the door before two beaded eyes caught my attention, and I was smitten. "This is perfect."

I handed Simon a small stuffed hedgehog sitting on the cash wrap. Its eyes were sewn lopsided, his felt nose a little small for his cute little face. I wondered if his boyfriend, the owner of Wildwood's craft store, Sew Cute, had done that intentionally.

"Keep it." Simon nodded, indicating for me to take the little critter before he began helping the next customer.

I left the store and found Jack leaning against the cherry-red 1950s Chevy, beautifully cared for and one of the perfect picture mementos for groups.

We continued toward our next destination with Pop Rocks, Nerf guns, and a disturbed hedgehog in tow. Campers were weaving in and out of the shops, with big grins and vivacious laughter, and it was like music to my ears.

I reached into my bag and fished out the weird little hedgehog. "This made me think of you." I mimicked a cartoon character and presented the cute little toy to a laughing Jack.

"Is my hair that fluffy today?" he asked, scooping the little guy up.

"It's always fluffy." I ruffled my hands through his hair, which always annoyed him. "What should we name it?"

He lifted it so that they were eye to eye. "Her name is Pearl. She's an old soul."

He squeezed it, and a sappy part of me wondered if she would be something to remember me by. I wanted to know, but I couldn't bring myself to say anything. Of course he'd be back. This was as much his family as it was mine. Jack wouldn't leave us like that.

"GO WILD," I told Jack, knowing he tended to ooh and aww at everything in the Treasure Trove, a mishmash antique and second-hand store located down a side street. He always found something, even if a fair chunk of the goods came from past campers' lost and found items that had never been claimed.

My bestie grinned at me, heading for the back corner where a painted pink dresser and sticker-covered filing cabinet leaned next to one another, along with paintings framed in large brass frames and, oh, the musical instruments.

Jack began playing with some bongos before spotting a harmonica, but we knew what we were looking for: the same mythical item we'd looked for every Town Day since Leo got it in his head that he'd be a one-man band. Today was made of gold and dreams and maybe even a little magic because there it was, nestled between a leaning keyboard and a kid's guitar with missing strings: a foot tambourine. I'd never heard of one before Leo had painstakingly and lovingly described it. He was going to flip his shit.

Jack halted his steps as he listened. His Cheshire Cat smile had me quaking with excitement. "No way."

I took my foot out of the contraption and handed it to him. He lifted his foot to his hip as he stuck his shoe in the curved thing.

"How did I not know you were this... Bendy?"

"Because you're not my girl, Autumn." He winked.

"Shut it," I told him with a playful shove. "I'm no one's girl." The words twinged with a surprising sadness.

Then why did Jamie's annoyingly handsome face pop into my head?

"You're about to forget all of that when you hear—" He stepped gingerly, and there it was: tambourine music? Noise? Whatever you wanted to call it.

I couldn't wait to see the look on Leo's face when we came back with this little beauty.

"This place is a national treasure." Jack's voice had no trace of sarcasm.

I looked around in the middle of this thrift store among broken and discarded things and wondered how one could even say that. But Jack was more of a romantic than I was.

He shook his foot again. And again. And again. The shop manager looked at him with a sharp eye, and he shot her his most ridiculous smile, the one that let him get away with way too much.

Then I heard it, the deep rumble of Jamie's laugh, the way it floated over me, delighting me. That laugh had always brought out my own just under the surface, one tiny nudge and I'd be giggling right along with him.

I pulled down my very inconspicuous, heart-shaped sunglasses and ducked behind a mannequin facing the aisle that Jamie, Ren, and Grant had just walked down. I glanced around it to get a peek at what they were doing.

"Hey, Jamie, what do you think about me wearing this?" Ren gleefully held out a beret. It was unconventional, but he could pull it off.

"That's perfect. It looks like something my nemesis would wear."

"No. Hey. We're nemeses now?" Ren gasped in mock shock.

"You know what you did."

I quickly went back to my hiding spot to avoid being seen as Jack picked up a ukulele and strummed a chord beside me. I put my hand on his forearm to stop him from drawing attention to us, but his phone vibrated, and we both looked at his pocket.

"Is it Gia?" I asked.

He shook his head. "Leo took gas back to the boat, and now it won't start. That man could touch bulletproof glass and it would break. You need anything?"

"I'm good."

He hit Leo's contact as he handed me the ukulele. "What did you do?" he said on his way out the door.

As he paced back and forth in front of the store, it was the best time for me to make my escape. Then Jamie approached Jack outside. So much for that. And why was Jamie talking to him anyway?

"Isn't he the best?" Ren's voice startled me. He popped up behind where I was still ducking behind the mannequin. Busted. His grin told me he wasn't the least bit surprised I was here. Ren wore the strangest mashup of clothes: some parachute pants, a leather jacket, and a beret.

I cracked a smile and shook my head at his ridiculousness. "Who?" I asked, remembering almost too late that Ren had asked me a question.

"Jamie. He's matured so much since high school, hasn't he?"

"You didn't know him then," I pointed out, but Ren was unfazed.

"Maybe not. But I do know that he is the most loyal man I've ever met. And he's reliable. If I need something, he's the first one I call. And there's no way he looked that good when he was fifteen."

Loyal? If he was so loyal, he wouldn't have ditched me the second he went off to college.

But I didn't contradict Ren, no matter how I felt about Jamie. "Why are you telling me this?"

"Because I think there are still feelings there."

And just like that, it was as if a bomb had gone off in my stomach. He wasn't pulling any punches.

I hesitated for just a moment, hoping I hadn't given him too much ground. "I think you're reading too much into this. I'm just his ex. I'm sure he's got a list a mile long of women he can date."

"And if he actually dated, I'd agree with you. But I've never seen him light up the way he does when he talks about you, and you know what that says to me? You should give him a chance. And something in your eyes tells me that maybe you want to."

Was I that transparent? And what would a chance even mean?

Because Jamie Davis had been trouble for me all those years ago. Now, all that trouble had only amplified. Because now I imagined dark, knowing eyes, and his sure-as-steel grip pulling me against him. The way he would have held me again, had we just...

No, I shook away those thoughts for the millionth time. No matter how sexy his laugh was and how intensely I could feel his eyes on me, that man was trouble for my heart, and I couldn't start anything with him ever again.

EIGHTEEN

Autumn

M OST CAMPFIRE NIGHTS HAD AN AGENDA, but Mondays were chill hangouts at the bonfire. This wasn't out of laziness on the camp's part. We'd just learned that people liked to unwind on their timeframe after a long day in town.

I stood victorious in a pile of giant Jenga pieces, holding back my fist pumps as Lamar shrugged in defeat. We bent over to pick up the pieces, and I used that time to covertly look around for a familiar face. Luckily for me, he wasn't here yet. Did I want him to show up? No. No, that was definitely not what I wanted. I just wished things didn't have to be so awkward.

I'd been ruminating on everything since our near-kiss, and I'd decided to put some distance between the two of us. It wasn't like I'd been trying to spend time with him before the almost-kiss fiasco. Okay, maybe I'd sort of tried a couple of times, but other than those, I'd been working like I normally would. It wasn't my fault I was intercepted by his gravitational pull like a planet orbiting the... Actually, that was a terrible metaphor. That would make him the sun, and he wasn't that important a presence in my life, previously or otherwise.

Dammit.

"Round two?" Lamar asked. When had all those pieces been put back together?

"If I spank you twice in front of all these people, I look like an asshole, Lamar."

He didn't argue. Instead, he rolled his eyes at my cockiness.

We were a competitive bunch at this sweet little camp, and we tried to harness that when guests were around.

Lamar looked for a new contender. "You." He pointed at an unsuspecting Ian, who promptly finished a s'more and stood up, brushing the crumbs from his shorts, determination in his gaze. This was shaping up to be something interesting.

I loved the atmosphere around the campfire. People were either relaxing or goofing off, and my pod was no exception. Laughter came from across the seating area. Kell-i, Kell-y, and Janna were having a good time, pointing at the clear alcohol-looking mess down the front of Kell-i's shirt. Then Janna snorted as she finished patting her shirt dry, and they were busting up again.

I scanned my surroundings and found my target behind the stage. He was standing in a group of women, their eyes rapt as he told some wild story.

I grabbed the bag that Jack had given me and pulled out the foot tambourine, dropping it to the ground.

Leo's head whipped around so fast I thought he might go full exorcist. I swear his ears went up like a dog hearing a squeaky toy.

I pushed it behind me to block it with my foot as he made a beeline for me.

"Autumn..."

"What?" I feigned ignorance as his eyes darted around. I backed my heel into the thing so that he heard a small jingle.

"I heard it. The call of the siren."

God, he was a nerd. I couldn't hide it any longer and bent down to retrieve the bright blue foot tambourine.

Leo's face was the epitome of happiness. "You found one!"

He tapped his foot, playing with it, dancing to the jingling beat. I began clapping to match his rhythm as we acted like kids at our first barn dance. We linked arms and started a little do-si-do, kicking out our heels and giggling together.

Once our dance was done, Leo threw his arms around my shoulders and gave me one of his famous squeezing hugs, nearly taking my breath away. "Now I'm going to win the talent show," he whispered manically into my ear, and I'd be afraid if I were competing this time around, but thankfully, this wasn't my week. "No, really, thank you."

He kissed my cheek and turned to his original location, kicking the tambourine up into his hand as he arrived, to the delight of his adoring fanbase. I rolled my eyes. Just what Leo needed: groupies.

Too bad for them. He didn't hook up with campers.

"If anyone could make a tambourine hot, it's that man," Emerson whispered beside me.

Sometimes, I forgot about Leo's allure, but I had to admit, the man was attractive. I'd probably notice it more if he didn't feel like my brother.

I turned back to giant Jenga and found Lamar flirting with his competition and wondered if this was a diversionary tactic and then thought better. I'd known him for the two years he'd been here and had quickly learned that he was the flirtiest of us all, but I never knew if he was looking for follow-through or if that was just his way.

The air felt heavier, more than just the smoke hovering around us. Or maybe it was just the weight on my chest. I sighed and couldn't figure out if I felt melancholy or relief. I'd had a good day today, but I still felt like I was drifting like embers in the fire. Smoldering wood and evergreen scents tickled my nostrils, the enchanting sounds of laughing campers and crackling logs my ambient noise. It still felt like something wasn't quite right.

The warmth overtook me and I noticed the fire was bigger than usual. Sawyer was in charge of the wood, what a surprise, and I was about to go tell them to tone it down when an unusually despondent Jack walked my way.

He sat next to me. "Hey."

"Hi, buddy. How're you doing?"

"I'm... Not great." His whole body sighed, and he looked as though he was deciding whether to tell me something. "Gia and I broke up."

"What?" I blurted a little too loudly, garnering the eyeballs of several campers before lowering my voice. "How did she go from having a migraine to breaking up with you?" That must have been a really nasty migraine.

"Actually, I broke up with her."

Oh.

Wait.

What?

How did I proceed when my best friend dropped a bomb like that?

Jack had been making plans. He talked about Gia like she was his world. There were times I'd seen them together when I was filled with this longing feeling, as if something in my life was missing. Like maybe I wanted... More. But if they couldn't make it, who could?

"Are you making s'mores?" he asked me as if the four components of a s'more in my hands weren't a dead giveaway and like he hadn't just flipped my world upside down.

"Yeah, you want me to make you one?" I asked, keeping my tone calm and sweet like a parent offering their kid a Fruit Roll-Up after a particularly bad day at school. When he didn't respond, I loaded up a stick and stuck it in the pit, making sure to keep it along the outskirts so it didn't catch fire, the way he liked. "You wanna talk about it?" I tried.

"I'm a little shell-shocked." He didn't continue, so I didn't pry.

I pulled his marshmallow out and built a s'more for him. He ate it as if it were an obligation. I'd never seen him like this.

Jack didn't operate by putting up facades. He was a light-hearted guy. He was the one everyone went to when they needed cheering up, not the other way around. This was new territory, and it was almost as if he didn't know how to be this way either. The only time I'd seen him down was when he'd been sick with the flu, and even then, he'd still made cracks about how he sounded like a foghorn every time he rasped, which made him laugh and cough harder.

We sat in a comfortable silence, watching people with their craft cocktails, talking and laughing as if it was a normal Monday night and someone's world wasn't falling apart around them. I truly didn't know how to proceed. I thought their relationship was going in a completely different direction, and the fact that he was the one to end it... It felt wrong, ominous.

So I did the only thing I could think of.

I shoved a marshmallow in my mouth. "One." Then I shoved three more in, struggling to get out a "Four."

Jack rolled his eyes. Chubby Bunny always worked with him, and it was going to work now. I counted three more and put them in my mouth.

"I don't want to play that stupid game with you," he said, waiting a beat before shoving five in his mouth.

I held up seven fingers and barely spewed out a "Chubby bunny" to prove I could still talk.

He topped me with eight, easily pulling off the same thing, but I was a competitive loser, no matter how many times he'd proven himself the victor. I added two more and spewed a barely audible "Chubby bunny" causing a muffled laugh to break through. The only thing keeping the spit in my mouth was the wall of marshmallows, probably on the verge of blocking my airway. Then a marshmallow plopped into my lap. I stared down at my legs as though it might have come from somewhere that wasn't my mouth.

Jack gave me a poor excuse for a laugh before raising his hands in victory, said "Chubby bunny" one more time, and popped one more in his mouth to be a jackass. Then he started chewing, his jaw looking like overstretched elastic.

There were no real winners in Chubby Bunny. Not when everyone ended up looking like an idiot.

Once he was finished chewing, he looked at me with a smile he couldn't conceal. He didn't say it, but he didn't have to. He was grateful for his amazing, brilliant, gorgeous best friend. He was in awe at my ability to bring joy to others, and my humility—my greatest characteristic.

He took my hand and squeezed, looking into the fire. I chewed quickly, prepared to ask him what happened, maybe about the logistics of her being here when they were no longer together, but he changed the subject.

"How are things going with Jamie?" Obviously, he didn't want to talk about his situation. Choosing to question my soft spot wasn't my preference, however. I'd call him a jerk if he wasn't so heartbroken. And why was he heartbroken if he'd broken up with her?

"There is no me and Jamie."

He nodded slowly. "That's too bad."

"You know I have a difficult relationship with him," I reminded him. "We broke up, remember?"

"Yeah, but you've grown. Both of you from the looks of it."

I wanted that to be true, but the only way we'd truly know if he'd grown up was by waiting for the other shoe to drop, waiting for him to break up with me again for no reason. Either way, breaking up with me wasn't even possible since there had been no discussion of our past or even a whiff of potentially dating. It was beside the point anyway because I wasn't willing to put myself through that again.

"We haven't grown much, Jack. He's still cocky as hell." I thought back to the night before, him stepping toward me, me staying still, waiting to see what he'd do next. But the truth was, I'd *wanted* him to do something. These were feelings I didn't even want to have, but there were little reminders of them prickling inside my chest. "He's still arrogant."

"In a funny way. You like that. Next."

"He's unreliable," I tried. Like when he'd forgotten to pick me and my friends up from a concert because he fell asleep. How he'd always bailed on my friends but would make time for his own. Or on our first-year anniversary, when he'd forgotten we had plans and went snowboarding instead. "You know how he bailed on craft night—"

Now I sounded like a child.

"That's a stretch."

"That wasn't the first time he's bailed on me."

"You're right, he did do that *a decade* ago."

"Fine. What about the fact that the man still only thinks of himself?" Okay, so what if I was being a little bit harsh?

"Come on, Autumn. You know you don't believe that." He placed his fingers to his temples as though he was at the end of his rope. He dropped them and turned to look me in the eye, more seriously than I was used to seeing him. "You may not realize, but I've noticed things. I see the way he is around you and his friends, and selfish isn't a word I'd use to describe him. He has no stakes here, but he still... Look, if he's only thinking about himself, if he had no reason to do something except in his own self-interest, then why didn't he use the information to further his chances with you?"

"What are you talking about?"

"Jesus, I'm going to break his confidence, and it took less than three hours." He shook his head, facing ahead of him, firelight dancing in his eyes.

I moved so that I could see him again. "Jack?"

"Gia cheated on me, Autumn, and that's why we broke up. Jamie witnessed it and had no motivation to tell me, someone he doesn't even know, other than to be a good guy. He even told me not to tell you it was him, probably because he's trying not to sway you one way or the other. That doesn't sound like someone who's selfish or looking out for his best interest. That sounds like a good man."

NINETEEN

Jamie

A GENTLE WIND swept through the abundance of trees as the crackle of the bonfire masked the sound of crickets and campers' conversations. There was something special about being here in this place. I could see why Autumn loved it. And yet there was still so much about her that I still didn't quite understand. Being self-assured and hilarious were qualities she'd always had, but now there was something freer about how she carried herself, something I hadn't seen before. The small-town comforts, the wilderness, and the bonfire smoke were all a part of her. It was like she'd always belonged here.

Fingers interlaced behind my head, I lay back and listened to the sweet sound of laughter as it floated through the white linen curtains over the bed. After a full day in town, I welcomed some alone time, content with the book in my hand, and the night's ambiance warming my cabin. After reading the same page over and over, I realized my persistence was futile due to the gorgeous blonde who kept popping up unbidden in my mind. I decided on a shower instead.

The water cascaded over me as I gave myself exactly until the end of this shower to stop obsessing about her. Turning off the nozzle, I felt clean but far from relaxed. I hadn't been able to stop thinking about the woman who'd turned my world upside down, not once but twice. Those hazel eyes and those distractingly bow-shaped lips I was too tempted to kiss.

Snuggling into the fluffy terry cloth robe, I headed back to my cabin. I made it to my room and fell back into the bed as if I were about to make an angel in fresh-packed snow. I wanted to get dressed, needed to, but I could also just lie here like this for the rest of the night and be content.

A fierce knock came at my door, and I scrambled up. Was Ren back already? When I pulled on the knob, my heart froze a beat as I tried to make sense of what was before me. Autumn. Those eyes set me ablaze. Wait, were those her *fuck me* eyes? Said eyes trailed unapologetically down my body. What the hell was happening? I was dreaming. Yes, that must be it. I swallowed hard under her perusal. Curse this comfy robe. It wasn't going to conceal the response I was having to that look for much longer.

Autumn gently nudged the door wider. My brain worked to catch up quickly. I wasn't about to question what brought her here.

"Are you going to invite me in?" Autumn asked enticingly.

I stepped back, and she strode inside. I was still trying to figure out what was happening. This wasn't how I thought my night would go.

Closing the door behind her, Autumn mirrored my movements as we looked at each other. It felt like we'd last forever in this standoff after several drawn-out seconds, but then she took me by surprise and reached for me, placing one hand into mine, its familiarity and warmth sending a shockwave through me. Already off-kilter, I was even less prepared when her other hand, full of confidence, found the back of my neck. An almost embarrassing sigh left my lips at that touch alone.

"What are you—"

She moved her hand from my neck, sliding it toward my mouth. A gentle finger pressed my lips together, stopping the question. Her hands found both sides of my robe, and my chest tightened at the movement, all questions leaving my mind.

Autumn's fierce gaze shone brighter than any bonfire ever could, and those flames drawing me in hadn't let up since she'd arrived. Filled with smoldering intensity, wrapped up in lust and promise. Her gaze dropped to her hands, which clasped my robe tightly. Steady and sure, she flicked her eyes back up to my face for confirmation, before her confident hands pulled my robe the rest of the way open.

Her eyes lingered on mine, then drifted down, down, down. Her gaze burned and caressed and demanded. I took a breath, realizing I hadn't breathed since her fingers touched my skin. Autumn tracked my movements and licked her lips as if she liked what she saw.

Another man would have been self-conscious about his ex-girlfriend taking his naked form in, but things had improved since high school. And the tongue between her teeth told me just that. I may have put in seventy-hour work weeks, but when I wasn't killing myself in the office, I was working myself to the bone in the gym. Apart from hanging out with Ren, it was my only pastime, and today, that didn't sound as pathetic as it was.

I pressed my body up against hers and glanced down at her lips, then back to her eyes. Not wasting any time, Autumn pressed her mouth to mine. Our reintroduction wasn't tentative. She kissed me as though we'd never stopped. Answering kisses became ferocious as she moaned into my mouth, her tongue dancing with mine. Lips finding their places, breaths finding their rhythm, it was all familiar yet sparkling new.

Moving fast and frantic, Autumn was ready for more. I used my lips to draw out apologies and promises along her neck and ears, before rising to her pace. I met her eyes again before my fingers found the top button of her jeans. I didn't need to know why I'd suddenly gotten so lucky. All I needed to know was that she was here, and she wanted me. I wasn't going to do anything to mess it up. I undid the button and moved my hands up her sides to cup her face, to kiss her, to taste her again. She went pliant and soft, warm in my arms.

Kissing Autumn tasted like everything good in this world. So much better than I remembered, but she also tasted like... Sugar? Marshmallow sweet, slightly smoky, tinged with artificial berry lip balm that made a heady combination, all pieces of my new heaven. We kissed until our cheeks were flushed. Our foreheads pressed together, we shared the same air.

Taking a moment to appreciate her, I leaned back, keeping our hips interlocked. Pink kiss-strained lips parted as we caught our breath together. Her flannel hung open, and hardened peaks stood out against the thin material of her tank top. I thumbed the fabric, immediately pleased as Autumn arched into my touch. Her hands found the back of my neck again as I leaned down and kissed her.

As I held my breath against her neck a moment later, the zipper's undoing became the only sound in the cabin. Autumn's hands kept possession of me while I hooked my fingers into her belt loops. Leaning back to meet her eyes again, I slowly peeled her hip-hugging jean shorts down. She stepped out of them, one leg at a time. Her fingers rested on my neck and urged me back up to her mouth. I gave a slight shake and dropped to my knees before her.

Leaning back on my heels, I smiled as Autumn pressed against my door, and when she returned the same fire and raw need, I let myself continue to explore her body with my mouth. Eagerness and desire greeted me as I trailblazed a path to her belly button, slowly making my way toward her hip. Peeking out from the waist-line of her underwear was the edges of a tattoo. *What have we here?* I grinned up to find Autumn watching me, rapt with my every move. Need to taste her again, after all this time, consumed me.

Her eyes were wide and certain, locked on mine and gave me all the encouragement I needed before my mouth came down on her with a little more power and purpose. Kissing her as if I'd never have this chance again because, in all honesty, I probably wouldn't. I wasn't going to waste a moment. I licked over her underwear-clad pussy. Autumn moaned, her fingers on my scalp encouraging me to graze my teeth over her. Her body writhed beneath me and put me in an awestruck state of being. I hooked my fingers in the delicate fabric and yanked them away, dropping them on the floor. Autumn shivered, her lips quirking up in an approving grin.

Gingerly, I traced my tongue along her hip to the exposed tattoo of a constellation I didn't recognize before I kissed it and made my way to the place I'd been dying to visit since she stepped inside.

Wild and tender noises made the best melody as Autumn met me with enthusiasm, her body reacting to every graze of my lips on her. I knew right then that nothing else would do it for me again. In all the years that stretched between us, nothing else had come close to feeling this good.

Desire was all I saw in the glance up at Autumn before I sank my mouth onto her, tasting her for the first time in way too long. This gorgeous woman was all about my tongue on her as she ground herself lightly against me, chasing her pleasure. Pulling her thigh up onto my shoulder, I opened her farther, giving in to the need to consume her. I dipped my tongue inside her core, pushing in and out a couple of times, tasting what I'd thought I'd never have again. My fingers took over, stroking inside of her as I swirled my tongue and sucked on her clit, wanting to remind her of all the ways I knew her. Her body was attuned to mine, soaking wet and shaking for me.

Autumn groaned, her pleasure building fast, coiled and ready to explode. If the way her hands tightened on me wasn't enough of an indication, the way her gasps became more guttural and raw was.

I didn't let up, pulling her ass against me, eagerly encouraging her with my fingers. I hung on to every moan she gave me, every ragged breath, every twitch. She was close, and I was dying to hear her say my name. I imagined how she'd half groan it, half growl it. As I swirled my tongue again and curled my fingers slightly against her front wall, Autumn stiffened against me. Her ankle dug into my back, as her orgasm rocketed through her. The crescendo of her pleasure washed over both of us as I devoured her.

Autumn melted farther into me, giving me the sweet nectar of her release, but I didn't let up. Soon, she became too sensitive and tapped me on the head, causing me to reluctantly pull away. She caught her breath before her leg fell from my shoulder, and she dragged me back to my feet.

Autumn stamped a claiming sort of kiss to my lips, and my heart pounded as she walked us back toward my bed. Her eyes fixated on me as though there was nothing else in the world worth looking at, and I knew without a doubt I'd follow her anywhere.

We were ravenous. I took her hips into my grip, and she pushed me onto the bed and planted her hands on either side of me, leaning down until we were making out again. She tore at me, shoving my robe off my shoulders, her kisses desperate again.

My inquisitive tongue and lips left open kisses over Autumn's collarbone and down to her still-clothed breasts. Her chest became the center of my focus as I was framed in flannel. I teased her stiff peaks through the thin fabrics of her tank top and bra. Autumn's gasp and impatient huff had me smiling. I took her shirt by the back of the collar and pulled it, restraining her arms and pushing her chest out toward me. Autumn made a half-hearted attempt to struggle with her limited mobility, but her sleeves subdued her wild movements and unleashed mine. I nipped at her collarbone and released her arms, yanking the shirt from her and finishing with her tank top.

Autumn let out a sigh of relief as she regained her freedom, unlatching her bra and letting it join the pile of clothing on the floor.

"Tell me you have a condom," she breathed. I'd never been more grateful for the one I carried for emergencies, and this was the sexiest emergency I'd ever had.

"On the nightstand. In my wallet."

She pulled away, lifting off me for an excruciating second before bringing back the foil package and ripping it open. The slowness with which she rolled it down had me questioning if she was torturing me on purpose. That was, until she lined us up and slid down on me as if she couldn't handle being apart either.

Our movements created a resolute well in me, and her slow intensity had me meeting her thrust for thrust. Nothing else mattered but the way she took me, her hips rotating and rocking against me. I worked myself under her, remembering this was her favorite position before. Was it still?

I trailed my fingers down her stomach. She'd always said I was good with my hands. I needed her to know that hadn't changed. Interlocked, I rubbed her sweet spot, encouraged by the sounds she made, and her hips shifted in time with my hand. The tension in my body built. I could only hold myself back for so long. It was becoming nearly impossible every time Autumn sank down on me. A sweaty palm pushed against my heart as she steadied herself and the intensity of her breathing and movements told me she was close.

"That's it, sweetheart." I groaned as she clenched around me. My thumb circled her clit in that way I knew she loved, and she threw her head back with my name on her lips.

Autumn's release decimated the last of my resolve. I was flying with her, enraptured by this free-spirited woman as I followed right behind her. Warm possession crept through me. How had I let her go before? Our ragged breaths filled the room as we embraced in the afterglow. She breathed out, and I took a deep breath, drawing it into my lungs and surviving on her.

Wrapped tightly in my arms, she settled against my beating heart. Autumn's body was relaxed and pliable against mine, her arms curling around and holding me as if she'd always been here, as if we belonged like this, free and entangled together.

TWENTY

Jamie

SUNBEAMS WARMED MY FACE, calling me to stare at the amazing wilderness outside my cabin window. I meant to cover my eyes with my hand but paused, realizing it was wrapped around the most beautiful woman I'd ever seen.

So it wasn't a dream.

I had Autumn in my arms on a resplendent summertime morning. I couldn't help but smile.

I realized we had never slept together before. We'd been together, but we had never lied about where we were and gotten a hotel or drifted to sleep after a quickie and forgot to go home on time. No, this was something new. I took a breath of Autumn's hair and pulled her in a little closer, determined to savor this significant moment.

Autumn's face was pressed against my chest, her deep breaths warming my skin. We hadn't taken the time to put on clothes. The most I'd done was take care of the condom and crawl back into bed with her, so we were sticking together in all the places we were touching. It was perfect except for one thing. I was famished.

I carefully kissed her forehead, lifting her so that I could slip my arm out to place her head back on the pillow. Jesus, she slept like a rock. She also didn't notice my removal of her leg from my shins or the noise I made as I pulled open a dresser drawer to get a pair of joggers, a shirt, and underwear. I thought about whether I should wake her up, noting that it was seven thirty, a first for me in I didn't know how long. Sleeping in felt amazing.

I stretched and gazed at her again. Her face was pressed into the pillow, tendrils of hair cascading over her face to show glimpses of her soft features. Her partially open lips, still red from our nightly activities. Her button nose led up to long eyelashes that drifted over her cheek. I could have stood there like that forever—which would be a perfectly normal fleeting thought *if* I had deeper feelings, which I didn't.

I opened the door to my cabin with as much finesse as I could muster, hoping it didn't creak like it always did and wake up the beautiful woman nestled in my bedding. Just my luck, it didn't. I thanked the door gods and stepped onto my porch, ready to get going on this glorious morning.

Ren's small but high front window curtain was closed. Curious...

After I did my business and brushed my teeth, my stomach rumbled. I moved to the mess hall with zeal, ready to load up on breakfast and bring it back to my cabin. I only hoped that she would still be there.

"No, they are totally doing it," one of Autumn's campers, whose name I thought was Irene, said. "She didn't come home last night."

Shit.

"How do you know?" Ian whispered.

Probably Irene grabbed a slice of spinach and feta quiche. "She's always in bed by eleven, and I'm a night owl. Plus, her curtains are open right now."

My ears tuned in. Were they talking about Autumn?

"You are so damn nosy."

"Are you at the same camp that I'm at? The gossip in this place takes me back to high school. It's like riding a bike," Irene mused.

Ian laughed. "I think you need to hook up."

"Believe me, I would. Unfortunately, everyone I think is hot has a ring on their left hand." She shrugged, picking up her tray and turning toward me. I waited for a flash of recognition to cross her face, but she didn't appear to recognize me or at the very least know me as the probable source of her gossip. Maybe I was drawing the wrong conclusions.

I walked by Autumn's pod. Her window blinds were shut, thank god. Maybe we'd gotten away with it. I knew this was ridiculous. We were grown adults, and she hadn't mentioned a rule about fraternization. But if I knew Autumn at all, we were walking a fine line between her freaking out and her being okay with what had transpired, and being found out would probably slant negative.

I tried to close my cabin door softly, but the thing wouldn't give without some strength, and I gave it a little too much, slamming it shut. Autumn didn't glance at me, instead speaking into her pillow, her words coming out muffled.

"You're clothed."

What I should have been doing was telling her to slip out as carefully as she could before the camp woke up. Instead, I dangled a croissant in her eye line. "It would have been weird if I showed up at the mess hall as naked as you are."

Her eyes snapped open. "You don't know that," she deadpanned, getting up and pulling the blanket over her shoulders to create a cocoon. She took the croissant and unceremoniously bit right into the center of the thing. Monster.

I sat the two plates of food I'd procured on the bed and handed her a coffee. She took it as though it was her only lifeline, looking over the rim as she sipped slowly. I looked out the window to avoid her gaze as it did something to me.

"You trying for round two?" she flirted. "That's the only explanation for this kind of treatment this early in the morning." Her stomach grumbled.

Couldn't I just get my girl a croissant? But that was the wrong answer.

"That's the only explanation?" I asked as Autumn beamed at me, patting the space next to her. I did as I was prompted, taking a piece of bacon and biting into it. "What about if I was trying to impress you?"

"Then it worked. But I'm more impressed by that thing you did with my leg over your shoulder."

"I've got more tricks up my sleeve, you know."

"Don't tempt me." Her eyes took on a dark quality that had me wanting to dive right into them.

I took a piece of bacon and held it in front of her lips, and she took a bite, smiling at me as if I were the damn sun. Apparently, bacon was the way to her heart.

"This is a lot of sweet things, Davis." She lifted her plate to demonstrate. "I don't remember you having a sweet tooth."

"I don't, but I was really feeling like s'mores for some reason." I paused as she snorted. "And since they don't have those this early in the morning..."

She didn't explain her burst of laughter, taking an apple chai scone and biting into it as though she was attempting to cover it up. Which reminded me of another thing she'd been covering up.

I tugged on the blanket and took a better look at her hip opposite her wildflower tattoo. It was a more subtle image, a small constellation.

"It's Phoenix." She watched as I traced the stars. "We each picked a constellation when we named the camp, and I chose this one because... Well, you're going to think it sounds stupid, but—"

"Starlight was your fresh start."

"Yeah." Her voice was just above a whisper. "It's my home."

I tried to imagine a younger Autumn starting this new adventure with the hope that it would stick, to the point of branding it on her skin. She'd taken a risk, and it paid off. I didn't think I'd ever put myself out there like that, and I couldn't imagine taking such a leap.

The silence stretched between us as I gazed at her skin to the point that I realized it had been too long. I looked up to find Autumn opening her mouth to speak before closing it. Then she went through the same motion before opening her mouth one more time and spitting out whatever she was thinking. "I'm not wrong. It got better, right?"

Ah, the sex. A perfect non sequitur. "Well, I hoped we'd improved since we were teenagers."

"I'd call it more than just an improvement. You've been practicing."

"That's not flippant at all," I joked.

"Fine, I'm proud of you."

"Not better."

She smiled from ear to ear, and I wanted to reach out and touch her beautiful lips, wishing they were pressed up against mine.

"So, no regrets?" I asked nervously.

"No regrets." It sounded like she meant it. "But obviously this can't go anywhere," she stated plainly.

I wanted to argue with her. It was where my talents lay. But in this case, she was right.

"I have to say, it was great connecting—literally."

She sputtered out a laugh, opting not to respond to my cheesy joke. Instead, she changed the subject. "What's your itinerary for today?"

"Well, to start: we're gonna be missing morning yoga."

Autumn's eyes opened with glee. "That's the hottest thing you've ever said to me."

A memory of more than one occasion where I'd given her a courtesy wake-up call so she'd get to class on time reminded me how much she detested mornings. I'd forgotten how bad of a morning person she was.

I placed the plate on the tiny nightstand and pushed her hair behind her ear. "Wow, I really had no game when I was younger, huh?"

She took my other hand and kissed my knuckles. "Your game was more like 'we have twenty minutes until my parents are home...'"

I cringed. We'd never had any time. "That's right, and you loved it."

"I wouldn't say 'loved,' but it was effective."

"Hey, Autumn."

"Yeah?

"We have an hour until your first class." I winked.

She pulled me to her and kissed me, her lips tasting like bacon and... Still, for some reason, marshmallows? It was oddly sexy. That made me sound desperate. Who cared? It was satisfying as hell.

She pulled away, tilting her forehead against mine. "Then we better make the most of our time."

TWENTY-ONE

Autumn

I was not freaking out.

And my hands weren't shaking. Neither were my thighs after an amazing night with my ex-boyfriend. That would be crazy, right?

Last night had been full of surprises. It was as if we'd picked up where we left off, but with maturity and much, much more skill than before. The things he could do with his tongue. The things he could do with his... Never mind.

I hadn't expected to jump him the way I did. But seeing his face, knowing what he'd just done for my best friend, it meant something to me. What mattered was that Jamie was acting in the self-interests of others and not just to gain favor with me but because it was the right thing to do. That felt different this time around.

He chose to alert my best friend despite the argument we'd had on my front porch, and it filled me with this fire I just couldn't tamp down. Maybe he had changed. Maybe it didn't matter since this was going nowhere anyway. Maybe I'd overreacted when he tried to kiss me. He sure didn't seem to mind when I mauled him immediately after talking with Jack around the campfire.

The first time we slept together had been in the back of his car. It sounded cliché, but back then, we'd been leading up to it for months, and we'd both known it was on the table. He'd brought pillows and blankets. Made it comfy. Had a new air freshener. I still thought of him whenever I smelled artificial vanilla.

"Um... Autumn?"

"What? Yeah?" I set down a bundle of paintbrushes in the craft shed and looked up to see the confused face of my fellow counselor. Apparently, I'd zoned out one too many times, and people were starting to notice.

Felicia looked at me as if I were sick or something. "I asked you if you could take over for my afternoon pottery class."

I pasted on a smile and tapped my chin with my finger. "Can't. I have ax throwing."

"On Tuesday? Since when?"

Shit. It was Tuesday. Yesterday was the day I'd decided to have casual sex with my high school ex. Yesterday, I knew he had changed, but it didn't mean anything had really changed between us. Yesterday, I decided to have a camp fling. That was all it was. If the gossip mill was correct (and it usually was), then camp flings were completely normal. No cause for alarm. But being brought breakfast in bed and waking up to his smiling face after the night we'd had was a different story. Feeling way too much for the man who'd broken up with me without so much as a goodbye was something to freak out about later. Now was the time to focus on what was important: this camp, my friends. Not gorgeous exes.

"I have a meeting in twenty minutes, but I think I'll be free in time," I responded. I'd already asked Sawyer to cover my morning class so I could meet with Joy and Marty, the owners of Foxglove Stables next door.

"Lifesaver," Felicia exclaimed. The light in her eyes was far too bright, as if I'd just agreed to give her a kidney.

"I prefer Skittles." I smiled at her for half a second, proud of my dad joke. I could have my meeting and then a two-hour break before Felicia's pottery class.

"Tonight, we're making weed ashtray pinch pots. Get it? A pot... For your pot." Whoa, pottery had changed since I'd led it. "The example is on the craft cabin desk."

I was wrapped up in an almost too-tight hug. Felicia always thanked me way more than necessary.

"Don't worry about the calendar. I'll update it. Go."

Loud laughter burst from outside, and I turned just in time to see Emerson gracefully lob a water balloon at Jamie. I couldn't look away as the balloon moved in slow motion through the air. His hands were outstretched, but his efforts were futile. The balloon burst all over his chest, inciting another round of laughter from him and his podmates. He looked so good in the outdoors with the sun on his face and a wide, uninhibited smile. I cupped my hands over my mouth and hollered a whooping yell their way. Emerson, Lamar, and Ren waved back before Jamie turned around and saw me.

His shirt was marvelously plastered to his chest, and now that I knew exactly what was under that shirt, how he'd flexed and moved under my hands, I couldn't look away. My body itched to run up and peel the wet material off him. Hand up high, he waved at me and called for me to join them right as Lamar pelted another one at his ass, and he shrieked. Jamie's happiness was a reminder that he belonged here just like all the other adults with too many restrictions and not enough fun in their lives. He'd finally found a spot to connect to that side of himself.

I waved him off, shaking with laughter, and left to make my way toward Foxglove Stables.

A STONE PATH lined the walkway to an adorable log cabin, what I'd been told was the home/office of Marty and Joy. I'd set up a meeting last week and was excited to finally visit the property that bordered ours. I'd never been here before, but I knew the couple in passing, because it was hard to live in a town as small as Wildwood and not know who people were.

Their camp was everything I expected it to be. To the right of the walkway was a demonstration on an American Paint Horse showing animal maintenance. Small children huddled around as a well-tempered animal's mane was brushed out, the kids' eyes rapt with attention.

The stables branched out over vast acres of pasture, woods, horse trails, and their own creek. Their website showed kids and teens coming for the day to ride horses and learn what life on a ranch was like. From trail riding to running obstacle courses and playing ball with furry friends, it looked like a place I would have loved to go as a child.

Joy met me on the porch with a buzzing sort of excitement. "Hey, Marty, it looks like summer's over because here comes Autumn!"

I laughed at the cheesy joke, enjoying the welcoming tone to start this meeting. It relieved some of the nerves I had about this pitch.

Joy welcomed me into her house. The door opened to a plant lover's dream, a warm space decorated with spider plants and pothos displayed proudly from ceilings in macrame pot holders much like the ones we did at camp.

Joy took me back to a whimsical kitchen painted in soft yellow and offered me a beverage. I asked for coffee because I noticed it was Beans and Beans's French roast—my favorite.

The kitchen appeared to be built for entertaining with a large island at the center, but the room mostly showcased what appeared to be pickling supplies and other various projects. Bright pink jars of what I assumed were pickled red onions lined the breakfast bar, their fermentation complete. Marty was writing names on hand-made tags as he caught my entrance. His face lit up when he saw me.

"Is it time already?" His eyes went from my navy-blue A-line dress to the folders in my hand. "So professional." Marty snapped the rubber band holding a tag onto a mason jar and walked with us to the living room.

We took seats in front of a wrought iron and glass coffee table hosting an antique vase filled with fresh indigo hydrangeas.

"It's so nice to have someone from Starlight come down here. It's been a while since we've seen Hazel and Leo." Joy's face softened at the mention of our camp's owners. They'd met with Marty and Joy when we moved in to promise we'd be good neighbors and had bumped into them in town, but we'd never had any issues with our noisy camp thanks to the acreage between us. "They're such a nice couple."

I nearly laughed at the idea of the two of them being interpreted as a couple. They would say that was crazy, but it wasn't like we hadn't all thought it. "Oh, they're not together."

Joy's face scrunched up. "Really? I swear they were finishing each other's—"

"Sentences," Marty cut her off.

Joy gave him a wry smile. "So, Autumn, as much as we like having company, you look like you're on a mission."

"I wouldn't call it a mission... I have a proposition for Foxglove."

"Ooh, we haven't had a proposition before." Joy's gleeful handclap made me think she wasn't thinking of the innuendo that posed.

I moved on quickly. "As you know, we're neighbors." Wait. That was obvious. "And we both have camps." This wasn't going well. "Sorry, I'm a little nervous."

"Nothing to be nervous about, sweetheart. We're just chatting."

"Right." I opened the folder and pulled out two sheets with facts and figures on them, passing them off to the couple. "So, Camp Starlight offers a variety of activities. As you can see, they're listed on the second page. We change them out every season and keep the most popular ones. I was curious, what days do you have camp running?"

"We host camps Friday through Sunday and Tuesday through Thursday," Marty explained. "But we're thinking of pulling back slightly because there's been a lack of interest."

I nearly bounced out of my seat. "That's perfect."

Joy looked over her sheet. "Perfect for what?"

"Well, I was thinking maybe we could partner with Foxglove. If you had, say, one day a week free, we could have campers from Starlight coming over here throughout the day to experience your ranch." I was practically crossing my fingers as I awaited their response.

Marty nodded in agreement. "So we'd be teaming up?"

"Exactly. We would pay to rent out your camp for the day. And we would provide staff—"

"We already have staff," Joy interjected.

"Then we could provide support. But the takeaway would be our campers getting a different experience and you getting the guaranteed business. And we were hoping, well, if you flip to page three, you'll see—" The flipping sound distracted me for a moment. "As you can see, sixty-seven percent of our campers have children. We were thinking that this would be an opportunity for you to showcase your camp to our campers and potentially gain business from their interactions as well."

"I like this idea, I do, but I'm not sure how beneficial it will be toward your visitors. We mostly gear our camps toward children," Joy observed.

"Most of our campers will probably have no experience on a ranch or with horses, and I think you'll find that our adults are children at heart. I know if I was visiting camp, I'd love the opportunity to ride a horse and participate in the activities you offer. We want this to be beneficial to both parties, obviously." They were quiet for a moment, and I wondered if I'd lost their interest. "If you don't mind my asking, how much do you make per day when kids attend camp?"

Marty whipped out an old-school ink printing calculator and typed in some numbers. He ripped off the piece of paper and handed it to his wife.

"You're not including staffing, Marty. But you can leave off food and beverage."

Marty nodded and went through a few more numbers before handing it over again. Joy amended it with a red sharpie and slid it over to me facedown. I smiled at the theatrics.

I lifted the paper and nodded, relieved to see that this was under my budget. "We could work with this," I said, tamping down my excitement.

Once the hard numbers were worked out, the couple agreed to come by Starlight to see our grounds and meet with Hazel, Leo, and me to iron out details.

Marty looked up from my document, his eyes sparkling. "This says you offer macrame? And they have pottery, Joy."

Joy nodded, suddenly all business. "I think we can agree to your terms, but I'd like to add an addendum. A monthly date night at Starlight for the two of us. I think that could be valuable to our partnership."

Two could play this game. I entered with the same tactics. Hazel and Leo would be so proud of me for negotiating other perks. "For a couple of jars of those pickled onions, something could be worked out."

I MADE my way back to the office to let them know how things went and deliver a jar of Marty's pickled onions.

The door opened with a small snick. We left it unlocked from sunup to bonfire so that counselors could pop by when they needed to check the schedule or ask a question.

I'd always loved their shared office space. Leo's area was bursting with color, little origami creatures and pictures everywhere. Hazel's had a much more minimal approach. With the exception of a random paper airplane, her desk only displayed two photos: one of her and Leo the year they'd met at a summer camp when they were twelve years old, and the first group photo Jack, Hazel, Leo, and I took together. The new Camp Starlight sign was displayed prominently, with the naked tree just in frame. We'd been red-cheeked and giggly from drinking the night before we opened to the public, and we'd had no idea what we were in for. Our smiles went from ear to ear, and you could see the excitement on our tired faces: dreams in our hearts, wide-open eyes, eager and ready for the adventure.

My hand was up on the whiteboard, writing my name in place of Felicia's, when Hazel stepped inside, her gaze landing on me.

"It really is a lovely calendar." I nodded at the giant whiteboard, lovingly referred to as our Command Center. We'd written the week's schedule across it with counselors in the first column so anyone could see where each of us was at any given time.

Hazel joined me at the board. "What's Felicia up to?"

"She has another date with that new librarian. They're going to lunch." The librarian in question was incredibly sweet, and nothing like Felicia's usual type.

"Really? I didn't see that one coming." Hazel looked deep in thought over the matter.

"Me neither, but you know who did?"

Hazel lovingly rolled her eyes. Of course, Leo had had a hand in their recent coupling. It was a strange superpower, to say the least. What would he think of Jamie and me? The thought lingered before I pushed it away. This minor, very tiny obsession over Jamie Davis needed to stop. Keeping it casual was one hundred percent the right decision, and I could do that. I'd set things into motion, and I'd deal with any consequences later, but the more I thought about it, the more I considered. What if there weren't any consequences? Just ridiculously good sex with a good man. That didn't sound so bad.

Hazel plopped down into her computer chair and faced me. She was the picture of cool in ripped cutoffs and hot pink nineties plastic bow barrettes clipped in just above a fishtail braid. She smelled like coconut and hibiscus and looked playful in the most summery way. My friend pushed her ever-present aviators onto the top of her head. "How'd the meeting with Foxglove go?"

"I think they're going to do it. With the number of horses they have and the number of campers we have, I figure we could have multiple sessions throughout the day and anyone who wanted to ride would be able to. They agreed."

"Really? That's great."

"I told them our campers will probably like the same activities as the kids do, with a steeper learning curve. Ooh, and they teach lassoing." I thought that through and realized one caveat. "We need to make sure no one is intoxicated when they go over there."

"Agreed. And Leo isn't allowed to go anywhere near me with one of those lassos."

"You sure you don't want to be caught, little darlin'?" I spoke in my best Western accent.

"What isn't Leo allowed to do?" He barged into the office and practically flew into his chair, spinning 360 degrees before Hazel gave him another spin. They were such kids. I loved witnessing their unadulterated joy when they were together.

"Lassoing," Hazel replied.

"Why not? I think I'd be great at it. I'm pretty sure I was a cowboy in another life."

"You think you'd be able to handle livestock? You're scared of squirrels, Leo."

"That's for a reason," he said through gritted teeth. "You know what, I can't let that go. You, me. We duel at dawn."

"I'll be there," she said with an eye roll. "If it seems like I'm standing you up, I promise I'm not. I'm probably running late."

"Something about that makes me not believe you, but whatever." He moved on, turning toward me. "Did you already tell her the news?"

"I was waiting for you." She shrugged, downplaying whatever had his seams about to burst.

"That's my girl," Leo said to castigating glares. "My woman?" he corrected. I snorted a laugh. "Fine, my patiently gorgeous genius."

Hazel nodded in approval. He always got her smiling. That was Leo, flirty, fun, and a very poor secret keeper.

"You're being so cryptic right now. What news?" I asked, matching both their silly grins. This was something good.

Leo spun his chair in my direction. "You're never going to guess."

TWENTY-TWO

Jamie

Dear Mom,

It's crazy writing this to you from summer camp. It still doesn't feel like a thirty-year-old man belongs at a summer camp, but what I've learned from this experience is that those things that I loved as a kid can be just as enjoyable as an adult.

I reread the words and shook my head. No matter what I did, it sounded like it was in the voice of a twelve-year-old. I'd never seen myself doing this in my life, but it was going to make her day. In the end, that was what mattered.

It was hard to get my mind off everything I'd been through in the past few days. I wanted to write my mother a reasonable but gushing letter after her kind care package, but there was a lot to put down on paper.

It's been kind of crazy how things have panned out. I've been spending a lot more time with Ren. We haven't been able to have this much fun probably ever. You were right in your letter. This has been really good for our friendship.

I was always honest with my parents. Our family didn't shy away from talking about our emotions and the things that mattered. It was a breath of fresh air compared to what I was used to dealing with in Seattle: shallow how-are-yous, guarded answers, and professionalism.

Other than that, I guess I have something kind of unexpected to tell you...

I stared at the words and scratched them out.

Remember the reason you had to fly down and pick my ass up off the floor my freshman year of college? She's here.

I scratched that out too. Oh god. How did you even broach this topic when you didn't know what it meant?

I think I have feelings for Autumn. Again.

I scratched the final line, staring at the disappointing sheet and crumpling it up before rewriting everything and changing the last line:

You'll never believe who's here.

That was it. I rushed through the part involving Autumn. Overthinking would get me nowhere. It worked. By the end of the hour, I had a letter that was ready to be mailed. I put a handmade bookmark made with dried flowers inside, hoping she would use it in her next favorite read, and rushed it out before the final mail call. More than likely, it wouldn't get to her before the end of camp, not that it mattered, but we weren't all that far from Portland, so there was a good chance.

I found Hazel carrying a beige mailbag, Santa style. She held it open for me and closed the bag when I was done. I nodded my thanks before she handed the bag to Lamar, who ran it toward the camp gate.

"Hey, Jamie, before you go—would you mind stopping by the office for a quick chat?" There was an excitement to Hazel's tone, which was the only reason I wasn't filled with anxiety over her question. It wasn't quite "we need to talk," but it was still slightly nerve-racking.

"Sure." I followed her into the main office.

"Hey, Zel!" Leo bounced excitedly as we slipped inside the doors. "Look who just sent us a birth announcement."

Hazel pulled the cardstock card from his hand, and her eyes crinkled from her warm smile. I'd only caught smirks and grins from her, never full-fledged smiles. She showed me the back of the announcement and then the front, running her fingers over the embossed words. I kind of loved being included, even though I had no idea who these people were. On one side was a happy couple holding a small bundle in a yellow blanket. On the other was a baby sleeping in a basket. It had been a long time since I'd gotten one of these in the mail. It just reminded me that my niece and nephew had been growing up faster and faster. It felt like every time I saw them a new milestone had been hit.

Autumn hung up a phone, making her presence known. She wrote something down on a slip of paper as she talked to Leo. "The winery has our order, but they can't get it to us in time."

He shook his head. "We can run over there and get it, but—"

"Who's going to do that?" Hazel interjected.

"I've got a couple of hours," Autumn started, and I wanted to offer to go with her, but that would look out of place. Plus, I had no idea why I was here. "I need to go get my purse. Hey, Jamie." She smiled at me as if she'd just realized I was there.

Leo opened a safe and grabbed a credit card out of its depths. They discussed the list, and she rushed out, not making any more overtures to me or Hazel. She was busy, but she was probably also trying not to draw attention to us, which was good. I had no idea what the implications were for her dating—no, *sleeping* with—a camper, but they couldn't have been good. Although they did seem pretty cool...

Hazel pulled out a seat for me before going to her desk. "So the reason you're here... We were thinking... I mean, you can say no if you want to..."

Leo cupped her shoulder. "This isn't something to be nervous over."

"I know, but he's here to have fun. And he's paying for it." Technically, that wasn't true. Ren had paid for our stay. And after he dropped a water balloon over my head, I would probably wait to pay him back just to be an asshole.

"I'm right here, you know."

She forged ahead. "Look, this is probably inappropriate, but Autumn told us that you might be willing to give us some legal advice. It'll be really quick. Probably. Or we could wait until you're back in the office and video chat or something..."

"How about you ask me your question and we'll go from there? Though it's important to remember, I practice corporate law. In Washington."

Hazel nodded as if she already knew. "We've had someone approach us about expanding." She delivered this as if it were bad news, but Leo's face was lit up. "To another state, probably Northern California."

He cut in. "We don't have any idea what we're doing. With negotiations and the contract, not with the camp."

"That sounds like a great idea. This place is magical," I practically blurted.

Leo smiled at her, and they shared something I couldn't explain before he looked back at me. "Thank you," he said humbly. "We were thinking this might be a good way to spread that magic, I guess, so that more people can attend. We've sold out for years now, and we only have so much space to spread out in—"

"And barely up-to-code cabins can be built in a day," Hazel deadpanned.

"She's joking," Leo corrected.

"Actually, if you're going to be our lawyer, we can disclose anything, right?" Hazel continued her joke as if Leo hadn't written the first one off. "Because those cabins in Orion are the worst ones. Like, we probably shouldn't even be using—"

He ignored her. "*The point* is, this sounds like a pretty cool idea, and we wanted to go over what you think we need to address with all of this."

They were right. This was my vacation, and work was the last thing I wanted on my mind, but I wanted to help them despite that. Not to mention the result would make Autumn happy. This was a no-brainer. Not that I was trying to make her happy or anything. I was being completely casual.

"I'd love to help. Tell me what you need."

THE REST of the day went by slowly without Autumn around. I went for a swim, and now I was turning the last page of my book in the Meditation Meadow. This shouldn't have been a momentous occasion, but it was.

I hadn't read a book for fun since college. I hadn't had time, and when I did, I usually spent it cleaning or sleeping. Even with the time I'd spent messing around with Ren and navigating this whole ex-girlfriend situation, I'd found the time to relax. It felt so good. It seemed like every activity I participated in, fun or mundane to most, made me reevaluate what I'd been doing with my life and what else I was missing out on.

As Ren had reminded me, that was just what happened on vacation. He'd also mentioned the fact that we'd probably need a vacation from our vacation, but I wasn't worried about that. What I was worried about was the dread that filled me at the idea of leaving here. I chose not to dive into that too much.

By the time I made it to the mess hall, I was rejuvenated and relaxed, but I was also starving. I got some food and sat on a bench next to Emerson, Lamar, and Sawyer. I pushed my roasted broccolini around my plate to mix with my mascarpone mashed potatoes and took a hearty bite.

"Has anyone seen Gia?" Emerson asked.

I nearly spat out my food, choking as it went down the wrong pipe. Emerson rubbed my back until the cough went away, but no one else seemed to notice my outburst.

"She left early. Wasn't feeling good," Lamar said as if it wasn't that big of a deal.

"Left as in *left?*" I asked. I wasn't surprised, not really, but it hadn't been my intention for her to remove herself from the premises when I told Jack. But I guessed the chips fell where they did, and I had to accept the consequences of my actions. Still, I'd done the right thing.

"Yeah," Sawyer said. The crowd in the mess hall drowned out their voice, so I leaned in to listen. "Apparently, she gets these bad migraines, and they weren't going away. It's probably the pressure or the altitude up here."

"She seemed all right to me," Lamar commented.

"Women are frequently able to cover that kind of shit up," Emerson posited, and Lamar nodded in recognition. Her eyes filled with sadness. "I just wish we'd gotten a goodbye."

I pushed down the snarky comment that Gia wasn't able to cover everything up and chastised myself. I had no idea if she was planning on telling Jack about what she'd done. I didn't know their situation, and it was none of my business. In my head, I just kept seeing Jack's dismay at her betrayal when I told him outside of the thrift store. It'd eaten at me after the scavenger hunt, and the only way I'd wiped it from my mind was by having sex with my ex-girlfriend. Like the true asshole I was, my mind went off track, and I started to wonder if that was the way to move on from most of my troubles.

"We'll get her contact info. It won't be over," Emerson promised. "Meanwhile, I can't wait for karaoke." She changed the subject, but she was clearly still hurt over Gia's lack of a farewell.

After we finished eating, we made our way to the campfire and found a couple of counselors setting up mics and messing with a portable karaoke machine. Someone passed a clipboard to me, and I quickly signed up. Ren had already added John Denver's "Take Me Home, Country Roads" to the list with his name next to it, and I was more than excited to see that show. I'd seen him do karaoke on rare occasion and it always made me smile. Most of our hangouts took place at our local bar, unless we were at my apartment watching basketball.

His vibrant and animated singing was just as amazing as I'd hoped. Grant gazed yearningly at my friend. He was the first crush I'd seen Ren have, and they appeared to be over the moon with each other.

Autumn's cohort must have arrived at the same time, because Kell-y and Kell-i went up and sang Beyoncé's "Halo" and were quickly followed by Janna singing Heart's "Barracuda." At some point, real instruments were being used, and Leo's tambourine made an appearance. We cracked up as one of the less musically inclined campers tapped the instrument in overly enthusiastic bursts.

Hazel and Leo went next. The other camp counselors stopped their side conversations and immediately turned to the stage. People were respectful enough to listen and cheer others on throughout the night, but laughter and general conversation still took place around the campfire. That wasn't the case here.

Leo carried an acoustic guitar, and they both sat on the edge of the wooden stage, no microphone or karaoke machine needed, apparently.

He began playing his guitar, singing an acoustic version of "Ho Hey" by the Lumineers by himself until Hazel came in. A sudden awe came over us as we listened to her ethereal voice mixed with Leo's dulcet tones, which created a perfect harmony, overshadowing the crackling of the campfire.

Their heartfelt rendition had me wishing for things I couldn't have. I searched for Autumn in the crowd and found her looking at me. Or maybe that was just wishful thinking.

I turned back to watch the couple who wasn't a couple and wondered if there was something I was missing. Leo watched Hazel with apt eyes as she wrapped herself in song, too focused to notice his attention.

When they were done, people remained silent for longer than made sense, before Lamar gave the couple a "Woo!" which reminded us to clap. We did, loudly. Cheers and whistles emitted from campers, and Hazel and Leo humbly smiled before leaving the stage.

"Okay, next up is..." Sawyer shouted as they looked at the paper. "Jamie."

"Fuck no," I blurted loudly without thinking.

The laughter that followed made my cheeks burn hot. I reluctantly rushed through the stands to avoid anyone seeing me, especially the gorgeous blonde, whose tear tracks were replaced with laugh lines.

"This goes out to my mom."

Scattered "Woo!"s came from the crowd, and I smiled as the karaoke machine started playing a very dramatic piano melody.

I sang the first line of "It's All Coming Back to Me Now." Three lines in, people started to laugh. I'd expected as much. That was what happened when your go-to karaoke song was an extraordinary ballad from a Canadian female pop sensation.

Then people started singing along, which was the goal. People were drunkenly raising glasses and shouting the lyrics when it was time, which was great because it covered up my voice cracking into the microphone. What can I say? The woman had range, and I did not.

The fire made it difficult to spot people from the crowd, and after a moment of searching for Autumn, I quickly gave up, gazing at the small prompter even though it was completely unnecessary.

When I finished, I received almost as many cheers as Hazel and Leo, which was unexpected.

Ren rushed me from the stage, throwing his arms around me and laughing as he almost took me down. "What the hell was that?" he slurred. He had definitely had too many s'more-tinis "Patricia would be proud."

"She loves Celine Dion," I admitted. I remembered nights

when me and Marley would go to bed and she'd play the music in the dark living room, prepared to come upstairs if we were too giggly and not going to sleep.

"Everyone's mom loved Celine Dion," Ren asserted, as though this were a fact, before he went to get another drink.

I looked around for Autumn and found her staring, her lip between her teeth. She sat down next to me.

"That's what does it for you, huh?"

"That's nothing. Imagine how hot I get over "My Heart Will Go On."" She waggled both eyebrows at me.

"Has anyone seen the Fritos?" Nat asked. She seemed fine, but I had no idea what the fallout was from last night's indiscretion.

"They're behind the bar," Autumn told her, seemingly oblivious to her connection to Jack. Nat left, thankfully, and I almost said something to my blonde counterpart before thinking better of it. That was up to Jack to divulge. "She melts chocolate and dips Fritos into it. Doesn't that sound so weird? It's a high snack if I've ever heard of one."

Jamie

I USED to think that sex in water always sounded better than it was.

Pool sex? Too open, frequently risky, very chlorinated.

Hot tub sex? Too many horror stories about bacteria, too warm, too... Man, I wanted her in a hot tub despite all of that. I had problems.

Now *shower sex...*

In a cottage-style communal shower building in flip-flops. That was surprisingly where it was at. I was being mostly facetious but more appreciative than anything. This was the last full day before we left on Thursday. There were already rare moments where Autumn and I had face-to-face time, but with our limited time frame until camp was over, it meant even fewer opportunities to come together. So I took what I could get.

And time inside of a gorgeous camp counselor with shared baggage was exactly what I enjoyed.

I covered her mouth as she moaned against my fingers. She used the wall to hold herself up, her back arched as I thrust into her from behind. I ran my fingers up her sides, across the goose-bumps I caused, and wrapped my hand around her breasts, tweaking her nipples. She pushed against the wall to give her leverage as she ground against me. It felt amazing. She felt amazing. I'd spent all day yesterday thinking about her naked and in my arms. I'd jumped at sleeping with her again last night, and when she offered to go to yoga with me this morning, I was the one who'd convinced her to first take a shower after a very dirty night that left us with a four-hour window to sleep. It was just enough time to feel like a too-long nap with a sleeping hangover, but it was worth it. She didn't even complain.

The showers were empty except for us, thankfully, since the stalls weren't soundproof. Autumn's breaths started to ramp up, indicating she was close. I kissed the tattoo on the back of her shoulder, a sunflower, just like I'd hoped when I'd seen her tattoos at ax throwing.

When we were teenagers, she'd told me that was her new favorite flower after we'd made out in a field lined with them. I'd given her the nickname to commemorate that special moment and now I wondered if it still held significance or if it was just a piece of art. But I didn't want to get distracted. Instead, I wrapped my arm around her and rubbed circles into her clit until she lost it, clawing for purchase against the shower tile.

There was no sound like her whimpering as quietly as she possibly could in an echo chamber like the one we were in. She moved my hands to her hips and squeezed them against her love handles. I gripped harder and thrust home, stiffening as I lost myself in her.

We both panted until she drew back. I listened for any sounds around us and rushed out of the stall, listening to her giggle. Her head peeked out from the door as I threw our condom into a garbage can and covered it with several crumpled paper towels. I rushed back inside, reveling in her beautiful ear-to-ear smile, and pulled her against me roughly.

"You think me running around this place butt naked is funny?" I kissed her ear. "Next time, it's your turn."

She lifted her chin so I could kiss her neck, my hands moving up her ass to her back. "Yeah right." She planted a kiss on my lips, grabbing my hands and placing them over her pebbled nipples.

"So it's like that."

She still had her eyes closed when I pulled her under the water, letting it wash over her until her hair covered her face. Her lips sputtered into a smile as she leaned away, pushing her hair behind her ears, pouring a liberal amount of bougie-smelling shampoo from the dispenser before lathering it into her hair. That was when we heard the footsteps from heavy hiking boots.

Then there was a chuckle.

She turned away from me as if the small amount of distance would keep someone from noticing the four feet in our stall.

"I only know one person who has black sparkle crocs in this place, missy."

Her whole body shook as she held back her laughter. "Missy?"

"You've been caught." Jack chuckled. "In the communal showers? Really? You have your own shower."

"You have your own shower?" I mouthed.

Her cheeks turned a whole other shade of red than they were under the warm water. She turned her head toward the curtain. "It was too far away from your cabin," she whispered, before speaking loudly. "Don't act like every corner of this camp hasn't been christened already, Jack. Move along."

He burst into laughter. "You haven't woken up this early since I've known you. Did you even go to sleep? Never mind. I don't need to know."

"That's right," she proclaimed, as if she'd won the upper ground.

"You're lucky I get stage fright, but if I didn't have to pee this bad, I'd steal your clothes as punishment for dirty deeds, Gardner." Jack's rushed voice alerted us to his departure, but Autumn listened until she was sure he was out of earshot, ignoring the shampoo bubbles dripping down her face.

When she came back to me, she was rolling her eyes through laughter. "Aren't you glad we don't have to listen to him peeing?"

"What are you talking about? That sounds hot," I joked.

"Gross."

I kissed the corner of her mouth.

"Please tell me—"

I kissed the other side.

"We do not need—"

Then the other.

"To invite Jack into our bedroom so you can hear him—"

I stopped her right there, kissing her straight on the mouth. She melted against me, and I forgot what we were talking about. Every moment with Autumn was better than the one before.

"You putting that image in my head makes me feel a little bit violated," I teased.

She kissed my jaw. "Leave it on a comment card."

It was unspoken that we spend as much time together as possible during this days-long casual hookup of ours. She told me last night that my body would need some decent stretching if I was going to bring my A-game today, but it was probably because she knew how important my routine was to me, and we'd already skipped yoga yesterday.

It was easier to leave the shower building than I'd thought it would be. No one seemed to be up for a shower at five in the morning.

She did surprisingly well during yoga—only falling twice which was an improvement.

When we arrived for early morning bird-watching, I nearly lost it. Jack had a comical bucket hat on his head, binoculars around his neck, and a neckerchief tied under his beige polo shirt. He looked like a Boy Scout who was also pushing thirty and could grace the cover of a men's health magazine. Autumn dramatically rolled her eyes, which pleased him, clearly eager to play the part. He probably needed the distraction after everything with Gia.

"He acts like this is a costume, but he loves bird-watching day," she whispered. "He's such a nerd."

"I heard that," Jack spoke under his breath without looking at her before turning to the crowd. "Hello, friends, and welcome to bird-watching." He was practically bouncing in his hiking boots. I tried to remember the last time I was that excited about anything. "Do we have any fellow bird-watching enthusiasts?"

A couple of people raised their hands, and he looked thrilled.

"That's wonderful. There are binoculars in the bin over there." He pointed. "Make sure to grab a pair because much of this can't be seen by the naked eye. They don't usually just fly up to us unless we're really lucky. I feel good about today, though. Let's go."

I tried to ignore the fact that the word *naked* only made me think of Autumn with water cascading down her body. She seemed perfectly normal next to me. I guessed only one of us was a horndog.

"We've got a bit of a hike to get to one of my favorite viewpoints," Jack started. "It looks like everyone took a Birds of the Pacific Northwest guide. If you see something, you can ask me or look through your book and venture a guess at what you're seeing."

The group took off en masse, and I bent down to tie my shoe. "You go ahead of me," I told her. "I'll catch up."

"If you think I'm going to let you use those binoculars to watch my ass, you've got another thing coming." She was too smart for my own good.

"Don't ruin this for me."

Autumn playfully bumped her hip into me, nearly knocking me over.

It took about twenty minutes for us to reach the point Jack was looking for, and he stood on the solitary bench telling us to spread out. It was a majestic overlook, a perfect view of trees, the mountain, and the sky. I reveled in the feeling of being a speck in this natural landscape. There was nothing like this in the city.

We all spread out across the vista, with Jack being the farthest away from us.

She pulled something out of her pocket and showed me, whispering, "He just got this thing. He was so excited."

"Then why do you have it?" I already knew the answer.

"I stole it."

I looked at the bird call, a wooden cylinder with a brass tip that twisted. "Autumn Gardner. Are you secretly a dick?"

"It's no secret," she deadpanned. That wit always got me. Trying to be as covert as possible, she put the binoculars to her eyes, speaking out of the corner of her mouth. "Stop looking at me. Use those binoculars."

"Fun fact: the migration patterns of birds have been changing due to deforestation and urbanization," Jack said facetiously.

Then the sound of a bird call came, followed by some shuffling as she shoved the thing into the back pocket of her jeans. I used one eye to see him turn. He turned again. Autumn laughed under her breath.

"Oh, Autumn," I chastised.

She glared. "Don't look at me like that. Once, he put all of my individual keys into Jell-O molds. And there was one time he put Vaseline on my doorknob. Oh, and he gave me a s'more that was loaded with toothpaste once."

I shook my head. "Wow. Are you two twelve?"

"That and we've watched *The Parent Trap* one too many times." She smiled shamelessly. "Let's just say there's a reason we shut down prank wars."

That had me losing it. "What even is your life?"

She shrugged as if it made all the sense in the world. Jack put his binoculars back up, and she waited a reasonable amount of time before using the bird call again. More shuffling. She looked completely neutral as she stared out of her binoculars. Then he closed in on us.

"Give it." He held his hand out and waited. Other campers

didn't seem to notice, looking through their field glasses and chatting among themselves.

"You need binoculars, Jack? You can have mine, and I can share with Autumn," I tried.

He saw the red string hanging out of her pants and yanked the thing right out of her pocket. She pursed her lips into a smile. "Just for that, you get to go to the front of the class, Miss Gardner."

I sputtered as he yanked her arm until she stood by him about twenty feet from me. She was barely keeping down her laughter.

"Kuh-caw." I cupped my hands around my mouth, doing a bad impersonation of a bird.

She snickered, her lips tilted into a smirk. Several people laughed. We were *all* twelve. I caught Jack's eye roll. Apparently, he was above such things.

Then came the subtle sound of wood being attacked by a beak.

Jack jumped and scanned the area. "You hear that everyone? In case you haven't heard that familiar sound, that's a sapsucker. Can anyone find it? First to do so gets a piece of candy," he joked.

It was enough incentive for people to move their binoculars every which direction until I found it on a lone fir out past a copse of trees. I called it out, and Jack confirmed my find after I pointed in the general direction. Everyone else followed.

"I see it." Janna beamed. "I've never seen a woodpecker before."

Everyone was genuinely excited. I could see why Jack loved his class so much.

He turned his back on me before walking away, and I realized I'd been shorted.

"Hey, what about my candy?" I sulked.

"Candy's for good children. Pretty sure you have two strikes against you. Make it three for even associating with her."

"I can't help that I knew her in high school. Don't hold this against me."

Jack flicked his hand in dismissal. "It's just a Snickers, man. Calm down."

I was starting to like this dude, but withholding chocolate put him on my shit list.

We hiked and found several unique birds before our time was up. By the time we made it down to camp, it was starting to take a toll on me. As much fun as I was having, I was also exhausted from being up all night and doing yoga this morning. Autumn had been up at the front of the group, but I'd lost her until a "psst" came from behind a tree nearby. She waggled her eyebrows as I looked to see if anyone noticed our disappearance.

I rushed to the tree she was leaning against, which was large enough to hide our bodies. I pressed my mouth to hers, knowing we didn't have much time and making the best use of it. Autumn whimpered into my mouth as my hands went to the small of her back, her body arching away from the rough bark without care.

"God, you feel so good." I moved to her neck and ran my hands up her stomach.

She giggled as I found her sweet spot, a little place above her collarbone that both tickled and unlocked something in her every time.

"Oh my god, Jamie," she moaned.

"I know, sunflower."

Suddenly, she stiffened, her hands dropping to her sides. I knew exactly what I'd done wrong.

Shit.

"You can't call me that," she said quickly, looking like she instantly regretted it.

The nickname had been on the tip of my tongue the entire trip, but I'd carefully avoided letting it slip. She was easy to scare when it came to our past, and remembering what it was like back when I called her that may have been the last thing she wanted.

"You're right, I'm sorry. I just saw the tattoo this morning and it was in my head. I won't do it again."

She used her opposite hand to touch her shoulder, almost hugging herself.

"I got that tattoo on a stupid whim when I was getting over you. It doesn't mean anything to me now."

I had a feeling that was the case, but the words still hit me like a punch to the gut. It might not mean something to her, but it meant something to me.

When we were younger, she'd fill with delight at the word, as though it always surprised her. And here I'd gone and reminded her of a time that she obviously still hurt over. A small part of me wondered if she had just been detached, compartmentalizing our moments as kids from our time here and ignoring the memories she'd tucked into a small imaginary box.

I pulled away from her and pursed my lips. A distressing look passed over her face. It went from incensed to crestfallen, and my stomach bottomed out as tears filled her eyes.

"Autumn—"

"We have to go catch up—" She gulped. "We have to catch up to the group."

I reached for her hand, but she pulled back from me. I looked deep into her eyes as a tear escaped, rolling down the side of her face. She quickly wiped it away.

In court, there were three possible ways to address a potentially damaging truth about your client. Deny, distract, or defend. You could deny reality and confuse the jury into seeing as many truths as possible. Denying was the easiest option unless the evidence was indisputable. If that was the case, you could distract the jury by drawing their attention away from the evidence and on to something more compelling. Or you could defend, which was the hardest option. You could make the jury understand why your client would make a choice to break a law and why you would likely make the same choice in the same situation and how, sometimes, the line between right and wrong was a bit blurry. I knew what I had to do.

"Go ahead," I implored. "You can ask me anything, and I'll tell you the truth." It was time for the truth.

I couldn't leave here knowing she had no explanation, no understanding of my regret, even if she slept with me and acted like closure didn't matter.

She looked into my eyes as if searching for honesty, and she must have found it because she finally asked the one thing she'd been avoiding this whole time.

"Why did you end it?" Her eyes were filled with tears, and it nearly broke me. "You can tell me if it was someone else. I... I'm more understanding as an adult than I would have been back then."

The pain in her eyes told me otherwise, and it filled me with an overwhelming sense of anguish.

"God, Autumn," I started, unsure how to even explain.

"You didn't say why, Jamie, not really. And I get that you were venturing off on your own and didn't want to be held back by your high school girlfriend—" Hearing the words I'd used took me back to the most painful conversation of my life. I was thirty, and I still felt like I was swallowing nails every time I thought about it. "It was so sudden. Like you didn't even try. Just confirm it for me, please. Put me out of my misery."

Autumn twisted her hands nervously. I knew what she was worried about but she was so far off base it wasn't funny.

"All this time you thought... There was no one else. There could never be..." I shook my head angrily, ready to rip the Band-Aid off. "I did it for you, Autumn."

The silence that followed was broken by a gust of wind wrapping itself around us and blowing a strand of her hair over her face. I almost reached out to move it, but I knew better.

"You..." Fury lined her features as she pushed it away, her voice breaking. "You did it for *me*?"

"No, I... What I mean is... Goddammit, Autumn." My lungs tightened. I'd been holding on to things for so long. It was time to own up. "I missed you so much. I know it had only been a few weeks—"

"We didn't last a month, Jamie..."

"You were talking about driving down to see me in the *second* week. You were barely holding it together." It was a harsh truth, but it had to be said. I'd been sitting in my dorm room every night thinking of my gorgeous girlfriend and how she'd been ready to give up her weekends to see me. During what was supposed to be one of the happiest times of her life.

"Neither were you." Her eyes flashed defiantly.

"I know. I know that. But I saw down the line. I saw your senior year going up in smoke, and what about when we only lived six hours apart? We had years where we'd be separated. *Years*, Autumn."

Our plan had been for her to go to Stanford while I was in LA, and if that didn't work out, she was going to go to the same school as me, or one nearby. Everything was based around me. Around us.

"You didn't know I'd get in." Her shoulders fell.

"I knew you'd get in." There was no mistaking my feelings on this. I was more sure about it than anything. She'd had perfect scores on tests, extracurriculars, internships, and amazing letters of recommendation, and all of this before her senior year. She was the smartest person I'd ever known. Still was. "I saw it. Your life would have revolved around me. You deserved better than that."

"And all you saw was wasted potential. What about now, Jamie?"

That hit me like a brick, knocking the wind out of me. "What do you mean?"

"I gave everything up. It's everything you just said you were trying to avoid. To many, that's a failure." She blinked away tears.

Of course, she thought I judged her. It was the first thing I'd done. But seeing her comfortable in her surroundings, seeing the way she lit up when she was doing her job, I'd immediately banished the thought. "It's not a failure to you. And definitely not to me."

Autumn had crafted this beautiful life where the only person's expectations she cared about were her own. It was awe-inspiring.

"I gave up Stanford. If you broke up with me like you're saying, that's what you wanted for me. So why would you think I made the right choice?"

I took her hands in mine and looked into her eyes. "You're happy. I love that you're happy. I see you work your ass off and still enjoy doing what you do. No one told us that that was the dream. They said that we needed to go to good schools, to be in good professions, but that was it. It's like our parents have the ideals of six-year-olds. *I want my kid to be a doctor. I want my kid to be a lawyer. I want them to go to Harvard or Stanford.* But why? They say they want the best of us, but they don't *know* what's best for us." I squeezed her hands. "I love the law, and I love being a lawyer. But that was all my choice, and my parents ran with it. I got lucky. I know the pressure you were under when we were kids. I can understand why the straw broke your back. There's nothing here to be ashamed of. In fact, I don't think I could be prouder of you."

Tears were streaming down her face, and a small sob escaped. "We were talking about forever. I don't care what my plans were, I loved you."

And why did that slice me through the gut? I'd earned her love at one time and destroyed it. I did that.

"And that's why I did what I did. Maybe it was the wrong choice, maybe it was unfair, but I did it, and I have to own that." I could have made it long distance for four years. Or six or eight depending on what she'd ended up doing. I'd loved her so much, I would have followed her once I graduated. But she'd been ready to do the same, and that truly hadn't been good for her. I'd meant it when I said forever, but sometimes forever wasn't good enough. "I said all that shit because I knew it would—"

"Break my heart?"

Tears spilled over my cheeks, and I didn't bother wiping them away.

Back then, I had broken my own heart in the process of breaking hers, but we'd needed a clean break. I wouldn't have been able to survive otherwise, but I hadn't known it'd be the last time I'd see her. Even knowing I did the right thing, it took its toll. After five days of ignoring all phone calls and skipping every class, my mom had shown up on my doorstep. I had only answered because I'd thought it was the pizza I'd barely managed to order. That was when I'd finally broken down.

Autumn never knew that. But my pain wasn't what mattered.

"You may never forgive me. I understand that, okay?"

Her silence killed me. The small sobs she emitted broke me down to nothing. But her words after a few deep breaths ruined me. "I do forgive you."

"You..." There was no way. "Really?"

She nodded. "I've had a long time to get over it. I don't like that you made that choice for me, for us, but it makes sense."

And while it made sense back then, I couldn't help but wonder where we'd be if I hadn't made that decision. Teenage love didn't typically last, but deep love, no matter what age, could sustain a relationship for decades until the end, and based on our previous moments years ago to now, our love had been profound. But I'd screwed that up out of a sense of my own righteousness, and I couldn't take that back.

TWENTY-FOUR

Autumn

So... That happened.

In the decade that had passed since our breakup, I had moved on, but our conversation had brought up old wounds that hadn't fully healed. His openness about what had happened brought me the clarity I needed to get to this place with him, and I was glad to move past it so we could enjoy ourselves in the time we had left.

"Meet me at the naked tree at noon," I said. After our heart-wrenching conversation, we could use a little fun.

He tilted his head, looking down at me quizzically. "Where you'll make all my wilderness dreams come true?"

I gave him a sweet kiss. "I'm taking you out."

"Like a date?"

"No, like an unsanctioned outing." I patted him on the chest. "Don't tell Hazel or Leo. Camp insurance will not cover this."

I APPLIED TINTED LIP BALM, popping my lips in the mirror. Grinning wide, I remembered how well Jamie fit in as we teased

Jack during bird-watching. How he'd laughed when I told him why we called it the naked tree, and no, it wasn't just because the bark was peeling but for the campers who had christened it during our first session. His face had said it all, excitement and anticipation showing through his voice. Everything about him gave away that he was looking forward to our date just as much as I was.

"Whoa," Lola exclaimed, taking a step back to give me a generous head-to-toe, and I knew I'd made the right choice with my low-cut royal-blue romper. Cinched at the waist and tight in all the right places, it was the ideal balance between comfort and dressy. "Who are you, you glamorous lady, and what have you done with our Autumn?"

"Shut it." I smiled. "Do you want a hand with that?" I reached for the boxes of wine she held precariously on her way to unload in the bar.

"Alcohol is flammable," she teased. "You touch that, *combustion*."

I smiled at the compliment, indulging her with a twirl.

"So, who's the lucky person?"

"It's just lunch and..."

Her eyebrows raised sharply, but she didn't push, likely knowing I'd cave soon enough anyway. I wanted to brag about him. I wanted to pretend he was mine to keep this time.

"Jamie hasn't been to the slide yet."

"Oh, I see." And I loved her even more when she didn't make a big deal over it.

"Figured it was time." I ignored the way my hands got a little clammy. Just pre-date nerves.

TEN STEPS away in profile stood the most handsome man I'd ever seen. He was effortless, classic charm on full display standing with his back up against our infamous naked tree. He looked so at peace as he gazed down the two-lane road that had brought him here only five days ago.

"You look incredible." He lifted my hand and pressed me up against the tree, kissing me as if we always did this.

The duality of this man stunned me. It was easy to imagine him committed to achieving his goals in a suit and tie from a high rise in the city, but I couldn't get rid of the idea of him in my cabin wearing flannel pajama pants by the fire, reading a thriller under my patchwork quilt.

"Hi there," I said timidly, after being jolted from my daydream.

"Hey."

"Fresh air sure does suit you."

He had a little bit of stubble, and there was a serious set to his jaw and a light in his eyes as he took me in. Jamie radiated not just his usual confidence and bravado but a bone-deep satisfaction. Satisfaction with where he was, what he was doing. His smiles were growing more and more frequent, and it was clear that he was enjoying these moments.

We made our way to the parking lot, and I tossed my keys to him.

"You'll let me drive Starla?" he asked in disbelief, as if I'd deny this man anything. He looked at my trusty blue Volvo I'd been babying since high school. "You never let me drive her before."

"You still get carsick?" I was surprised when he came around to open my door, kissing my cheek before I got in. He seemed stunned that I remembered how sick he'd get when he wasn't driving, but how could I not after that time we road-tripped to Pacific Cove Beach? I'd made him roll the window down in the hopes that the breeze would do him some good, and he'd vomited on the side of my car. Thankfully, I was a little less hardheaded now.

Four minutes later, we pulled up to the Wildwood Ski Resort —a mountain staple. Attractions such as skiing, snowboarding, and snowshoeing offered an array of winter entertainment. Different lifts would take adventurers and families to different levels of ski routes from the bunny hill to the double black diamond runs. During the offseason, the Alpine Slide was the main attraction.

Wednesday afternoon around noon was the sweet spot, apparently. No lines for the ticket booth. No line for the slide.

Jamie's head tilted up toward the mountain peak. I maintained my forward gaze, leading him toward the ski lift that would take us to the top of the slide.

"We're going up there?" His voice was equal parts fascination and excitement.

I reached for his hand, not thinking about it. Dark brown eyes snapped to mine as our fingers interlaced. He held on to me and lifted the back of my hand to his lips.

I resolved to do this. Together, we sat down on the lift as the attendant nodded at me. Jamie didn't let my hand go. He held on like we might never part, like everything would end if he did. Indulging him, I gave his warm hand a little squeeze.

"Amazing. Autumn, check it out." He waved over the tree line.

"Uh-huh." My gaze locked onto the man at my side. His eyes crinkled playfully as he took in the scenery. I felt us lift and didn't move. One hand on the ski lift's sidebar, the other holding on to the man who suddenly looked ten years younger. Fun and foolish and all mine.

"You're giving me a lot of eye contact right now." His amusement was clear.

"In order to know that, you'd have to be giving me a lot of eye contact." I willed my voice to be steady, breath calm.

"Autumn, are you all right?" His eyes searched mine. I wondered if he could feel my clamminess. If not that, he definitely felt the shiver that went through me as the lift took us higher and higher.

"I'm just enjoying the view." It wasn't a lie. But not wanting to admit the reason I hadn't been up to the slide in my time on this mountain.

Then I saw the recognition on his face that I didn't want to be here. I didn't think it would happen like this. I thought I'd get over it. But the last time I'd been on a ski lift, I'd been left up for an hour because the lift had stopped working. And I hadn't gotten over that fear with age.

I glanced at my shoes and watched my toes as they dangled... Dangled. I was going to be sick.

"Hey, it's okay. I'm here." Jamie's lips pressed gently to my temple, then my cheek. Calm enveloped me at his tender words.

I squeezed my eyes shut, and he took my hand. "Yup, I like you here."

He shifted us closer. "I like being here."

I couldn't believe my stupid anxiety-ridden brain. Tempted to look around, to gauge how close we were, but I forced myself not to. Instead, I took a deep breath before focusing on him again.

"I'll let you know when it's time," he said, not making a big deal of it. He really did know me.

After that harrowing experience, we made it to the top. I'd never been so happy for my feet to hit the ground.

With jagged reluctance, we finally unlocked our hands when we were told it was one adult per slide. But I held on to that warm feeling as he settled onto the toboggan. It was a sled-like cart with wheels and a single handle riders could use to go faster or slower. The slide was set up for racing. I lined up in my cart in the lane next to his, prepared to launch at the same time. Jamie's smile told me this was a date he'd never forget. I settled into my cart, all fears gone. Turned out, I was only afraid of heights when I was on a wobbly, open-air ski lift. Being up on this devastatingly tall hill about ready to slide down the mountain filled me with the nervous kind of energy but not fear. Energy that made my stomach swoop and tumble, like it did whenever he smiled at me like that. We took off, and his smile swallowed up any residual nerves.

"I'll be waiting for you at the bottom," he called over to me, but he was underestimating my competitive nature.

I blew him a kiss before leaning back and slamming my control handle to make the cart go as fast as I could. His rapturous laughter told me he was close but not ahead of me.

My body jostled from side to side. Tilting my head back, I soaked in the rush of adrenaline, and everything felt liberating. A scream of elation left my lungs as I plunged down faster and faster. Adventure called, and I let it lure me. Laughter spilled unbidden the whole way down, even as my stomach rode high in my chest. My heart thundered, and dampness gathered in the corners of my eyes as I reached the bottom just behind him. I felt myself being pulled up, then out of my cart. He tucked me into his warm muscular chest and I took in his spicy scent. Insatiable, I looked up at him. His eyes were alight and full of joy.

"Again?" I asked, and Jamie nodded into my neck.

THREE RIDES down the slide later and my cheeks hurt from smiling. My voice was slightly raspy already from the yelling and cackling that came with each exhilarating plunge down the slide. Every time we rode up in the ski lift, our hands locked together, and Jamie's lips coaxed me into comfort. I felt all the security I needed to try again, but I reminded myself that I couldn't fall for him.

I hoped that wasn't a fool's errand.

He looked at me honest and open and like he might just have the same thought that neither of us was brave enough to whisper.

We settled into our seats beneath an ivy-covered pergola on the patio. Raphael's Trattoria was where I'd chosen to go for the next part of the date. Raphael greeted us with a friendly wave, tucking his prematurely graying hair behind his ear before leading us out to their patio seating. The smell of fresh greenery and Italian food mingled pleasantly as we sat at the picnic-style table with the magnificent view of the mountain.

We placed our drink orders, and our server left us alone to get settled in. Bench seats were covered in crocheted pads for each of the tables. Our table was embellished with a brilliant maroon and yellow mandala-like pattern stitch, and carnival glass votives took the restaurant ambiance from nice to cozy. You'd never know that just last winter these tables were built with love and the proper amount of frustration by Jack, Simon, Lola, and me. Long hours and energy had gone into sanding and staining them the right shade to match the bar inside. We'd been happy to take on another way of expressing our love and loyalty to this one-of-a-kind town. We'd always be there for our town, just like they were always there for us. Two years ago there had been a rough storm where we needed a sandbag barrier, and Raphael had used his truck to load, deliver, and unload them, saving our camp from potential water damage from a creek that ran near the mess hall.

We ordered the famous fried ravioli appetizer that I'd dished about as our drinks came out. His Aperol spritz was good of course. My Bellini was better.

Our server came back a moment later with our appetizer and took our orders. Then it was just the two of us.

"What do you think—" I started just as he began, "How do you feel—"

We both laughed, and I reworked my original thought. I couldn't say that.

"What do you think about the ravioli?" I chickened out, yes, but in my defense, he was leaving tomorrow, and that was going to have to be okay.

"You know me so well. Am I that predictable?"

"When it comes to food, yes. When it comes to life decisions..."

"What are you saying?" He folded his arms, and his lips quirked in a sideways grin.

"I didn't mean it like that. I just... Kind of thought you'd be taken by now." I hoped I wasn't overstepping. But I couldn't say the thought hadn't been eating at me. "I've always thought of you as a relationship guy, that's all."

Jamie's shoulders dipped, but his smile didn't disappear. He'd always appreciated my directness. "What makes you say that?"

Had I just dug myself into a hole? Yes. And the darkness was closing in around me.

"I mean, every girl you'd dated you'd ended up in a relationship with. Case in point." I touched my collarbone. "Not to mention you were so good with me. Not that there wasn't room for improvement."

He chuckled. "I'm never going to live down our first anniversary, am I?"

Back then, I'd let the fact that he missed our anniversary go, but I liked giving him a hard time about it now.

"I never told you, but I'd had every intention of being home in time for our date. The only reason we didn't make it back by then was because Gabe disappeared after he'd found some local, and hooked up. We looked for him for hours, but we had bad cell reception. That's why I wasn't talking to him the week after."

"What? Why didn't you tell me?" I was flabbergasted.

"Because it didn't matter. I'd still fucked up. I never should have gone in the first place." Jamie paused for a long moment, as if pondering what to say. "I am a little more responsible than I was when I was in high school. I guess the reason I haven't settled down is that I just haven't met the right person since you. But what about you? What are you looking for in the future Mr. or Mrs. Autumn?"

He may have glossed over that declaration, but I still caught it. I decided to let it go, and redirect the conversation. It hit a little too close to the line we'd been toeing.

"Well, they've got to be funny."

"Of course."

I tapped my finger to my chin. "I need someone I can go toe-to-toe with. Who isn't judgmental, and supports me in my decisions. And they need to get along with my friends because they're also my family." Wait, was I describing him? "And, good hand-eye coordination is a must. Especially with axes."

Jamie burst into laughter, garnering the attention of the tables surrounding us, as well as our server who'd just arrived with our food.

A beautiful plate brimming with rich pesto-covered linguini was presented in front of me, and delicious looking chicken marsala was set down in front of him. Still coming down from our slide-induced high, I let the hot, comforting food and the reality of this moment with this man in front of me sink in. We could be happy here. Us, together, weeknight dates in between camp sessions and his day job, like it was our normal.

A small dab of marsala sauce glistened in the space between his lower lip and chin, and I licked my lips as I stared at it. His lips curved up at me when he caught the movement, and his delicious smile made me grateful we were sitting down. Jamie leaned closer. He was stunning as I caught the faintest smell of his amber and spice soap and him, that perfect combination that had my heart spinning and my instincts to lick that sauce off him kicking into overdrive.

"What's going on in that beautiful head of yours?" he asked, drawing my eyes to his.

Guilty as charged, I was staring as he licked his lips. Our eyes locked together for what had to have been the billionth time. I grinned. I shouldn't divulge these tempting thoughts to him. The man's ego was big enough as it was.

"There's a little sauce right there." I ran my finger along my lip, miming.

Jamie grinned at me. "Maybe you should lick—"

"Don't you dare finish that sentence."

His eyes went wide before he slowly blinked, feigning shock. "You'd let me just walk around like this?"

"Will it get you to take your shirt off again? I know how you are with unruly sauce."

"It was *everywhere*, Autumn." Jamie's face was full of humor and sweetness. "I had to take matters into my own hands. You saw…"

I leaned over our table and swiped my thumb lightly across the space between his lower lip and chin. Bringing it back to my mouth, I sucked the sauce off my thumb, staring directly into his eyes. He stopped mid-sentence, all his attention focused on that singular motion, and I recrossed my legs at the heat in his eyes. We were too far away from the privacy of my cabin. And my bed. Jamie Davis *in my* bed. Heat pooled low and hot, but I tried to ignore it, to push it aside like I'd done before.

My throat suddenly felt dry as a desert. Grasping for redirection, I took another sip of my Bellini. "Cooking with you in that class reminded me of your mom. Does she still make her famous zucchini orzo dish?"

His smile broke out again, then a look of something more tense passed over his face before he took a bite of fried ravioli. "Yeah, I think so. I haven't been back home in a while."

His gaze was far away, and I wondered not for the first time just how different our lives might have gone. I squeezed his hand across the table.

Jamie weaved his fingers with mine. "She would love this place. I should bring her for her birthday next year."

I couldn't contain my smile, stretching wide and unashamed for it. He was going to bring his mom here to tell her all about his time at Camp Starlight. Would he tell her about me? About this?

Hand in hand in the comfort of the candlelight, Jamie chewed his food quietly and didn't pull away. Eating and drinking one-handed came naturally to me, but Jamie struggled to use his fork because I held his dominant hand. This man was making me smile more than I had in a long time. He brought out my snark and my sweetness. He killed me with his humor, and our shared past was still not as dangerous as the undeniable thing he was doing with my heart.

After a while, I excused myself for the restroom before I could say something really stupid. My thoughts were a chorus of "Tell him," and "No, it wouldn't be fair." Maybes and what-ifs ran wild through my mind as I struggled to articulate what he was starting to mean to me... Again. Splashing water on my face in the restroom, I'd completely forgotten about the light makeup I'd applied and took a little bit of time with a wet paper towel to fix it. Moments later, I approached our table.

"Yeah, no, great... Thanks, Margaret, for the call." He paused as I sat back down across from him. "Uh-huh, you do the same." He looked flabbergasted as he seemed to gather himself before another smile made a home across his face. "That was my boss. I got the promotion."

My smile matched his. "You got it?" I screeched. "Jamie, that's wonderful."

He took another bite of his dinner, delighted in my excitement over his news. "It's everything I've been working toward, all the long hours, all the missed... Just, everything."

I stood up fast, with all the enthusiasm I had bursting at my seams. "One sec." I waved our server over with excitement. "Can we please get two glasses of champagne and your famous cherries jubilee?"

"Jubilee?"

"This calls for a celebration. You're incredible."

FULL OF CHAMPAGNE AND NOODLES, I led Jamie along the busy street toward the viewpoint. It was still warm and bright outside as we walked in a comfortable quiet. Taking in the laughter around us, the out-of-towners and locals darting in from shop to shop.

His eyes lit up as we walked past Beans and Beans, as they damn well should. Every town should have a treasure like this even if we weren't indulging tonight.

"Here we go." I motioned for Jamie to sit down on a bench in front of the forest.

He slid his arm around my shoulder and pulled me in tighter to his side as I opened the lid of the to-go container of jubilee, then scooted closer to him.

Velvet sweetness sat rich on my tongue and tried its best to comfort me. Watching his face light up as our server lit the rum and kirsch into the sweet syrup, then poured it over the ice cream was permanently part of my favorite memories. He took the offered bite of dessert, holding my eyes as he licked his lips. Neither of us spoke, letting the moment rest peacefully between us for a breath, then two, and then his liqueur-sauced lips were on me. His tongue was a mixture of hot and cool as it slid across mine. My heart raced. My hands found his neck, and the to-go container was carelessly moved behind me. We pulled toward each other, and the kiss was everything we could and couldn't say.

"What was that for?" I asked a grinning Jamie.

"You had sauce on your lips."

I smiled into the thin slice of space between us. I pulled away gently and leaned my head onto his shoulder. All earlier thoughts of what-ifs were gone in the harsh reality of one phone call, and now I needed to do my best to be happy for him. He fit here, sure. I wanted him here, but none of that meant this was home for him. Maybe, in a parallel universe, he'd stay.

After seeing what Jack went through all year trying to make things work with Gia, a long-distance relationship was out of the question. And yet why was it suddenly all I could think about? The clock wouldn't stop, no matter how good things were between us, and Jamie didn't fill the silence. Instead, we stayed like that, my head on his shoulder, our hands still clasped in the end-of-summer breeze.

"I didn't think I'd ever see you again. I'm really glad you came."

He wrapped me into his side. "I'm glad too."

I didn't know what he was thinking, but he seemed to have a lot on his mind despite this positive development. Instead of saying something, he reached beside me to reclaim the opened to-go box. He offered me the last bite of the cherries jubilee, and I took it.

I'd take what I could get from him. I always had. Syrupy richness collided with the bittersweet reality that this, right here on this bench, was as good as we were going to get, and that had to be okay.

TWENTY-FIVE

Jamie

"IT IS A BIG DEAL, EM." Ren sat between Grant and Lamar, scooting as close to Grant as he could. I'd just returned from my date to find my friends huddled together. "It's our last night." Ren had always been a little nostalgic, but I couldn't help but agree with him here. "This place is delightful, and I want to document it."

Lucky for him, Jack walked by, and Emerson flagged him down with gusto.

"It is," I agreed, and Ren looked at me with a strange sort of pride. "Come on, everyone, mush."

Ren picked up the Polaroid camera from the middle of the table and handed it to Jack to take a photo of our pod. He shook it out, and we all watched with excitement as it developed over the next minute. There we were, a toothy bunch of friends gathered around for our last pod hangout. We had all grown from strangers into friends in such a short amount of time. It was impressive. Tomorrow would be a frenzy of packing and goodbyes, but right now, we had some final memories to make with each other.

I was still full from my late lunch with Autumn. We had walked back to the car, and I'd felt full in a soul-deep satisfied sort of way, not just from the cherries but from Autumn's confidence in me. Her eyes had sparkled as I told her the big news. I'd gotten the promotion. It still hadn't sunk in that I'd have the future I'd worked so hard for. So why was I second-guessing myself?

"We're going to keep in touch." Emerson's words brooked no argument. She might act as cool as her perfectly coiled curls, but I'd seen how tightly she'd hugged Lola and Tara when she spotted them earlier. This place was special, and this group of people were once-in-a-lifetime friends.

Today's buffet spread was extra camp-themed, as silly as that sounded. There were hot dogs, burgers, mac n' cheese, chicken salad, twice-baked potatoes, and yet everything was elevated, gourmet style with a unique and delicious flare mixed in.

Unfortunately, I was too full to try much of anything. I made room for a Shooting Star Shooter that a mischievously grinning Lamar brought and even drank himself despite his strict *superfoods only* diet. We reminisced about the good times, ending when Emerson had a little too much that first night and serenaded our pod with eighties jams until we were all singing along.

"Of course we'll be in touch. Outside of my family, you all are my favorite people," I confessed, feeling more open around them than I'd ever imagined I would be after only a week together. Even though this week was nearing its end, it felt like I'd known them for a lifetime and that I'd keep getting to know them. This was far from over.

"I'm going to miss all of you—" Lamar started as Sawyer came by and playfully flicked his ear.

"Gonna miss you too," they called back as they sauntered off to join their pod.

There was a buzz around the table over this almost goodbye. We had time, but not much, and I knew they felt it too. We weren't going to waste a minute.

After swapping stories and drinks, Ren mischievously pulled

me toward the zipline, one of the few events I hadn't done yet. "Look, there's no line."

We watched as Nat sang a song from the platform with Monica and Marisol.

"See you on the flip side!" Monica yelled out, arms extended as she launched herself, still singing her duet with Nat until her voice got too far away.

Marisol couldn't wipe the smile off her face while Nat got her situated into her harness. Then her walkie went off, signaling that Monica had landed. She gave Marisol the go-ahead, and she sent herself flying, no doubt trying to catch up.

Looking up at the platform, I couldn't help but think of how it felt to ride the ski lifts with Autumn. Had she ever ziplined? Based on her reaction to the ski lift, my guess was a big nope. I could imagine her suiting up, her cheeks red as she talked herself into it, then the smile that would take over her face once she reached the end, jumping into my arms to kiss me.

"You two coming?" Nat yelled down at us.

"Yeah, you're right. We gotta do it." I gathered myself and climbed the ladder to the top.

Ren's grin spread wider as we stood on the landing harnessing ourselves. Nat's long dark hair was trying desperately to escape the red bandana it was trapped behind as she inspected us. Her cheeks were apple-pink, kissed by the friendly sun, which made her freckles stand out. I remembered her kissing Gia in the dark, fierce and unrelenting. But here in the sunshine and on her platform, she seemed carefree and giggly. There was a Bluetooth speaker blasting K-pop hooked up to her bejeweled cell phone, a hot pink water bottle covered in flower stickers, and a small cooler I assumed was chock full of snacks. She danced around wearing faded rolled-up shorts and a tied-off oversized T-shirt that slightly contradicted her sparkly diamond necklace. Her attitude made me wonder if she was aware of the effect she'd had on Jack, or if she just didn't care.

Quick as a breeze, Ren leaped off backward because Nat mentioned it was "the most badass way to go."

A few minutes later, her walkie went off again. "And you're good to go."

Flying above the grounds was surreal. I'd been feeling this warm sense of wonder, of something fitting just right all day, but seeing the full view of camp from above was something spectacular.

Autumn was everywhere I looked, from the mess hall and location of my unfortunate sauce explosion to the craft cabin where we participated in Paint and Sip. The zipline didn't go over the lake per se, but I could just spy the dock where we'd talked alone, naked and laughing. The campfire was quiet at the moment. Soon, it would crackle and pulse as if it were the heart of this place, calling its amazing counselors and the eclectic, fun, and sometimes rowdy group of campers together.

The mess hall had campers going in and out of it still. Some stopped and waved up at me as I whooped at them, waving back. It was hard to believe that soon, I'd be back in Seattle while Autumn was here planning for the next summer of campers. The image filled me with a bittersweet sort of joy. I could never ask her to leave this place, but I also couldn't stay.

Once the ride ended, we planted our feet back on the ground. All in all, the zipline went by too fast. Just like everything else here.

Ren's face matched mine, our smiles wide and carefree. My cheeks were getting used to it, but smiling this much was still quite the workout. We set a slow pace as we meandered back, taking in the scenery. We walked past the Meditation Meadow, witnessing a serene sight: a couple of campers sharing a blanket. The man appeared to be napping, his head resting on the woman's lap as she turned pages in her book, her back up against a western hemlock tree.

"Hey, man, I have something for you." Ren's tone was far more earnest than I was accustomed to.

"Yeah?"

"Well, I just wanted you to have this... It's not a big deal or anything."

I stared down at the braided friendship bracelet he placed in my hand and met my best friend's eyes. I stopped in my tracks. "You made this? Seriously?"

The bracelet sat nicely in the palm of my hand. Braided colors, a mix of blue, gray, and yellow, woven together into intricate little diamond patterns.

"I love it." I hugged him and put it on immediately, wishing I had something to give him in return. "Before I forget, I wanted to tell you about something." I rubbed my hands back and forth. "Margaret called earlier today, and I got the job."

"Oh, that's great. Are you gonna take it?"

I half-laughed before realizing Ren was serious. I was floored. "Why wouldn't I take it?"

"I just thought—"

Before Ren could finish that sentence, my phone started blaring the loud and happy ringtone I'd assigned my sister. He raised his eyebrow just like he did every time he chastised me for my inability to abandon technology. "I went off the premises," I whispered, like I owed him anything. I answered the phone to Marley's wide smile as she hugged Savannah so they filled the screen. Ren nodded in understanding and left without a word.

"Look at you and that scruff. So, are you, like, Paul Bunyan now?" Marley asked.

"I haven't chopped any wood, and they probably won't let me go near an ax since mine ended up in the lake."

"What? How?" she asked through a peel of laughter.

"Well, you remember Autumn? It was all her fault."

"Autumn... *Autumn*? As in your high school love Autumn? She's there?"

"Yup, she's here." Stunning as ever.

"Weird coincidence that you two would attend the same camp

at the same time. What's she up to now? She become a fancy doctor like she planned?"

"Actually, no. Get this: she's a counselor here."

Marley's eyes bugged out of her head, giving Savannah a chance to speak.

"Hi, Jamie the Lumberjack." Savannah spoke loudly over the children screeching in the background. That house was always chaotic. I loved it.

"I don't chop wood all day. Have you two ever been camping?"

"I thought what you were doing was *glamping*." She stuck her tongue out at me like a rotten little sister. "So, what do you do all day, then? What's it like there?"

How could I even put into words what this had meant to me?

"It's unbelievable. You would love it. Mom and Dad would love it. In fact, I was thinking we should treat them to a week here, maybe for her birthday? There are all kinds of arts, crafts, and games. The cabins are charming and cozy like you wouldn't believe. The food is amazing, and there's an open bar. We have campfires every night that bring everyone together, but really, it's the people. The counselors make it even more magical. People come from all over to be here. There's nothing else like it."

Marley made a hmm noise. "Camp's really stolen your heart, then, huh?"

"Yeah." I paused. "I guess it has."

TWENTY-SIX

Autumn

"I JUST WANT ONE SELFIE, Sawyer—get back over here." Nat chased an oblivious Sawyer down and pulled out her phone, ready to snatch a photo with them.

This was the last day for our campers, but our staff was also running out of time. Most of us would be separating after our end-of-summer reset once campers had left on Thursday. Some staff might return next year, but the majority would probably move on.

Move on. That was a painful pill to swallow.

The counselors had all gathered for a quick fifteen-minute huddle before dinner. Hazel organized stacks of photos for each of us. I drew little swirls on my notebook, like I wasn't saying goodbye to all of these people I'd grown close with for the past several months.

I was terrible at goodbyes.

Lamar cleared his throat beside me. "Looking forward to the offseason?"

"Yep." I nodded. "There's a lot to do during the year, but it's nothing like this."

We hosted Outdoor School for local middle schools and held corporate retreats, and then there was recruitment and setup for next year. Jack would work on new cabins, and I would run events alongside Hazel and Leo. It wasn't better or worse than our summer sessions. It was just different. Quieter.

Sometimes, I liked the quiet, but this time, it felt like it would be harder to enjoy.

"What about you? Where are you off to?"

"I have a job lined up with an adventure excursion company." Lamar dipped his head, but I could tell that mixed in with the ennui was excitement. "I think this is my last season here."

I nodded regretfully, knowing that was where this conversation was headed thanks to the guilty look on his face. Lamar was a popular counselor and had been with us for two years before this. He worked in eastern Oregon during the offseason, and he loved it there.

"You're going to love that new job. Do they have river rafting?" I'd learned asking questions was the perfect distraction from dealing with sorrow, and this was no exception.

"That'll be my role, actually. Full time during rafting season and camping during the rest of the year. Who knows? Maybe I'll pick up a new hobby like free climbing while I'm at it."

"That sounds amazing. Minus the camping in the rain and snow."

"Come visit me and we'll see how you feel about it after."

"Or I could do anything else." I preferred enjoying the wilderness from the comfort of my cabin during the rain and snow seasons. I smiled at him and took his hand in mine. "I'll come visit, though, I promise."

Lamar had been one of my favorites. He was funny at all times and a great listener, and he made the best chili I'd ever had. He always had dog videos to show me, and I wished I had one of those right now because my eyes were starting to well up.

The atmosphere was mostly cheerful, which had me in a different mode, like I was on a sitcom where the main character was looking back on both sad and happy memories leading up to the big finale. But there was no big moment for me. I would be staying back and working my dream job. It was just the people that would change.

Thank goodness Hazel, Leo, and Jack were staying too.

Things were wrapping up, and we were about to go over announcements, but in a rare show of indifference, Jack turned from Nat as he saw her approaching him and walked away from her. A look of dejection spread across her face, but she played it off, turning to Felicia and walking arm in arm to the other side of the table. I tried to get his attention with my eyes, but he slumped into his seat beside me and stared at his pile of photos.

"Okay, everyone, we are in the home stretch. Last day, last dinner, last campfire." Hazel walked behind us, passing out the remaining bundles of photos for counselors to hand out. They took painstaking effort to make sure every camper left with images of their friends and their best moments captured at camp. "I know there's a wave of melancholy going through this group right now, but our focus needs to be on a positive end to this session and the season. Then, at *our* final campfire, we cry." Like there was any choice in the matter. "Once we finish with housekeeping tomorrow, we'll break for staff dinner and campfire. Now, does anyone have any updates?"

AFTER A MOSTLY CHEERLESS MEETING, I headed to my cabin to get a refresher, maybe even a mini depression nap before dinner. That was, until I made it to my pod.

They were already waiting for me. Shit.

Kell-i, Kell-y, Janna, Irene, and Diego were gathered at our small campfire, laughing and crying with each other as I approached.

"There she is," Kell-y shouted, already a little sauced, if the two empty bottles of wine situated on the outdoor table were an indication of anything. "Autumn. Sit down." She sounded exasperated, with flawless drunk girl desperation.

I plopped into an Adirondack and was handed a cup of the good stuff.

"Kell-y was telling us about your camp boyfriend," Janna slurred happily. "We heard you went on a date today."

Of course this had made its way through camp. Was I expecting any less?

"Not my boyfriend," I corrected half-heartedly. I was never going to be able to call him that again. That filled me with a sorrow I hadn't anticipated.

"We know," Kell-i jumped in. "It's just camp love."

I forced a smile. Camp love. Love that lasted a camp session and then went up in smoke the moment you returned to the real world. That was exactly what was happening to me, and it didn't sting any less as an adult.

"Nothing happened between us," I lied.

Kell-y raised her eyebrow, but the rest of the group nodded as if they believed me. They overlooked my glare-down with the incredulous blonde, which was good because I lost.

Fine, one camper knew. Not a big deal. Why was I even bargaining with myself? She'd be gone in a day.

"Did you hear about Diego and Breanna? They hooked up last night."

"*Since when did we involve me in this?*" He groaned.

I wondered if I should add that to the shipping board but opted against it since it wouldn't be enough to sway the results. Man, if I had gotten to be the one to pry that trophy from Leo's hands...

"Was it good?" Irene asked.

Diego was all smiles. "It wasn't *not* good... Okay, it was great. I didn't know it was possible to do that with your tongue—and I'm cut off." He dumped his remaining ounce of wine into the small firepit. The whole group busted up laughing.

One of the only drawbacks of being with Jamie throughout this session was that I'd had fewer of these moments with my pod. Less sitting around late at the campfire and seeing who was grumpy and who had bedhead in the mornings. I had spent my time with them in activities and dinners and campfire moments, but it was just slightly less thanks to my preoccupation with my handsome ex.

Had it been worth it?

My pod was great, but the truth was that campers came and went every week like clockwork, but he'd only been here for the limited time I'd had him, and so much of that had been wasted.

Kell-y was buzzing with excitement. "Oh my god, you know who I saw leave Ian's cabin this morning? Sariah!"

Why was the good stuff just coming out now?

Kell-y's eyes went wide. "I thought he was with Becca."

Janna looked mischievous. I loved mischievous Janna. "Not since Monday after..." She paused a beat, considering if she should tell us of her misdeeds or not. "I may have seen Peyton and Braxton go into her cabin for a late-night rendezvous. I wasn't peeking into their rooms, I swear! His window faces the pathway to the bathrooms, and he didn't even draw the blinds. And if I'm gonna see what looks like a threesome, I'm gonna watch for at least a minute or two. You'd all do the same."

Kell-i leaned in. "So did it *look* like a threesome, or..."

"Oh, it was definitely a threesome," Irene confirmed.

I hid my laughter behind my wine cup. I had really been behind in the chatter, and either some staff were hiding their knowledge of hookups (which was poor form) or they'd been shirking their responsibilities as camp gossips as well.

"That's nothing. Once, there was a full-blown orgy." Well, shit. It looked like I needed to be cut off too.

Kell-y's eyes went wide. "Wait, what constitutes an orgy?"

"I think more than two people," Diego contributed.

Kell-i had her phone out and was reading it to us. "It looks like it needs to include five people or more, but that's just Yahoo Answers, so..."

That got some laughs. Until Irene's lips twisted. "Well, shit. Then I've definitely been in an orgy."

Guess I got to cross that off on my bingo card.

"Okay, tell us, Autumn," Diego started. "Where the hell is there enough space to have an orgy in this place?"

"Does that mean you're looking for one?" Janna asked

I cackled. "Let's just say it was under the open air and leave it at that."

Autumn

"Did you hear they arrested the devil? Yeah, they got him on possession."

Mixed laughter and groans emanated from the crowd during our last campfire as Lamar delivered dad jokes like he was a stand-up comic. He did this every other week to raucous applause and eye-rolling. Most of them were pretty funny.

"A friend of mine didn't pay his exorcist," Lamar said to literal crickets. "He got repossessed."

Most of them.

We'd learned a long time ago that the last night of camp was filled with mixed emotions, most of them sadness. That was why we did a talent show on Wednesday nights. It was a great distraction from the inevitable. And man, did I need that distraction. So, what qualified as talent? We weren't picky. If you had some sort of skill, weird or not, we extended an invitation to make yourself look outstanding or silly.

We saw plenty of contestants, but typically, the best performances of the night were from the staff, who'd honed their crafts over dozens of talent shows throughout the summer. Hazel and Leo always took part, and as for the counselors, we split off doing the talent show and alternated, with three of us going each week. This week, I was off, thank god, because I had plenty of things to think about, and I didn't want to be distracted by winning the whole damn thing as I deserved. Okay, maybe not winning. The voting was biased toward the campers. It was a rigged system.

"What kind of drink can be bitter and sweet?" Lamar asked the audience.

"What kind?" someone shouted.

"Reali-tea." Lamar looked pleased with himself as the crowd burst into laughter. At this point, they were just laughing at him and not his jokes, but I wasn't about to tell him that. He thrived on both applause and boos.

Our emcee, Sawyer, waved goodbye to our opener and moved through the rest of our participants. We saw multiple singers, a very impressive doo-wop group, and two jugglers who used hacky sacks to juggle with each other. Braxton and Peyton, one of this year's returning couples, did a surprisingly good hula hoop routine, but my personal favorite had been a group of dads who somehow knew the dance moves to NSYNC's "Bye Bye Bye" to perfection. Hazel also did a magic show where she made cups disappear and ended her set sawing through a pink-wig-clad Leo in a box. He wore the wig every time, and she never asked him to do it. We still didn't know where he'd gotten the damn thing, but he brought it out frequently.

Jack was on the docket this session, but he wasn't in the front with the other contestants, so I assumed he'd discussed skipping this week with Sawyer.

I found him sitting in the back row with his elbows on his knees, watching one of his pod members singing a fairly decent "Music of the Night" as the Phantom.

"Oh, come on, you love *Phantom of the Opera*."

"That was before I died inside."

I fought back a laugh because he didn't look like he was joking. There was no light in his eyes, no laugh lines on his face. I realized then that most of the time, even the way he sat was funny, as if he were ready to deliver some joke or was bracing himself to laugh. He loved to laugh.

"Is this because you're sad about being broken up or because you get angsty when you watch musicals?"

He turned to me with a half-hearted smile. "Can't it be both?"

"Yes, it can." I lifted a yo-yo in front of him. "You know, if someone asked me what I'd like to see most tonight, it'd be yo-yo master Jack Hawthorne."

"Ooh, I like that." He clearly approved of his new moniker with as close to a Jack grin as it seemed I was going to get.

"You can use it. Tonight, even. I don't know if you know this, but I have an in with the emcee."

Jack forced a chuckle.

"I know you've been knocked down, but you always get back up again," I tried. "But if you don't feel like getting back up again right now, you don't have to."

"You think I can get back up again?" The disbelief in his voice cut deep.

"Of course I do. But you can also just be sad." He nodded without looking at me.

He tossed his yo-yo between his hands. "I don't want to be sad."

The theme of the night.

I didn't want to be sad either. I wanted to use my time wisely. Wasting it got me nowhere. Sitting in my sadness got me nowhere too. God knew I was going to be doing it for the next week. No, month. Months. It didn't matter. I wanted to be with Jamie, not sit apart for appearances or because he wanted time with others, whether or not I was being selfish. I wanted to get the hell out of here.

By the time Crispin was done singing "Call Me Maybe," Jack was on stage, and he was amazing. Doing tricks we'd never seen before, including one using multiple yo-yos. He looked both amused and focused, great at getting laughs and applause from the rest of us. But no matter what, he was in his element. It made me want to do what I was good at too—sleeping with my ex-boyfriend.

Just not on a stage.

Cheers and applause broke out, echoing off our little slice of nature to where I wondered if we were spooking the horses at the camp next to us. Maybe we *were* about to have our first noise complaint from Marty and Joy.

Slips of paper and pens went out with a reminder that staff were (unfairly) not on the ballot.

I sought Jamie out again, finding his eyes as he both looked at me and whooped with the crowd.

He met my gaze with an intensity that had me hot and wishing I could take off my flannel and fan myself with it. I tilted my head away from the campfire, and he nodded, not even indicating to his friends that he was leaving. We met at the back of the wooden bleachers, garnering the notice of nobody, and he took my hand.

We didn't speak as we made our way through the woods to my cabin. I didn't even know when we decided that was where we'd be going or who was leading, but that was where we ended up. I fumbled with punching in my door code. I'd done this a thousand times, but it didn't matter. I was too nervous.

He touched my hand again, calming me, and I managed to remember the code, opening the door as though nothing crucial was about to happen. Just a friend helping a friend.

When we got inside, I was hit with a wave of lavender from my favorite wax melt, but it was overpowering. All I wanted to do was rest my nose on Jamie's collarbone. I didn't want to smell like me. I wanted to smell like sex and sweat and him.

Suddenly, the air felt heavier.

That was the best way to describe it. Like the tension had wrapped itself around both of us, and we had to push through it to get to my bedroom.

We didn't even turn the lights on. The third time we bumped into something, I felt his smile against my lips.

"You've accumulated a lot of clutter in this place."

I would have been mock offended at his jokingly judgmental tone, but then he kissed my neck.

"Clutter? Like furniture?" He was sticking his hand up my shirt, and I barely got the words out.

"If this were an open area, I'd already have your clothes off."

"I'm getting rid of it all tomorrow," I said feverishly.

Since we were getting nowhere like this, I decided to take fate into my own hands and turned around, grabbing his fingers to lead him to my bedroom. The lack of lips on mine was killing me.

He paused at the door. "So this is your room?"

"Less talking." I tugged at the hem of my shirt and tore it off. "More getting naked."

He threw his shirt at me, and it landed on my head. Damn lack of night vision. I threw mine at his head to even things out.

"You are so sassy. Have I ever told you I like you this way?" Jamie's voice deepened as we came back together, reaching for each other's pants, only to realize that they couldn't be removed at the same time thanks to clashing limbs. I let him take mine off first. I was generous like that.

"I'm always sassy."

I heard his zipper going down, and the sarcasm disappeared as the sounds of him pushing jeans down his legs overhauled my brain. My eyes had adjusted enough to see him kick them off. Reaching his hand out to pull me to him, he kissed the inside of my wrist and blew on the wetness there. I had no idea that was an erogenous zone, but it set my body alight.

He sat on my perfectly made bed, tugging me onto him, grinding my hips against his cock and making me wish there was no fabric between us. He ran a hand up my throat to the back of my neck, pulling me to him for a consuming kiss.

In the years we'd been apart, I'd forgotten how overwhelming his kisses were. When his lips were on mine, nothing else existed, not homework or friends or parents. He could kiss me in a hallway, and I'd miss the bell. But the way he cradled the back of my head as he kissed me soft and slow, as if we had an eternity to gratify each other's needs... It wrecked me. Tore me from the inside out and turned me into a blathering, needy mess.

I spoke between breaths. "Jamie, I—"

He ignored my half-spoken plea, pushing my hips down against him. I had to be soaking through my underwear to his boxers, but I didn't care. He was bound to find out what he did to me sooner or later.

Jamie reached behind my back to unhook my bra, sucking gently as each clasp released. The straps fell down my shoulders, and his grip tightened around my back.

I tossed it away and pushed him back against the bed, reaching over his shoulder to grab a condom from my nightstand drawer. As I held myself up, he helped remove my underwear, sliding them down my legs until I shook them off my feet. We worked together to take off his boxer briefs, but I almost went off course as his cock sprang free. His powerfully hard erection had me salivating and licking my lips, and the effect wasn't lost on him. He lifted my chin and looked me dead in the eyes.

As if reading my mind, he said, "Not tonight."

If not tonight, then when?

If I had forever, I'd give him all the attention he needed.

I wiped the thought from my mind and told myself to live in the present. Here, I was with him. Now, I had him to myself. Tonight, we'd make a new memory that would hopefully last. Even if that wasn't what was best for me, it was what I longed for.

Jamie unwrapped the condom and rolled it down his shaft as I held myself up, immobile. He was right there, and I couldn't make contact. Thankfully, he took over.

He pressed his fingers into my hips and lifted me so that we were lined up before lowering me slowly. I snapped to attention, spreading my thighs to better accommodate him. Jamie let out a low groan when we were flush against each other, and goosebumps dispersed across my skin.

All my senses were heightened. Every touch, every tingle he left in his wake. I loved the way he reached one arm around my back and held me tightly to him. I relished the way he groaned as I deepened our kiss.

It was surreal, a decade later, riding the man who had been all of my firsts. Everything about him felt different and somehow still the same. He kissed my shoulder, and I was transported back to us as teenagers, gentle but rushed, desperate and horny. But now we weren't breaking any rules. Now we had time, if only for one night. I wasn't about to waste it.

In these moments, it was easy to forget all the facts and the baggage. How we were about to say goodbye. How this was probably the last time we'd ever be together. It started a fire in me. It caused me to go slower, to envelop him. To savor him.

Our bodies spoke their own language, the words leaving our mouths more timid than before. Moans and whimpers but never promises. And I fought the urge to beg because I wanted those promises. Jamie moved inside me, and I arched, dropping the thought along with one hand to clutch his chest and the other to his lips. He welcomed two fingers into his mouth, sucking and licking them until I was satisfied enough to touch my clit and rub circles. The feeling set me off like a spark. He looked like he was about to go off from that movement alone, but instead of exploding, he arched to drive into me deeper, holding me as if the only thing tethering me to this world was him. I knew in that moment, in different circumstances, if given the chance, he'd never let me go.

That was enough for me to lose myself. He ground up as I rode out the wave of pleasure, unleashing a frisson within me. And when I was almost finished, he gave in himself, clinging to me as he looked deep into my eyes, begging me for something I couldn't decipher.

I rested against him, as I tried to catch my breath, and Jamie ran his hands through my hair, stroking it as though it was precious. As though I was precious. It made me feel dizzy, like I couldn't tell up from down. And a part of me wondered if I'd been searching all this time for this. This feeling of security. And all I could think was that the word *falling* was such a relevant word, it hurt.

Or maybe the word I was looking for was *fell*.

I snuggled against his chest without thinking and prepared myself for the inevitable pulling away that would occur once he realized this wasn't casual hookup behavior. But I wasn't ready for the moment to end. Sex that amazing felt more like a welcoming or a necessity than a goodbye.

Jamie kept a loose arm around me, palm holding firm against the small of my back as we caught our breath and relaxed into each other.

"That felt…"

"Incredible," he finished, joyful eyes searching mine.

"Different." I let the smile touch the corners of my lips as I pressed a kiss into his throat.

"Different?" He tilted his chin down, but I kept my lips on his neck, not meeting the gaze I could feel. "Different *good*, though, right?" His unflinching confidence seemed at odds with his sudden need for reassurance.

"Incredible," I agreed. "I've never had sex like that before."

Love-infused, intense, and so passionate. Most of my past hookups had been satisfying, but only on a physical level. Sex with Jamie was mind, body, and soul-shattering. Nothing would compete.

"Mm-hmm, damn right."

Giggling softly, I let my fingers trail up and down his ribs. I knew I'd be exhausted. Tomorrow was going to be one of the busiest days of the year, but stealing a few more minutes in his arms would be worth the extra caffeine I'd consume to make up for it.

"So, what are we going to do now?" he asked.

"Never have sex this good again with anybody else, that's for sure." The words fell out of my mouth without thinking.

Jamie tightened his hold on me. I let myself savor the warmth, his spicy scent, and all the safety he wrapped me in. Was this feeling what Sawyer meant when they talked about being completely present? No thoughts of the past or the future? It felt too good, being in the here and now with Jamie Davis.

"We could do this, you know," he started.

This time, I did look up at him. "Again? We just—"

"No, although, very, very, tempting." He punctuated each "very" with a kiss to my forehead and then my nose, making me smile. "But I mean *this*, you and me."

I paused and took a breath. "We could *what*?"

"Seattle isn't that far, I could visit." It was a tempting thought, one I'd almost entertained a few times, but it wouldn't be enough.

"We can't." I sighed, feeling a burning in my throat. How he was even suggesting this, I didn't know. "You'll be busy with your new role, and I'll be here, wondering when you'll have had enough."

There it was. The thing I felt hidden in my heart. I couldn't be the person he used up and discarded. No matter his intentions, that was where this was going. It was practically a guarantee.

A seriousness passed over his face. "I can't get enough of you, Autumn. I don't think I ever will."

That nearly broke me. Jamie voiced the same thing I'd been wondering the past several days. Could I get enough of him? I hadn't thought so back when we were teenagers, and it was even more obvious now. But I was an adult who had to make adult decisions for my well-being. And, apparently, his.

Thoughts of visiting him for a week in the coming months popped into my head, but it would only make things worse.

"This needs to be a clean break, Jamie. It'll be too hard otherwise."

And this was a terrible time to be having this conversation. I had a lot to deal with. There was cleanup. Preparations for our winter retreat season. We were expanding. I could distract myself. I could get over this.

Except that I was falling in love with him again.

Not puppy love, not superficial love. Change-your-life love. Rip-your-heart-out-love. But I couldn't do that. This was my family. This was my home. I wanted to choose him, but if I did, I'd only have him, and I'd sink into the depression I'd been in before I'd found my life's purpose. That was what this was. I belonged here.

I needed to think. But I didn't have time to think. We never had enough time. And wasn't that always our problem?

Jamie nodded in understanding, and I could practically hear his thoughts bouncing around in his head. Then he said something I never expected. "What if I turned down the promotion? What if I didn't stay in Seattle?"

What if he didn't stay in Seattle?

He couldn't mean that. He'd be giving up everything he'd worked for his entire adult life. I couldn't let him give his dream up. A memory of the first time we broke up crossed my mind. Perfectly juxtaposed with how I felt in his arms currently. He'd told me that back when we were kids, he'd ended our relationship for me. He'd seen a future where I'd change my plans for him. Where I'd mold my goals around his. Now, he was here offering to do the same for me. I'd disagreed with his methods and reasoning back then, but in this moment, I saw it through another lens. For the first time, I completely understood his motivations. He'd wanted what was best for me back then. He'd seen more potential in me than I had seen in myself. And now I wanted that for him.

"You were meant for big things."

"That doesn't make this a small thing," he declared as if he was willing to fight over this, but I wasn't going to argue with him. It was true. He would make an amazing boyfriend, but I couldn't let him trade in his future and his dreams for mine.

"We said for the week. And it's been a wonderful week. Let's just leave it at that."

The silence was deafening.

He looked like he had so much more he wanted to say, yet he just held me. What if *I* left? I let myself consider it for a half second before knowing deep in my bones I couldn't leave Camp Starlight. This place meant so much more to me than any job ever could. And this was my family. I loved him, but I was doing what he'd wanted me to do all those years ago. I was forging my own path.

I was choosing me. Even if it meant breaking my own heart.

TWENTY-EIGHT

Jamie

A SLICE of sunlight peeked down at me, and I blinked back the haze of sleep. As I propped myself up, my head whipped from side to side before I realized Autumn wasn't in bed with me.

Usually, I'd toss and turn until sleep decided it'd had enough of my antics and would pull me under. Last night, everything was different. My instinct was to hold on to her tightly. The woman who'd stayed beside me all night, warm and cuddled close.

She had a lot to do this morning, and it was probably the explanation for why she was out of bed this early. That didn't negate the emptiness I felt with her not here.

And that emptiness didn't go without notice. Why was I feeling this after what could probably be labeled as a second-chance fling?

Feet down on the woven rug, I looked out the window. It was early, yoga early. I watched the mist on the water outside of Autumn's window and wished it'd be a frequent occurrence.

Mindfulness be damned, I showed up to sunrise yoga anyway.

Sawyer's untamed curls fell into their face as they moved like liquid from one pose to the next. Yoga flow was something I'd usually been good at, but since I hadn't slept more than an hour last night, nothing felt right. I had been counting on the movements to keep me grounded, but found myself barely able to go through the motions. I tried not to replay the words over and over, what we had confessed and reasoned with each other in the dark of night. Words like "we can't" and "clean break." She'd been sound and certain, and yet I kept wondering, *what if I had said this?* Was I wrong in suggesting I stay? Or that we see where this could go? Offering for her to come back with me was a nonstarter, but it felt wrong to throw this away. Maybe I was the only one feeling things.

Forty minutes later, the sun was up, and Sawyer had the seven of us dripping in a cleansing sweat, ready to be dismissed for the last time, which filled me with a sense of sorrow. Spiraling seemed like today's reality, but I was doing my best not to let that last longer than this class.

I took a deep breath, got out of the shower, and set back to my cabin to pack up. Tossing my clothes and things haphazardly, I was surprised at how different the suitcase was now compared to the tidy and careful way I'd packed before coming. Today was the last day, and how I packed didn't matter. Seeing Autumn before leaving did. She couldn't leave, and I couldn't stay, but I could find her some coffee.

Still early, the mess hall was buzzing. Campers were saying their goodbyes and taking photos before their scheduled departures. I was grateful for the pod dinner yesterday and the time I'd had with Ren and then with Autumn. Picturing Autumn's blonde hair bouncing against the contours of her neck as she pushed it behind her ears and smiled down at me. Hovering over me, knowing we'd never do it again.

I could still feel her hands on my chest, her hips in my hands, her lips on my mouth. In between the banter and fun, we'd had moments of unchoreographed affection as we whispered and rocked together. In the bliss of our recovery, when everything had become clearer than a line in the sand, I felt like I'd lost the tug of war in my heart.

I made my way toward the espresso bar. I'd watched her make her coffee a couple of times and was pretty sure I had the hang of it. I grabbed a pink mug off the caddy that reminded me of her, ground the beans, and added the hazelnut flavoring to finish. The French roast was her favorite, and it smelled amazing. As I waited for the adorable mug to fill, I leaned into a calf stretch, the lack of sleep catching up a bit. Autumn had already mentioned the last day of camp was the craziest, so with all that work she'd put in last night, I wasn't about to let my girl—who wasn't my girl—go into a caffeine-starved deficit.

Mugs in hand, I went searching for her, checking her cabin first. Maybe she had come back looking for me, but her cabin was empty, nothing out of place. I humored the idea of not finding her before I left, and it hurt. What if I didn't find her in time? What if I had to leave without saying goodbye again? I wondered briefly if this was how she'd felt when I'd disappeared on her all those years ago. That must have felt awful. I couldn't let that happen again. I shook the thought away before making my way over to Jack's cabin.

I set one mug down and knocked twice, glad when he opened up. He looked like he'd already been working half a day and needed a shower. His messy blond hair was contained in a backwards cap, in natural waves at his shoulders. He had a towel and a toiletries bag in hand, and I wondered why he wasn't using his own shower because Autumn's cozy cabin had a bathroom. I shrugged. None of that mattered.

"Hey, man, is Autumn around?"

He set the toiletry bag down on the porch banister and met my eyes. "No, she's been zooming like a hummingbird. Go, go, go. It'll probably be like that all day. You might be able to catch her over at the office, though."

I thought about making the trek, but if I went over there, I'd just be interrupting her focus. I met Jack's eyes again. He looked at the steaming mugs I held, his face full of longing.

"That makes sense. I don't want to bug her." I grabbed the cute pink mug off the railing and held it out to him.

His eyes lit up as though it was the best thing he'd ever seen all week. "Come on in."

As I took in his living space, I wondered if he had time to do anything but work. There was an overflowing basket of laundry on his couch, dishes in the sink, and more than a week's worth of mail on the floor, probably from falling after being carelessly tossed onto the table.

Jack took a swig of Autumn's coffee and winced at its sweetness. He probably took it black.

"Is it strange? Becoming friends with people, only to have them leave in a week?"

He looked contemplative before he shrugged. "I wouldn't have it any other way. There's no other life like it, you know?"

"Yeah, I've been thinking of this place and how it's so different from my real world. It makes you never want to leave."

His eyes met mine. I knew it was all over my face. Yearning to belong here too. Even if I never would.

"But you are? Leaving?"

I didn't know what to say. For a minute last night, I'd thought she might agree to a relationship, that she might want me to stay. Autumn had hesitated, and I'd held my breath along with the words I'd been desperate to let go. *Let me stay. I want to be with you.* Those thoughts weren't helpful now. In the aftermath of everything, it just wasn't an option.

"What makes you ask that?" I inquired, my tone neutral as I let my curiosity build. Had she said anything to him? Maybe she'd want me to extend my time here. I could take another week off work before starting the promotion. Maybe they'd let me if I asked. My mind flitted to the possibilities, before I reminded myself, no, I wasn't staying and she wouldn't have mentioned that to Jack without telling me.

It's been a wonderful week. Let's just leave it at that.

A pang hit my chest again, her words echoing in my mind as if they hadn't fully seeped in.

He opened his mouth to speak. "I was just thinking that you—"

Radio feedback startled both of us before we realized what it was. "Leo for Jack" came over the line.

He reached for his walkie-talkie on the dining table and pressed the button to reply. "Leo, what's up?"

The last time I saw Hazel and Leo, they'd had big smiles on their faces. I'd told them to reach out to me directly when the next set of paperwork came through for the second camp. And I was happy with the knowledge that they could rely on me. In that way, I'd still be part of Starlight even after leaving.

"Hey, so I hate to be the guy who only calls you when there's a problem—"

Jack grinned. "Spit it out."

Leo continued over the line. "The disposal is backed up. There's this grinding noise akin to a banshee's wail, or maybe a haunted... Anyway, it scared Bobby half to death. Could you come by and assess its viability, maybe give it an exorcism?"

Jack shot me a quick look, a smile still tugging at his lips. He didn't need to say anything. I was already getting up and grabbing our empty mugs.

"It probably doesn't need a full-blown exorcism. Maybe sage will be enough. "I'll be right there." He threw on his tool belt and boots before reaching for his keys, and I followed him out. He paused at the doorway. "I've been thinking a lot about second chances. Like, if people deserve them or if it's worth it to try again. I guess what I'm asking is, do you think she's worth it?"

It wasn't even a question. "Of course she's worth it."

"Then maybe letting her go again isn't what's best for her. Thanks for the coffee. See you around." He tossed me a wink, as if we were in on some joke, before taking off in a light jog.

I wanted to ask him to look out for Autumn, to take care of

her. But none of that needed to be said. She'd take care of herself, and as her best friend, Jack had already been doing all those things before I came around. He'd continue looking out for her, be there for her when I couldn't.

As I walked back to my cabin, groups were reminiscing, laughter lacing the air. It still hadn't sunk in that I was leaving. I'd be going back home, but my condo didn't appeal to me like it had before. A sterile open floor plan and walk-in closets felt useless and emotionless. None of it felt like home when I thought about it. Guess it was time to redecorate. Yeah, that's what I'd do.

TWENTY-NINE

Autumn

FIRST, it was a kitchen fire at six in the morning.

It was small, but it left our culinary student, Sebastian, freaked out. He'd only been in a commercial kitchen for the summer, and his mistake had him reeling and thinking he could never be a chef, which I persuaded him was not true, and distressed that he might be fired (also not true). He was also troubled about the kitchen itself and the oven that was badly damaged and needed to be sorted through insurance. That left us an oven down for family breakfast, but it wasn't the end of the world, just a lot of worrying by a twenty-one-year-old over quiche.

The fire fiasco was followed by a rogue opossum blocking access to the west bathrooms. No joke, he literally ran back and forth, hissing at anyone who tried to enter. And how did I solve this problem? Bacon. I could honestly say I solved a problem with bacon, and if that didn't belong on my resume, I didn't know what did.

I'd just told Hazel I'd been putting out fires all morning when, ironically enough, a pipe had burst in the east showers. I met Jack to see what a "small leak" meant and learned that "small" actually meant "big," and "leak" was more relative to "flood."

I looked at three campers standing helplessly with toiletry bags. "Y'all can use the west showers for now," I spat out, exasperated.

A towel-clad Jack cursed with a clothed Cherry Lips Cheryl as they tried to quickly tighten a bolt with a wrench. I was busy wondering where he had pulled out the wrench when I snapped into action.

"So all those times I asked if there was a wrench in your pants or if you were just happy to see me, there was a literal wrench?"

"Shut up, smart-ass. The shut-off valve is out back." Suddenly, three other showers were spraying water outward and up to the ceiling.

"I'm gonna—" I rushed outside to shut off the water supply. I came back to find water sputtering until it stopped spraying and dripped off. I held back laughter, taking the wrench from a soaked Cheryl and turning back to him. "Were you taking a shower when it—"

"Yep," he said bitingly. Jack may have been our handyman, but he was bad at taking care of his own problems, so he was likely showering in the guest showers because he still hadn't fixed the pipe to his bathroom. Now he was probably regretting that fact.

He went to turn the water supply back on once it looked like things were under control, and despite not being knowledgeable about plumbing, I chose to look up into the shower head right as water splattered out, spraying me in the face.

Jack came back to the mess and cracked up at the image of his best friend taking on the appearance of a wet dog.

"Your towel is slipping."

He grabbed it quickly and glared when he realized I was just fucking with him.

Felicia walked in and whistled until she saw our soaked faces. "Why aren't you using your shower?"

"Plumbing issue," he said wryly. What a joke.

I pushed back a lock of dripping hair. "Cancel that shower, Jack. This place is underwater as it is."

It wouldn't be the last day if it wasn't a shit show.

ON THE LAST day of each session, we made enough food for families to join in for breakfast, which meant that many arrived early. After greeting newcomers and helping people load cars, I caught my breath next to the welcome sign. It only took a moment for me to realize I hadn't heard from my bosses in a while, which could either be good or bad.

"This is Autumn for Leo."

"Leo speaking."

"Did you need anything—Mom?"

I recognized that bob anywhere. My stepmom had passed me by, turning as she heard me. She held hands with my dad.

"I'm not your mom, Autumn," Leo returned. "In a better world—"

I lowered the sound on my walkie and turned to the woman pushing her sunglasses up onto her head. Her face brightened when she saw me. She looked pristine in her signature floral scarf and her favorite silk top and Bermuda shorts combo.

"What are you doing here?" I said, exasperated, all tact gone.

"We waited fifteen minutes to park, Autumn," my dad griped, his face a twinge redder than I was used to. Great. This busyness was normal on the last day, but this was not the first impression of Starlight I wanted for my parents after they finally visited. Arriving during a clusterfuck, just the thing to make this place look reputable. Why were they here?

"I know, Dad."

"What kind of place are you running here?"

My stepmom tried to appease him. "Take a breath, Robert. I'm sure there's an explanation..."

Fantastic. I felt like I was sixteen years old again, explaining how the pot ended up in my possession. To this day, I didn't know which person put that dime bag in my ceiling vent. Okay, I did. It was me. Past Autumn had been too stoned or stupid the *one* time she'd tried weed to realize that marijuana had a very distinct smell and ceiling vents blew out air.

I scratched my head and took a deep breath. "We're just busy, Dad. That has nothing to do with the running of—never mind." I hugged each of them and tried again. I stifled my anger, knowing that if I had shown up to my stepmom's job unannounced, she would have killed me. "Are you here to visit?"

My dad folded his arms across his chest and scanned the area. "Well, you've been talking about this place for years, so we figured we'd come see what all the fuss was about."

Great timing.

I forced a smile. "That's so... Nice of you, but this isn't the best time, and I—"

"Is that Jamie Davis?" My stepmom cupped her hand over her brow to shield her eyes.

My god, what were the chances of this?

Crispin rushed up to me. He looked frantic.

I jumped into damage control mode. "What's wrong?"

"My son is missing."

"*What?*"

"He's six..." The hopelessness in his eyes nearly had me breaking "His name is Josh."

I nodded quickly. Suddenly, I forgot about my parents, about my ex-boyfriend, about everyone who wasn't a small child. I got some details out of Crispin and turned my walkie back on.

"Attention: this is an all-hands message. Drop what you're doing. We have a six-year-old missing. Last seen near the parking lot. His name is Josh." I thought to the worst possible place he could be. "Sawyer, are you still near the beach?"

"Been here for ten minutes. No sign of him, but I'll stay to make sure."

I breathed a sigh of relief. Thank goodness.

"This is Leo—near the ax range."

"Oh my god, are there axes—" My dad's eyes were practically bugging out of his head.

I didn't explain, just shook my head no.

"Hazel, are you still at Cygnus pod?"

"Yes. I'm looking here now."

"Jack, I need you at the loading bay. Felicia, Lamar, spread out."

I turned to Crispin. "We'll find him," I promised, touching his shoulder.

"How can we help?" my stepmom asked.

I climbed on a bench. "Can I get everyone's attention!" I shouted. "We are missing a six-year-old child." The place went silent. "Please look for him. He's wearing—"

Crispin jumped in. "A blue sweatshirt and green shorts. He has blond hair—"

"Wearing a blue sweatshirt and green shorts with blond hair," I relayed into the walkie.

Dozens of adults dispersed immediately, abandoning bags and cars to find the missing child. I looked for a moment for my parents, but they were gone.

I held down the parking lot and found the rest of our staff's locations via walkie. Lamar checked the zipline area. Sebastian, Azalea, and Bobby had all spread out. After five minutes, he was finally found walking in the woods at Delphinus pod by Nat. There were cheers, some choice words to a child who "should have known better," and an order to head to the mess hall to have a breather as every staff, camper, and family member carried themselves as if they had a weight lifted off their shoulders.

I didn't see my parents, and I fought the urge to run and hide. There was no avoiding the inevitable. Everyone was heading into the mess hall for family breakfast, and apparently, my parents got the memo because I found them talking with Hazel at the entryway.

"She's a wonder," Hazel was saying. "You have no idea how happy we were to find her. With Autumn's logistical mind and quick thinking... She's such a great assistant director. We'd be lost without her."

Assistant director? I'd never heard that job title before. I *liked* that job title, but we didn't exactly have business cards. I didn't care. I was going to get them made. I'd hand them out to squirrels if I had no one else to give them to.

Hazel went on. "Autumn told me you're a sales manager, Mr. Gardner. Tell me you were the one who taught her to use spreadsheets because no human should be as good at them as she is. I assumed she learned it in the cradle."

He laughed. "We did have some sessions when she was a preteen so that she could organize her schoolwork."

That we did. It was a surprisingly happy moment in my childhood that I looked back on, not that there were many bad moments. But we hadn't had tons of time together when I was younger. They'd both been so busy that I had to get organized or I would have floundered or, worse, needed to have my hand held.

"You've got quite a resort here," my stepmom observed. "We've only seen a bit, but it looks like a place even I'd like to visit and"—she leaned over to whisper—"I hate the outdoors."

Hazel did a full belly laugh and tapped my stepmom on the shoulder. "You're invited any time. We have plenty of bug spray."

That made my stepmom wrinkle her nose, which led to another laugh.

"Why don't you go get some food and I'll be right there?" I tilted my head toward the breakfast bar, and they did as asked. That left just me and Hazel.

Hazel smiled. "Didn't mean to force your hand there but I think it's time for a title bump, don't you?"

"I mean..."

"With this potential expansion for Camp Starlight TBD, we'll need extra help running things. I have no idea what starting another venture simultaneously will be like, but we know we can rely on you to help us see this through. There will be a pay bump of course. And with that will come different responsibilities—things you frequently take up on your own anyway, so if you're interested..."

"I'm interested! I'd love to do more."

"I hope you realize we couldn't do any of this without you." She grabbed my hand and squeezed. "You are integral to the running of this place, and we enjoy having you here. We love you, Autumn."

Warmth filled my chest. I swallowed and nodded without saying anything. It made me think back to the early days when we were setting up camp. When Jack, Hazel, Leo, and I lived in tents until we had Jack's cabin up and running for us to sleep in. Before we had functional spaces for each of us, we'd stayed in what was known as the bunk cabin and slept in the same room. They were some of the best moments of my life, staying up telling ghost stories and giggling like we were at an actual slumber party until we inevitably crashed early. They were messy and exhausting days, but they were also fun. Nothing bonds a team quite like sharing the same bathroom.

"I'm gonna go tell Diego's kid to get off that table. The apple clearly doesn't fall far from the tree." She laughed. "Now I wish I'd thrown Diego into the lake like I threatened." In true Hazel fashion, she sounded completely serious. And how many people did she threaten to throw into the lake?

I was stunned. Not about the kid on the table but about my new role. This was more than I'd hoped for. We'd been solvent for a few years, but now there was a second camp which hadn't even been on my horizon. And to have this new role added to our staff. I'd felt like a partner in this venture, sure, but now I was going to get more responsibility, more buy-in. It made things feel more concrete. I didn't know if I realized it before today, but I'd always been worried that this would be taken away, even now.

I didn't even pay attention to what I loaded onto my plate, finding my stepmom and sitting next to her in a daze.

"That was quite a spread." She took a bite of bananas foster French toast and placed it delicately on her fork. "You sure your camp can afford this, honey?"

"Yes, Mom, we can afford it." I tried to hide my annoyance. "Where's Dad?"

"He went to say hi to Jamie."

Fuck. I scanned the room and found them by the kitchen shaking hands.

"So, are you seeing each other again? Is that why he's here?" She didn't look excited or disappointed. Just curious.

"No, he's here as a guest. It's a coincidence." They seemed to be having an easy conversation. There were no angry faces. Then I thought about it and realized there was no reason for either of them to be angry. I just felt like I was a kid again. I thought a decade would be enough of a gap for me to move on from that feeling, but it wasn't working with my dormant feelings for Jamie either, so...

"That's some coincidence."

If she only knew.

"What are you doing here, Mom?" I asked again, trying to sound as interested as possible, rather than annoyed at the fact that they'd just dropped in without asking.

"Oh, we were visiting the wineries in Emerald Falls and decided to come around the mountain to see where you worked. Today might not have been the best day, though. I'm sorry we didn't ask first."

I should have been angry at the situation. All these years, I'd come up to visit them, but they'd never seen where I lived and worked. They'd barely shown interest in my life once I changed the plan we'd been working toward for so many years.

"Yeah, today is the last day of the summer session. How long are you here for?"

"We found a cabin a few miles away. Figured we could stay a couple of days. I know you're busy today, so we can leave after breakfast, but if you want to meet up tomorrow—"

"Yes, that's perfect," I started. "I can take you on a tour and show you my cabin. There's a bunch of things to do around here. You can visit town and..."

As Jamie and my dad made their way to us, I pushed my hair behind my ear and licked my lips in preparation. We hadn't had a moment all morning for us to see each other, so this was looking like it was it. I'd planned on bringing him coffee, but I'd ended up skipping it to deal with this dumpster fire of a day.

My stepmom jumped up to give Jamie a big hug, nearly knocking the tray out of his hands as he smiled warmly at me. "Are you going to eat with us?" she asked.

"Oh, Mom, I'm sure Jamie wants to eat with his—"

"I'd love to." He didn't take his eyes off me. I was starting to wonder if I had something in my teeth. I closed my lips and licked my teeth to make sure.

"So, how are you doing?" she asked.

"I'm great," he assured, though the words felt half-hearted and almost like they were laced with something different. Something like sadness. "Life has been really good to me."

"And your parents?" My stepmom's eyes lit up as she inquired about Jamie's mom. They had always gotten along but stopped seeing each other when he broke up with me.

"They're living in Portland now, to be nearer to my sister and my niece and nephew." He pulled out his phone and showed them his background screen with a photo of Erin giving Adam a piggy-back ride.

My stepmom smiled wide. "Aww, how precious."

My dad took a breath and turned to my ex-boyfriend like a man on a mission. "Can I just say, I know we weren't really supportive of your relationship at the end and we want you to know that it wasn't about you. We just wanted what was best for Autumn."

Back then, my parents had been rather strict about our relationship, especially in Jamie's senior year. They'd told me constantly that we might end up at different schools, so there was no point in being that serious.

"So did I," Jamie agreed without a hint of frustration. He still would have made that decision, and it was for the best. It was so much better to know what I hadn't back then. "And I understood, even then, though I appreciate the sentiment."

My father smiled, patting him on the back. "Jamie was just telling me he's getting a promotion in his law firm back home. He graduated summa cum laude. Are you surprised?"

I smiled at my ex-boyfriend. "Definitely not."

I beamed. I was astonished that there was barely a sting. It felt as if this conversation was entirely about him, not about me in the slightest, and I was grateful for the respite from the "what have you done with your life" conversation.

"Autumn's been helping run this resort for five years now, though I'm sure you know that. She was always outdoorsy, so I don't know why I was surprised. Can you believe this place?" The genuine delight in her voice caught me off guard.

I dropped the remaining corner of my sandwich, my eyes growing wide. Finally. Finally, they were realizing what this place was. You call it *camp* and people don't take you seriously. It was the primary issue when it came to recruitment in the early stages, but it had changed thanks to five-star reviews and adjustments to marketing materials.

"I know, it's amazing." Jamie squeezed my hand and didn't let go. It was an innocuous gesture, but I leaned into the little bit of contact I had with him. "My friend Ren convinced me to come, and it's been one of the best decisions I've made in years." He looked at me with a wistful look in his eye. "Seeing Autumn in her element has been an added bonus."

My parents didn't pick up on the undertone of his words, but I knew what they meant. He was happy we'd gotten time together, no matter how short. The feeling was mutual. I didn't know how I'd be able to get past this amazing week. It was gratifying to move on from something that had hurt so badly so many years ago. It was unbelievable to feel what it was like in his arms again, to be adored in the small window we had. I would never forget it.

"I'm truly surprised at how different this was than expected," my stepmom observed. "She's done a wonderful job."

My eyes went glassy, and warmth filled my chest. Maybe this was on me too. I didn't exactly invite them to come down to visit. Part of me never expected them to appreciate all the hard work I'd done. Nothing ever felt like it'd be good enough once I dropped out of Stanford, but I'd worked my fingers to the bone for this place. I might not have gotten the sought-after degree my parents had wanted for me, but I'd done something that mattered.

My dad patted my shoulder. "We're really proud of her."

"We'll talk on the phone" and "I'll call you" and "It was really great to meet you," along with other similar sentiments, swirled along the breeze as campers hugged and smiled, cried and packed. Normally, big emotions on a vacation would be overkill, but after spending 24/7 with this group, they'd become an extension of family.

Some balanced precariously packed bags, no doubt bigger than they'd come with after spending time with Autumn or Felicia in the craft cabin, making beeswax candles or pressing wildflowers for bookmarks. Memories made here were the kind to stay with a person. Relived over and over each time they brought a friend to visit or when they'd hear a song we'd belted out at karaoke or smelled a burnt marshmallow.

Glad I'd already packed, I was free to roam among the chaos. There was still time to catch Autumn running around, no doubt saying her goodbyes and helping campers with whatever they'd need before heading back to their regular lives. That life still seemed like something Future Jamie would need to deal with, but Future Jamie was quickly becoming Present Jamie again.

I looked around for Ren and Autumn through the crowded

entrance as campers and their families packed their cars. Sure enough, she was there—directing, helping, and doing an on-the-fly secret handshake with one of Grant's kids once bags were loaded.

Her smile still spread across her cheeks as she tucked her hair behind her ear.

"Why don't we have a secret handshake?" I asked.

Autumn's laugh seemed to burst out of her. It was the sweetest thing. "We were busy doing other things..."

Now it was my turn for my cheeks to blaze. I looked past her to regain myself, distracted by Robert's and Nancy's laughter as they chatted with Lamar. It was amazing how quickly the camp staff had ingratiated themselves with Autumn's parents. I watched a moment as her parents took in the madness that came with today. At least now they knew what camp was and the effect it had on people, and I'd bet now that they'd seen the place, they'd want to visit her more often. Breakfast between the four of us had gone so well, it was clear that all remaining resentments had dissipated.

Talking about our present and future had left more room to understand each other. I wasn't the class clown they'd probably remembered me as, and they didn't seem as severe as I'd remembered either.

Catching Autumn's eye again, I took a deep breath, preparing to... What? Say goodbye? Tell her it was great getting to know her again? That it was even better getting my world rocked by her? Genius. My chest ached at the thought of leaving her behind again. But after I'd laid my cards on the table, after everything we'd been through this week, she wouldn't let me stay. And there was no way I'd try to take this away from her.

The crowd faded away as her eyes met mine again and she took a step closer to me as if she could feel this pull between us too. "Hey."

"Hi."

Autumn smiled at me, bright and reassuring as the sun. I was at a loss for words. What if I didn't get them back?

"You and Ren heading out?" she asked.

I took another breath. Right, *casual*. I could do this. "Yep. Meeting here in a couple of minutes."

Smooth. I tried to make more words happen, but I just got lost in memories of the past week. When she rescued my ax from the lake or when she teetered in yoga and my fingers itched to take her hips in my hands and balance her. I took another step closer, then hesitated, and Autumn's hand clenched at her side. I should have dipped her into a big, romantic kiss or tried to make her laugh. That was what I should have done. Instead, I took the hand she offered me and shook. She must have seen the confusion across my face because she redirected and patted my forearm.

"Jamie, it was so nice to see you again." Robert came up beside Autumn and reached to squeeze my shoulder.

I plastered on a mostly genuine smile. The timing of her parents was impeccable as always, and I struggled to keep the exasperation out of my voice. "You too, Robert, Nancy."

As we hugged, I looked over Nancy's shoulder to see a torn Autumn. I wanted more than just a friendly goodbye. I wanted to wrap her tightly in my arms. She didn't look impressed as her dad lingered.

"We'll see you tomorrow for brunch, honey."

"Yeah, Dad. That sounds great." She didn't even look at him, still maintaining eye contact with me.

Autumn and I stood again, not quite saying goodbye. This was goodbye, though, and I'd be damned if I fucked it up again. I kissed her cheek, and she smiled at me.

We spoke at the same time.

"Can I call you?"

"Let me know you got home okay?"

So that was that.

I gave her a nod and a friendly wave as Ren came up and said goodbye to Autumn, too, starting their own secret handshake. *Are you kidding me?* She shrugged as if reading my mind. A moment later, I was wrapping my arm around Ren's shoulder, and we were off.

A few minutes later, on the same winding road headed back to real life, I remembered how I'd been twisted up with excitement and anticipation when we'd first started on this drive, and now I was dreading leaving. A week hadn't been enough time, and yet it was enough time to change everything.

THE DIAMOND PATTERN OF GRAY, blue, and yellow brought a smile to my face as I glanced at the friendship bracelet Ren gave me, finding it comforting.

I caught Ren staring and lifted my wrist, wiggling it at him. "Best friendship bracelet I've ever received. Thank you."

His eyes went wide as I pulled a matching one from my pocket. It was a little wonky, some of the diamonds were more square-like, but he smiled anyway so I didn't care.

"Anything for you, Jamie."

I smiled at the way Ren said my nickname. There'd be no going back to James, for him anyway. James lived to work, and Jamie could work to live. Friendships hadn't been a priority before. They'd needed more time and energy than I'd been willing to invest back then. A week ago, Ren and I had been a little more than work friends, but now, judging by his goofy grin, it was safe to say this relationship would be worth everything I could give it. There was no way I'd let Ren slip away like I'd let all my friends from high school and college. I pictured my phone filled with all of my new camp friends and knew I wouldn't go back to that life.

"Don't think I let just anyone call me Jamie."

"Yeah, good thing we're best friends."

"Bracelets don't lie." I grinned.

Miles stretched as the music turned hopeful and reflective as we drove on. Ren was unusually quiet for the last several miles. He and Grant had spent most of the morning together, and silently hugged before separating, mirroring the mournfulness between me and Autumn just moments before. I could see the pain in his face at having to part.

I pulled into the parking lot of Wildwood's two-pump gas station, and Ren dashed into the convenience store for more snacks while I pumped the gas.

Ren came out a couple of minutes later carrying... Everything. He'd obviously learned the importance of snacks from his camp boyfriend. There would be no shortage of food in the event of an emergency, no fight to the death.

"Didn't you eat before we left?" I asked.

Ren tossed me a bag of Funyuns, my favorite, the motion almost causing him to drop the rest of his stockpile. "I mean, we were kinda busy."

Ren tried to regain control of the precariously balanced snacks. I opened the door for him, and he sorted through the bounty.

"Making the most of the time? I get that," I said. "I went looking for Autumn, but she was so busy today. Found Jack instead."

"How was he?" Ren asked around a bite of a rocky road protein bar.

"He was okay. It'd be difficult living their life, making friends, then watching them leave over and over. The strange thing was, he talked with me as if he'd see me again soon. He was kinda surprised that I was leaving today," I admitted.

"Maybe he's onto something." Ren shrugged. "I almost thought I'd be heading back on my own today."

"Really? You think I'd miss the first week after being promoted? That doesn't sound like me."

"So you would never, you know, decide to go back... It was just goodbye?" he asked, mouth full again.

I shook my head, shoving away thoughts of Autumn in the

slice of moonlight in her cabin as the painful decision to not continue was made. Then I pictured her in our final moments. This was going to be harder than I thought.

"Yeah, of course I'll visit again." I tried to skirt the issue. "I have to after such an awkward goodbye. I mean, her parents were there, and if there isn't anything that kills the mood like parents..."

"Man, if my parents had shown up, I would have been running up that mountain in the other direction. But then maybe I would have been able to stay." There was a wistfulness to his voice, and I knew, like me, he wished we could go back.

"Funny how quick it felt like home or something, right?" I tried to put into words all the mixed-up feelings I had about leaving where we'd been growing closer, where I'd gotten back in touch with my lighthearted don't-have-to-live-to-work self.

Ren waved his protein bar in the air. "I know what you mean. I mean... How am I going to go back to a non-communal shower?"

I chuckled. That was probably the only thing I wouldn't miss about camp. But the people...

Ren completed my thought. "It'll be the people I miss the most. They make you never want to leave."

I knew he was mostly talking about Grant, but my mind helplessly wandered back to Autumn. Was she still assisting campers? Or maybe partying in celebration of a hard-worked summer? A day hike daiquiri in one hand, giddy as she swapped her ridiculous pod stories with the other counselors?

"At least no one fell in love though, am I right?" Ren trailed off. I wasn't sure if he was talking about himself or me, but those words punched me right in the gut.

"Yeah, that would really suck," I agreed.

Pulling out of the gas station, I let the thoughts mingle as the deep forest green of the trees became swallowed by pastures and fields. I was going to miss it. I'd just have to visit again. I had to keep Autumn in my life.

There had to be some way to make that happen, but the idea

of taking more time off once I was responsible for upcoming junior associates was nerve-racking. Sure, I'd have vacation days, and while I'd rarely used them before, that was going to change. It was time to prioritize myself. I wanted to spend more time with my family and to watch my niece and nephew grow up. That was what mattered. I'd already missed so much by overworking and I was done offering excuses. This time around, it would be different. I was different.

Ren's playlist started, and the road stretched out as memories of Autumn filled me. She'd been everything to me before, and I'd messed it all up. And here I was again, knowing what I felt, knowing what I needed, and driving away from it.

THIRTY-ONE

Autumn

I ALWAYS SAID things have to get messy before they get better, but this was past messy. The craft shed looked like a bomb had gone off, and I stared at supplies with no clue how to start or why I was choosing to do this to myself now.

It may have been because I couldn't even walk near his pod without tearing up.

Today, our cleaning staff jumped right into tearing down cabins just like they did every Thursday. Only this time, they winterized everything. There were no more sheets and pillows, no welcome baskets replaced for incoming campers. Every step was taken to prevent varmints from taking residence and locking us out. We almost gave a cabin to a nest of squirrels one year. True story.

Our day-to-day staff was cleaning individual buildings, pulling in supplies from activities, and making sure everything was locked up, not to mention packing individual belongings since most staff would be leaving tomorrow because the season was over.

Everything was over.

He'd been gone for two hours. And I was struggling.

I stared at the floor littered with macrame rope and pots, mugs for marbling, vases for painting. Pick one thing and start there. That was the best way to tackle any project.

I grabbed the leftover Mod Podge and started marrying jars together.

This was cathartic. Liquid poured into liquid until it transitioned into globs from the almost-dead containers. I leaned all of them against a shelf so they didn't fall over and allowed the slow process to continue. Then I moved on to the yarn.

Most years, I found piles of it that needed separating and threw out the truly severe cases, but today, I started rolling them into balls, following colorful strand through colorful strand as if it were punishment.

We didn't break up. We just went our separate ways. I'd known this was going to happen, and I was still torn up. So I separated yarn, even though I had months to do this. I looked at my task and figured that was how long it would take to make a dent and chuckled to myself, dropping the rat's nest into the basket.

"Hey, Autumn, I've got the paint supplies you—Oh." Nat looked as though she'd driven up to a car crash and didn't know whether to call 9-1-1 first or jump out and do some triage.

"I have this handled." My voice cracked. "The wind did this."

She rolled her lips in as if she didn't believe me. With a sharp nod, Nat toed aside a box of wax for a make-your-own candle DIY that had been a hit this year, walking inside one more step. She picked up a pile of boards for our string art kit and put them into a box with even more boards.

I stared at the box, knowing she'd done it right, and even though she was doing a nice thing, it annoyed me. That was how I knew I was not doing okay.

"Thanks," I muttered under my breath.

"I'm guessing you have a system for this..." She carefully swiped her hand through the air.

"Yeah." I nodded, my voice softer. "I start with an explosion and then trap myself in my man-made cave for the winter."

She chuckled. She found a few more wood boards on the other side of the room and put them in the same box, straightening them when there was no need.

It seemed like she was working up to asking me something, so I cut that off at the pass. "I never asked. What brought you to Starlight?"

She didn't make eye contact, just ran her hands along the box. "Oh you know, running from a breakup... It's a tale as old as time." It wasn't an anomaly. She wouldn't be the first staffer to work here on the heels of a breakup.

"Was it because of the traveling?" Nat was a travel influencer. The photos she posted were filled with interesting experiences, and her happy face was front and center in all of them. Other than that, I didn't know her much. She and I just didn't cross paths very often. There were only six counselors, but that wasn't our entire staff. I was friends with everyone, and she and I were more like acquaintances. "Sorry. I shouldn't have asked that."

"It's okay, I'm not afraid to talk about my breakup. My ex and I had been at odds for a while. I loved what I was doing, and he didn't love that I loved it," she said, wistfully. "The trips led to fighting, and the distance thing... It's hard."

I nodded, twisting a piece of yarn around my pointer finger until it cut off circulation and the tip of my finger turned an angry shade of red. I quickly let go, and the throbbing sensation disappeared.

Nat dropped her eyes from my fidgeting and her tone took on a hard edge. "But then he forced me to choose between what I wanted and what he did."

"Jamie would never make me choose," I said without thinking, wishing I had a filter.

Nat didn't take offense, opting for the tea instead. "So you two *were* a thing."

I didn't need a reminder of that, but it was the truth. "We were more than a thing. We have... History."

"Ah." She nodded in understanding.

"Do you ever feel like you made the wrong choice?" I didn't want to pry, but I had to know. Maybe she understood what I was feeling and could make it make sense.

"I know I made the right choice but it still hurts. I'd built something I was proud of and I just wasn't ready to settle down. There's still so much adventure out there."

I tried to relate, but I'd had my adventures. I knew where I belonged, but with Jamie leaving, it felt like I was being split down the middle. Did that mean I'd always be alone? Was I *choosing* to be alone?

Nat clarified her previous statement. "Not that this is the same thing, I'm sure it isn't, I just... I know this feeling, that's all. That life won't go on. But it will. Sometimes things have to get worse before they get better."

She didn't act like my week with Jamie was too short, like I was being overly emotional. She just gave me her experience and hoped it would help. It made me want to hug her. But hugging would lead to crying, and crying would lead to me on the floor, unable to get back up again. So I just went with the simplest way to show my gratitude.

"Thank you, Nat."

Our situations weren't the same, but there were parallels I couldn't ignore. Either way, I wouldn't find the answer at the back of this tragic craft shed, so I decided to leave it and go clean my pod.

WIPING away the sweat of a hard day's work, I took a solidifying breath and stared out at my favorite lake. The sun was starting to lower in the sky, but it still shone on dancing waves from the rushing wind that was cooling me and my damp face. It was hot in those cabins, but it wasn't nearly as bad out here.

"You look like you've never seen that lake before," Leo said from behind me.

Jeez, was everyone looking for me today?

"Just marveling at the beauty of nature and shit."

He sat beside me and smiled ruefully. Did he know exactly how I felt too? Had I been hiding it this poorly? "You know, I wouldn't give up on your happy ending just yet. You could even say I'd bet on it."

I shrugged, then I understood. "You bet on us?"

Leo looked proud of himself. "I started the side bet."

So my coworkers knew. And they'd been rooting for us. They did it so quietly... I guessed I'd been too wrapped up in bliss to notice.

Now I had to deal with that aftermath.

"Unsanctioned betting is not allowed when it comes to shipping," I deflected.

"I'm the boss. I can break protocol." Leo's crooked smile almost won me over.

"Y'all are unrealistic. How could you believe that would work out?"

He looked determined. "I'm great at being unrealistic. But you should check my track record. You'd be surprised at how often I'm right."

My stomach clenched, as though it were empty and I was still about to lose my lunch.

Leo started doodling in the dirt with a stick. "You know, we could work with you, right?"

"What?"

"You don't have to be here all year. We'd need you during the summer, sure, but the rest of the time, you could telecommute and travel like you frequently do already." The doodle turned into a star and he smiled.

I loved Leo for his optimism. He wasn't thinking about the fact that summer for us meant May to September, five long months of camp that I couldn't exactly leave for more than a week-long jaunt, max.

"Hazel and I can do the event stuff during the year, and we could give you something else, like... Budgets or..." He shivered. We both knew we couldn't steal budgeting from his counterpart. She'd have a conniption. Not to mention, that was a minor thing, and for me to be a full-time staffer, I'd need to do work around this camp throughout the year to prepare and keep things running. It just wasn't feasible.

"I love my job, Leo." I had a new role and plenty of buy-in. I wanted to help this place thrive, and I wanted to witness the fruits of my labor. It just didn't work.

His soft smile held love and satisfaction. He wrapped his arm around me and pulled me into a hug like he would a sister. This was so much more than a job. That was one of the things I loved about this place.

This was the right thing to do. Jamie already had a life. He could find someone who he didn't have to give everything up for. I knew I'd have a hard time reconciling that, so I shoved it down deep.

"You can love other things too," Leo said.

I sucked in a short breath, making it hard to swallow the lump in my throat.

I'd been so sure that turning Jamie away had been the right thing, but my heart was fighting my decision, and my friends weren't making it any easier. But that was the thing about life. Nothing was cut and dry and you had to deal with the conse-quences. I imagined a different world, one where I made the other choice, and wondered if I'd still feel the same. Because the lingering feeling that I'd just made the biggest mistake of my life was eating at me, and I wasn't sure if it would ever go away.

THIRTY-TWO

Jamie

"Take that exit." Ren pointed to the sign indicating we'd be getting off in a quarter of a mile. "We need to make a quick stop."

I tilted my head as I read it. I'd taken this stop a number of times. But that was just a coincidence, right?

Wrong. We ended up in front of the place I knew well.

Stepping out of Ren's car to head up to my parents' home was a visceral experience. I was hit with a familiar scent: wings on the charcoal grill mixed with the floral perfume of the rosebush my mom had transplanted from my grandmother's house.

I should have known my devious friend had something up his sleeve.

"So, I know we didn't discuss it, but this was your mom's idea, and I told her I could strong-arm you into a stop. Surprise!"

I couldn't help but smile. "Thanks for doing this, man." I patted Ren on the shoulder. He didn't need to bring me to my parents' house. We could easily have just gone home, but I had learned he was pretty selfless when it came to me.

I didn't mention it, but I was grateful for the comforts of my family when I was going through a breakup that wasn't actually a breakup. Somehow, it felt worse than a breakup.

"No need to thank me. I'd travel hours just for a taste of your dad's marionberry cobbler."

His cobbler really was that good.

"Uncle Jamie!" Adam ran down the porch stairs and threw his arms around me. The kid was downright angelic, from his toothy smile to his curly blond hair. He squeezed me as though he hadn't seen me in years, but maybe to a little kid, six months felt like a lifetime.

Had it actually been six months?

I thought back to the last time I'd seen everyone for my dad's birthday in March. I had missed Mother's Day and Father's Day because of two big cases I'd been working on that had me working through the weekends. Man, I'd been a terrible son.

"Where's your mom?" I lifted him onto my shoulder so that he could spread his arms and fly like an airplane. He pointed forward, so forward I went.

We made our way to the back deck, and I teared up. My entire family was here. In the middle of a Thursday.

"How are you all here?" The lump in my throat made it hard to speak.

"Well, Marley and Sav had extra vacation time, and your dad and I took half-days," my mom explained. I couldn't believe it. Taking time off and throwing a BBQ all because I'd be in their area. "There's my favorite second son." My mom embraced Ren, bypassing her own child. They'd only met in person a few times, but there had always been an easy rapport, and obviously, they'd been conspiring against me for this trip. Ren reached for a slice of watermelon, but she smacked his hand away from the bowl, and he shook it out as if he'd been burned. "No dessert before dinner."

"I'm a grown adult, Patricia." He cowered behind Erin, who already had a slice in her fist.

Marley came up the deck stairs, laughing. "A grown adult hiding behind an eight-year-old." She tickled the bottoms of Adam's feet, causing him to squirm on my shoulder until I set him down. "Hi, big brother." She kissed me on the cheek just as Savannah came up and opened her arms.

"Did you get shorter, Sav?" I ran my hand from the top of her head to my collarbone like the world's worst measuring tape.

She elbowed me in the ribs. "Did you get snarkier?"

"Oh, you have no idea." Ren leaned forward as though he had hot gossip. "*Jamie* here is basically a whole new person."

My dad turned from the grill to raise an eyebrow, but his curiosity shone through.

I tried to get ahead of the situation. "I don't know what he's talking about."

"What did you do at that camp?" Marley pried.

"You know, normal stuff. Hiking, bird-watching, swimming."

"Crafting, ziplining, making moon eyes at past girlfriends," Ren added.

That got everyone's attention.

"Autumn was there?" my dad asked. Obviously my letter hadn't gotten back to my mom, or he would have known this information already. But him jumping to which specific girlfriend was telling.

Ren's look of surprise put me in my place. It said, "You really only had one girlfriend?"

"I dated other people too," I answered without his asking.

"It *was* Autumn, wasn't it?" My mom vibrated with excitement.

"She was there. You wouldn't believe all the stuff she does for the camp." I picked up one of my parents' linen cloth napkins we'd found at a yard sale probably twenty-five years ago, twisting it in my hands. Way to give myself away.

"I haven't thought about her in a long time," Dad mused. He turned back to the grill and flipped the meat, running a brush over them with his famous wing sauce.

My mom didn't say anything, but the opposite was probably true. Every time I showed up without a date to a family function, she brought up how good a boyfriend I was and how I deserved to be happy. The only person I'd dated that she'd liked was my high school girlfriend. Go figure.

"Who's Autumn?" Erin inquired. She looked just as interested as the rest of the group. I felt like I'd shown up with a dog to show and tell. Except for my dad, no one's attention was on anything else.

"You know that photo of James before his prom? The one where he's laughing like a fool?" Dad supplied, turning back around to give me his full attention too.

My parents still had a photo of the two of us in their photo collage in the hallway. She'd worn a chartreuse strapless dress that she'd hated. She'd pulled the thing up all night because it kept sliding down. Autumn hadn't been super into dresses back then. I wondered if she was now. I also wanted to find that picture and remember better times. I knew I'd look at it later to torture myself though.

"Ooh, she's pretty," Erin said. I wondered if she actually knew the photo they were talking about or if she was just taking part in the conversation to feel included. Didn't matter. It was still the truth.

"Tell me you didn't just let her go." The seriousness in Marley's tone had me feeling like the chastised teenager I was back when I'd dinged her car.

"Oh he did," Ren cut in. "And he's in love with her."

"Dude." I elbowed him before addressing my sister. "She lives in Wildwood. What would you have me do?"

"I don't know. Maybe *try*," my mom interjected, eyebrows narrowed. "You were hung up on that girl for years. Tell me different."

I thought about arguing, but she was right. And she probably already had a presentation with bullet points in her head for why we belonged together.

Ren watched with apt eyes as my family tore into me. I didn't think this had been his intention, but it was happening, and I'd chew him out later.

My mom continued. "You've been so focused on that job that you've forgotten what matters."

I wanted to shout. I'd been reevaluating everything and knew I'd had my priorities out of whack and needed to rectify that. But even though I was feeling a change, it wasn't obvious. I'd have to put my money where my mouth was.

But this was my family, and as much as I hated to hear it, they knew what was best for me. I hadn't been with anyone in years, hadn't even humored the idea of starting something with someone because I wouldn't be devoted to them, but the idea that maybe I could have a family of my own wasn't so daunting anymore. The hard truth about that was, it was only after spending time with Autumn, after falling in love with her all over again, that the thought even crossed my mind.

But that wasn't what she wanted.

"I loved my care package," Ren tried, finally stepping up and being the friend I needed. "Thank you so much, everyone."

"Did you get my drawing?" Erin asked.

Ren squeezed her hand. "I did. I'm going to put it up in my office."

"I packed the Warheads." My dad came up from behind me, placing the wings on the table. We all sat down and started loading our plates. "Reminded me of when I went to camp as a kid."

"Way to rub it in our face, Dad. I always wanted to go to camp." Marley whined.

Ren attempted to make her feel better. "Well, now you can. But Camp Starlight does have a bit of a waitlist. Although you may have an in..." He looked right at me and so did everyone else. So much for that friend save I'd been hoping for.

I HAD to force myself to get in the car after chatting with my family. Leaving them was hard enough. Leaving Oregon was like admitting that I wasn't going back.

The wave of sadness that hit me when I pulled away was flattening. We drove in silence for a while before Ren pressed continue on the playlist he'd curated for our drive. The upbeat tunes we'd belted on the drive down now felt demoralizing.

I needed a reset, and I think Ren knew that, because he changed up the music to a playlist of ballads. Instead of sounding comforting, it just sounded like heartbreak. Physically, I had to drive between the lines, but emotionally, it felt like I was all over the place. Like I was experiencing the five stages of grief all at once.

Denial.

I knew denial well. Sprinkles fell on the windshield and I waited long enough until it was difficult to see before turning the windshield wipers on. The water washed away days of dirt and grime, which just reminded me that washing away camp meant washing away Autumn, and I wasn't okay with that. This wasn't happening. I had only known adult Autumn for a week, and that wasn't enough time to re-fall in love with someone. I had been constantly busy during long Autumnless windows of time, so it made even less sense for these feelings to be true. This was just a figment of my imagination, something I was building up into more than it was. I was remembering past feelings and present, which created a cocktail of confusion, but confusion didn't equal love.

Anger.

It was easy to be angry over the way things played out. I gripped the steering wheel a little too tight, until my knuckles went white. She didn't want me, and that was good to know, but it didn't take away my frustration. We had something, I knew we did, even if she was too stubborn to see it. I was mad at Past Jamie for the way he treated her and wondered if I had earned back that trust in the small window of time I'd had her. But if she held my past mistakes against me, mistakes that took place ten years ago, then there was something wrong with her. I didn't need her.

Bargaining.

Or... I could pull over and call her. Or text her. I hadn't done so at my parents' place because I wasn't sure what would happen. She could respond, which might break me, or she could ignore me, which might be worse. What did opening the lines of communication even do? Maybe I could visit her again next summer. Maybe things would be different. Maybe she would see that this was real then. But that would be months without her. Months I didn't think I could take.

Depression.

What hurt the most was the fact that I had offered to stay and she'd said no. Even if that seemed unbelievable, I was willing. "Total Eclipse of the Heart" poured through my speakers. It was probably one of the most dramatic songs in music history, and it was screaming inside my head. Bonnie Tyler really understood me.

The only thing driving me to get home was the fact that I could sleep all weekend. Nap away this sadness. In my cold bed with my cold sheets. A bed I could spread out across because I had no one to kick me with their cold feet. God, was I missing bruised shins? I was truly pathetic.

Acceptance.

The drizzle came to a stop and sunbeams broke through the clouds. I could get over this. I had to.

But maybe I shouldn't.

We had gone years apart, and after a short period of time, this wasn't something that happened every day. Something that could even be guaranteed to happen again. No one was like her, and no one would ever live up to her. When it came down to it, all of these emotions only solidified what I had to do. Resolved, I wasn't about to let love slip through my fingers again, not after years of knowing what I was missing.

THIRTY-THREE

Autumn

Everything had fallen into place.

That was what I told myself as I sat in front of flickering flames at the staff campfire, clinging to a cup of hot cocoa and Baileys as though it were integral to my survival.

I had my dream job, and it was only getting better. After years of seeking their approval, I had my parents' support. They'd been proud even. I'd never seen that coming.

I had my friends, the family I'd made. I had the outdoors and sunshine and tears in my eyes. I—

I was going to be fine.

The chaos from this summer session was finally winding down, a feeling I both enjoyed and lamented, but overall, it meant good things. I'd have some time to work on making Camp Starlight better, something I loved to do. I could get organized—and finish cleaning up the craft shed, because that was already driving me crazy. I'd be able to work on building cabins with Jack. I had a new role, and I was incredibly excited to hit the ground running. Plus, I'd get an actual break at some point. All good things.

It just felt like my heart had driven away from me hours ago.

I imagined Jamie's hand out the window, dancing through the wind, a smile on his face as he looked at his best friend, passing rock walls and ravines filled with trees.

This had been temporary. We both knew that. So why did it feel so terrible?

I remembered the way he'd made me feel at sixteen. Like everything had been full of promise. Like he'd never let me go. I remembered the second I'd realized I was in love with him. The way the feeling had wrapped around me like a warm blanket. But there had also been fear back then. Fear at curbing the many emotions I hadn't known how to handle. Fear that I'd never feel like that again. And yet, here I was, sitting in sadness, wondering how he was, even though I'd seen him hours ago, and he probably was getting back to his real life and already forgetting me.

But a lingering sensation told me that wasn't true and had me questioning if I was making the right decision. Maybe this wasn't the life I was supposed to lead. I could give up my dream job, right? It was barely a job, anyway, when you thought about it. Because you weren't supposed to love your job like I did. I could live in the real world with its pantsuits and noise and fast food within a twenty-mile radius. I—

I let out a sob. Quietly. Like a lady.

This was so unfair. We hadn't even broken up. We'd just gone our separate ways, like we'd planned on doing from the start. But images of Jamie flashed before my eyes. The anxiety in his eyes as I picked up an ax after throwing a bull's-eye. The way we held hands in bed. The way he looked in that robe.

I could call him right now and fix this. After all, this was a mess of my own making. And once we found each other again, we could... What could we even do?

I sobbed again. Thankfully, no one noticed.

They were too busy using aerosol marshmallow whipped cream over spiked cozy beverages, laughing and smiling, because this was a happy occasion. The end of a successful summer. An uplifting, joyful, fun-filled summer with ups and downs, with mistakes and problems that had all been solved, because in the end, everything worked out for the best. I was fine.

"Sawyer. You're too old for a keg stand," Azalea yelled.

They flipped upside down, and Leo and Hazel rushed to their side to hold them up.

"I'm not responsible for anybody today," they shouted. "I'm gonna live foreverrrrr!"

The group burst into laughter as they let out a belch and rubbed their stomach. What possessed them, I didn't know, though I understood their need for recklessness.

More than anything, I wished I could share in their joy.

"Hey, Autumn, who won the shipping board?" Leo asked.

I tried not to roll my eyes. I was hoping I could get away without having to say anything. He looked on expectantly. He was never going to let me go without announcing his continued reign as our shipping board king.

"Well, I think it's obvious who won so yay—" I spouted off quietly, but Leo cut me off.

"Autumn."

I raised my voice and walked to the stage. Leo met me on the side, as if I were the emcee of this show and he was about to deliver his acceptance speech.

"All right, folks, the season has come to an end, and the winner of the shipping board competition is..."

People reluctantly patted their thighs to make some noise, but they increased it to a more enthusiastic rhythm because they couldn't help themselves.

"Leo Lovejoy," I proclaimed with as little fanfare as possible.

Hazel whistled, and she seemed to be the only one who was excited for him to win. The rest of us were poor losers.

Leo tried to nonchalantly hand me the busted-up kid's soccer trophy we'd bedazzled a few years ago. The head was superglued on after we'd found it barely hanging on, the nameplate reading "Kevin Blevins." We thought it was hilarious. Poor kid.

I took it from his hand and gave it right back to him, leaving my place to go back to my seat.

He lifted it high into the air. "Who wants to kiss it for good luck? There's always next year," he gloated—a true asshole. Then he gently petted the top and spoke into its plastic ear. "You're going right back where you belong." He kissed the statue before cradling it in his arms.

Hazel looked appalled. "You know we got it at the Treasure Trove, right? I can only guess how many grubby hands have been on that thing."

Leo shrugged it off. "Yeah, but glitter negates bacteria."

Nat's arms crossed her chest and she spoke under her breath. "Maybe he'll contract some disease and then someone else will have a chance at winning next year." She'd come in second place, and wasn't taking it well.

I let out a watery chuckle.

Before long, Lola and Luis were back at it again, making drinks even in their off time, like they truly loved to do. It was on nights like these that their playing off each other's unique tastes led to incredibly random drinks Frankensteined together to eventually become the new camp sensation. That was how our PB&J cocktail came to be and the reason our secret menu included Paradise Mountain: a mixture of Mountain Dew and Malibu rum, which was surprisingly good.

Leo tuned his guitar while Hazel and Nat laughed at Lamar, who'd been sprayed with whipped cream by Sawyer. Felicia and Bobby were by the fire, roasting marshmallows. And Jack? Well, I couldn't find him among the smiling faces.

"Hey there, stranger." My best friend placed his hand on my shoulder, and I turned to face him.

"Hey." Not sounding like myself, I cleared my throat.

"So he's gone for good, huh?" Jack seemed surprised.

"Why wouldn't he be?" I sounded despondent, but like I said, I was fine. "He doesn't even live here."

It didn't make sense for him to live here, after all. He didn't have a reason beyond being with me, and that wasn't sustainable. Relationships didn't last when lawyers left new opportunities to stay with their ex-girlfriends after a week of bliss.

That was just a general circumstance. Nothing specific about that at all.

"You know what I mean." Apparently, he didn't come here to play.

I said nothing. I didn't have an answer for him.

He sat next to me and put his hand on mine on the bench. Leo started to play background music on his guitar while everyone continued talking. It smelled like smoke and the wilderness. It sounded like happiness. It felt like pain.

I stared at the fire like you weren't supposed to, seeing little stars as my eyes protested. I turned to Jack again, only to find him with cheeks stuffed, holding out a marshmallow bag. "No," I tried.

He reached in and grabbed me a marshmallow. Then a handful. It was incredibly unsanitary. I took them anyway.

The music stopped for a moment, and then Hazel's striking voice started singing our goodbye song—"Don't Stop Believin'" by Journey. A wave of pain washed over me. Goodbye.

Jack handed me another marshmallow, and I took it as a tear ran down the front of my stuffed cheek. The music filled my ears as everyone else sang. This campfire was the hardest one because it was the last, a culmination of everything from the entire summer. After this, some things would be in the air. We didn't know what counselors would come back. Sawyer could be gone next year. Or Nat or even Jack if he found someone else. But I'd still be here. It was where I was meant to be.

Didn't mean I wasn't going to cry about it.

Jack shoved another marshmallow in his mouth. "Four."

"That isn't going to work on me right now. Can't you see I'm wallowing?"

"You can marsh-*wallow*," he literally spat out, elbowing me as if he was proud of himself, and I couldn't help but smile. He had me. I took four marshmallows and stuffed my face.

I wondered how many marshmallows Jamie could fit in his mouth.

When I was emotional, the tears always flowed over the dumbest shit. I wiped them away, but they were too quick to keep up with. Jack narrowed his eyes. He looked like a sad chipmunk. He handed me two more marshmallows, and I shoved them in my mouth, turning back to the fire. And maybe the sugar rush gave me the clarity I needed.

All those years ago Jamie had been sure about what direction our lives would go, and what was best for me. I'd hated it back then, even if he'd been right. But things were different now.

It was hard to imagine a world in which I could live without Jamie. It had only been hours since he'd left, and it felt like I was having trouble breathing. I wish I could blame the marshmallows blocking my windpipe, but I knew that wasn't the case. He was my person. He'd always been my person. Even Leo knew, and that had to mean something, right?

I didn't have to do this.

I blinked back my tears, unfisted my hands, and pushed against the bench, ready to leave, ready to go find him and fix this. I still had a chance.

But Jack tapped me on my shoulder, pointing through the flames. I blinked, wondering if I was witnessing a fire mirage of Jamie walking in my direction. Now I was just delusional.

Silence crept up on us, and I wasn't sure if it was because my coworkers had seen him and gone quiet or because the world had fallen away.

It was just him and me.

He got on both knees and held my hand, kissing it. I started to speak and remembered how stupid I looked.

Oh my god, I was going to spray a cocktail of marshmallows and spit at the feet of the man I loved.

A stream of tears fell down my face, probably smearing the light layer of makeup I was wearing. I tried chewing, looking away from him toward where Jack *was* sitting, but he'd abandoned me. I turned back to Jamie, swallowing, and started the process again.

"Autumn—" he started. "Oh my god, I can't talk to you when you look like that."

I sputtered. "You can't make me laugh, idiot!"

I tried chewing again, covering my mouth with my hand as my jaw worked overtime before finally, finally swallowing the last bit.

He wiped the tears from my eyes and smiled gently. "Hey, sunflower."

"What are you doing here?"

Jamie's eyes softened. "I was really craving marshmallows." He squeezed my hand, and my heart fluttered. "Unless you ate all of them?"

I laughed again, and I swear the tears on my cheek flew from my face. I was a fucking mess.

He looked at me somberly. "I didn't want to leave."

He said it as if it was so easy. As if there weren't a million things stopping him from being here.

"So you came back? Don't you have to be at work on Monday?" I clutched his hand, unable to let go. I wondered how long I'd have him for. A few hours? A day? Would I have to say goodbye all over again? I didn't care. I would take what I could get.

"I do. But that leaves us a whole weekend if you're willing to drive me home. Then I'll go back, I guess. For a month or so."

"*A month*?" I practically shouted, gripping his shoulders. "What about your job? What about Seattle?"

"I don't care about the job, and I don't care about the place I'm living. I only care about you." He pushed a strand of hair behind my ear. "I'm going to quit and get my ducks in a row. But only if you want me—"

I practically jumped him, kissing him as though my life depended on it. Suddenly, I was standing up, his arms wrapped around me as he deepened the kiss.

"I want you." I peppered him with kisses. "I want you so bad."

"Yeah? Well, we can't do that here," he joked.

"Please don't do that here," Ren said from behind me. I hadn't noticed he was here. Had they even made it home?

I ignored him and stared at the man in front of me. "I love you," I blurted. "I think I always have. That sounds so ridiculous, doesn't it?"

"I think I'm the only one who understands what you mean."

"You do?"

"I feel like I've loved you for my entire life, Autumn. There's nothing I want more than to make you happy. The moment you kicked my ass in our first debate, I knew I was done for."

He kissed me again, and we only stopped when we heard cheers and claps. I turned to see every one of my friends, my chosen family, with the happiest smiles on their faces.

Epilogue

JAMIE

EIGHT MONTHS later

It was always a good sign when the drive down Highway 26 changed from civilization to an evergreen-surrounded winding road. After many trips, it felt like they were welcoming me with open arms. Sun shone through the needled trees above me, reflecting off my windshield as I drove the curved highway. Soon, I'd be home.

Now, if you'd told me a year ago that I'd run off to live in the forest, I would have laughed in your face, but some things in my life still surprised me.

Living with Autumn at Camp Starlight had been many things but especially a learning curve. Who knew you couldn't get food delivery at all hours of the day unless it was from a guy named Herb in his nineties-era Dodge Neon, *if* he wasn't stoned? Or that you could scream at the top of your lungs with no one noticing? That one was a little nerve-racking. A lot had changed since I'd moved away from Seattle. I'd found myself going on adventure after adventure, and Autumn was always game.

I'd put in my notice the second I'd touched Seattle soil. Clint and Margaret were more than surprised at my leaving. They'd likely thought I was losing my mind when I opened with "I'm running off to live in the wilderness," or something to that effect, but they'd been supportive, even offering to refer some Oregon clients to me when I was ready once they learned I was opening my own firm.

I hadn't even researched taking the Oregon State Bar Exam before quitting. That was how unprepared I'd been. But I'd jumped, and Autumn had been prepared to catch me. I had to remain at the firm for three long months to finish my cases and sell my condo. It hadn't been lost on me that we'd had to do long distance again during this process. I'd been grateful that she took a month off to help me settle affairs, so we got to spend time together, alone and happy. The other two months were difficult, but still less of a struggle than when we were teenagers. While it was nice having her with me through that process, it was clear where we belonged. I'd had my fill of Seattle, and she wasn't meant to live there. Autumn was like a baby bird who'd left the nest and fell right into a puddle of water, getting out and shaking the liquid off before waddling away all disgusted.

I knew I'd made the right choice.

Once I moved to Oregon, I spent my time studying for the bar exam around the clock. I'd be taking it in July, but I was already getting inquiries about the firm I planned on opening. There was a lot of interest because, it turned out, there weren't any lawyers in the sticks. I anticipated having clientele coming from all over, and planned to expand my repertoire to include land disputes and agricultural business pursuits, as well as general law. I avoided giving legal advice, but I did help a particular camp with its expansion.

Another thing that had changed? The amount of time I spent with my family. It took a little over an hour to get to Portland, so I did it frequently. Watching my niece and nephew grow up from a short distance away was the icing on the cake, especially since I'd barely been there for the first years of their lives. I loved being an uncle, and even though there were stressors from starting anew, I still found time to spend with them. They'd even come to stay at Camp Starlight for a few days this spring.

But my favorite moments had been with Autumn. When I moved to Wildwood, she offered me one of the other counselor cabins until the new season, but I'd spent so much time at her place, I was basically moved in already. We'd spent our days getting reacquainted, but the more time we had together, the more it felt like things had never ended between us. Every day, I was still just as excited to see her, and living with her only made it better.

Eight months together went by quickly, and I learned how much I loved taking in the seasons with my girlfriend. Winter found us cozy, huddled happily under her patchwork blanket, sipping cocoa at the bonfire and cheering on Leo's shenanigans until our sides hurt from laughing. Spring was a whole other beast. Autumn increased her time working with Jack and his small team to finish the next round of cabins—which were to be opened this week. There were many nights she came home sopping wet, dirty, and happy, and I loved to see it.

Meanwhile, Jack had been a bit of a workhorse to meet his timeframe, and it wore on my girlfriend. She'd told me she was worried about him being down, that he hadn't been the same lighthearted guy she'd known, but she attributed it to the deadline, assuming that he'd come back around to his old self once camp restarted. I hoped she was right.

Today, I was touring the building I planned to operate out of. It was a small location with a single back office and space for two small desks in front, and it fit me perfectly. My future office was nestled between Beans and Beans, my favorite Mexican/coffee shop hybrid, and Wildwood's craft store Sew Cute. It was also right next to the bench I'd done some important thinking on, and now I couldn't wait to spend lunches sitting there and looking at the forest.

The realtor had just walked away when Ren called. I sat down at a squeaky chair and hit answer.

"How was your trip?" he asked.

"Good. How was yours?"

He and Grant had gone to the San Juan islands for a getaway. They'd been together nearly as long as Autumn and me, but they'd started out the normal way, meeting each other for dates instead of moving in a month after connecting, which was progressing pretty slow, if you asked me.

"It was amazing. The water was as blue as Grant's eyes, I kid you not. And we saw whales, Jamie. Real whales. They're the cows of the sea."

I didn't think he realized "cows of the sea" kind of downplayed the wonder. "That's really cool."

"How's my favorite ax-wielding blonde?"

"She's good. I'm excited to see her, but I had to stop by the new office first."

"Always got that nose to the grindstone." There was no real judgment in his tone. He knew I was pushing myself to the limit, but he was always there to remind me that things would work out. I wiped a layer of dust from the desk where my future assistant would be working. "You're one to talk."

Ren had been studying for his LSATs, and we had regular calls for me to help him practice. He had continued working at our firm and was gelling with his new associate. I was so happy for that (mostly) seamless transition.

"Hey, I have my reasons," he said. "For one thing, Grant gives me sexual favors if I answer enough questions right."

"There's a joke in here about Pavlovian responses," I started.

Ren cackled. "It's definitely training me to *enjoy* work."

It was hard being away from him, and there were times I felt that four and a half hours of distance, but he and Grant were planning on coming back for another summer session in a month, so I had that to look forward to.

After our call ended, I wrapped things up with the realtor, and I took my trusty notebook outside to do some brainstorming while

I waited for Autumn. It wasn't long before arms wrapped around my shoulders from behind.

"Hey there, stranger." She kissed me on the cheek.

"Excuse me, miss, but I have a girlfriend. She runs that summer camp across the highway, and she's scary good with an ax."

She came around the bench and fell dramatically so that her head was in my lap. "She sounds hot."

I ran my fingers through her hair, her murmur sending a tingle straight through me. I tried to think of other things, but it was difficult with the love of my life hovering over my junk. "She's actually got a pretty big ego, if I'm being honest."

She blew her bangs out of her eyes. "Which contributes to the hotness."

"Sure," I deadpanned.

She ran her fingers up my neck and massaged my scalp. I released a groan at the feel of her fingers on me again. It had been too long. "How was the dinner?"

I spent last night at my family's home to avoid driving late after my sister's birthday dinner. I'd missed these kinds of events the last couple of years because I was working. Back when I didn't know how to take time off. Autumn had wanted to be there, but she was knee-deep in preparations for the new season, which started tomorrow, and I'd planned to spend the night in Portland, so she'd stayed back.

"It was great." Except for when I was playing with Adam and he dropped off a swing set. Thank god Autumn didn't want kids either, because holy fuck, that feeling that I'd almost killed a child was still eating at me, and it was a complete accident. "I have something for you."

She bounced up, reaching for the container I was pulling out of my bag. "Tell me your mother's blueberry cheesecake is in there."

"My mom's blueberry cheesecake is in here."

She kissed me hard on the mouth. I was going to thank my mom for that later, in a way that didn't reveal just why.

Other than the swing set scare, being a more present uncle came to me pretty easily, but not as easily as becoming an auntie came to Autumn. I'd fielded questions about where she was the entire time, especially from the kids.

"Come on, let's get some mocha-ritas," Autumn joked, her hand warming mine. My lunchtime vice had been coffee and enchiladas while I studied and Autumn frequently met me at Beans and Beans on her lunches, which gave me something to look forward to.

Autumn spoke quickly once we started moving, waving her hands with more vigor than usual, a nervous energy I suspected was due to her starting camp tomorrow as an assistant director. I could only imagine how she'd been without me here.

"Hazel and Leo just got in yesterday."

"Cutting it down to the wire?"

The camp directors had been getting the second Camp Starlight location up and running after I'd helped them negotiate terms with their investor.

"Yeah, but I could have handled it," she said, more to herself than to me.

"I know you could, sunflower. You're ready."

"I'm ready." Her voice was laced with humble confidence.

I didn't think she'd had time to overthink this one, because she'd been so busy getting ready, our cabin was covered in a variety of sticky notes, and I could see the traces of her brainstorming through each activity we did, whether it was eating, snuggling with a movie, or walking through the wilderness. There was even one time I'd been kissing down her neck and she mumbled the word "registration" as if a lightbulb had gone off. I'd flipped her on her back and gone down on her after letting her write it on a Post-it to truly take her out of her head.

Based on what I'd learned about her new role, Autumn had

been doing some aspects of this job already, just not continuously. She'd always liked taking on more each year, and Hazel and Leo were smart to put more responsibility into her hands in an official capacity.

"So my dad called today." Autumn's tone didn't give anything away, but it still had me wondering if this could be good news. The mile-wide smile on her face told me it'd gone well. "He wanted to wish me luck on a new season."

This was a first for her, and I was so glad it was happening. She'd been speaking with her parents a lot more often than before, and they'd even joined us when my family was visiting for my birthday. Her dad and stepmom had been surprisingly supportive of our relationship and with me starting a practice. I'd half worried they'd take issue with me leaving my former law firm and starting something new. But I felt brave, just like Autumn, jumping from a plane without a backup parachute, never knowing what the next day would bring.

Autumn wrung her hands together as our first drinks were delivered—surprisingly without us ordering them. My girlfriend didn't notice, but I nearly jumped in my seat. Was I a local now?

"Things are going to be fine." I pulled her hands apart and squeezed one of them.

"It's just first-week jitters," she reassured me. "I know we're ready. The axes are sharpened. The glitter is glittering. It's going to be a good year. The real question is, are *you* ready?"

"What do I have to be ready for?" I asked honestly.

"It's a big change, going from living alone to moving in with your girlfriend to living on a campground with forty-plus people at a time. And that's just one session."

I took both hands into mine and squeezed. "Autumn, we may be moving too fast."

She pulled me into her and kissed me. "You're a little late to be giving that feedback, handsome. But if you want, you can leave it on a comment card." She smiled that shimmery smile I'd loved since we were teenagers.

"I thought all the ones I submitted were getting thrown away."

"Not true. I keep them... If they're sexual in nature." Okay, maybe I'd given her a couple of those. Ten tops. She looked at me with an expression that said "duh," and I burst into laughter.

"Oh, so you do read them. What did you think about that pretzel thing where you... Actually, never mind. I'll just show you later."

Autumn's eyes shone with happiness, and I couldn't help getting lost in them. She took my hand in hers and squeezed. "For real, though, it's your first summer camp season. Are you ready?"

I kissed her hand, and she melted against me. "When I'm with you, Autumn, I'm ready for anything."

Want more Autumn and Jamie?
Sign up for our newsletter for a bonus chapter and to stay up to date with the Camp Starlight universe:
elliebelmont.com/bonus

Acknowledgments

After years of dedication and hard work, it's finally time for us to acknowledge that we finished! We wrote this for us, thinking it would be really cool if anyone else in the world liked it enough to read it. At the time we didn't know what kind of adventure we'd signed ourselves up for. We loved spending time at Camp Starlight so much, we can't wait to go back.

Now, to thank the people who made this dream happen:

To our editor, Sara. Thank you for adding all the red marks across our document (red means love, right?). Your expertise has taught us a lot and made our story better. To Kristen, thank you for your willingness to make this happen within our timeframe. We appreciate your amazing feedback and the outstanding research, as well as your strong suggestion to use less exclamation points! (Sorry). Thank you to our amazing cover artist Andra, you created such a beautiful cover (some of us still have it as our phone background).

Camille, Camille, Camille. You had no idea what you'd signed on for when you agreed to beta read for us, now, did you? You have a brilliant mind and amazing questions. Hannah, and Jessica, thank you for being fantastic beta readers and taking care of our characters.

Sho and Alyse, our world would be bereft without you in it. Thank you for creating a community and space we love, and for letting us use that space for writing. We loved rewarding ourselves with a book when we finished a draft or needed a pick-me-up, and you always cheered us on. To the Maggie Mae's book club ladies, your excitement has only encouraged us to keep going, even on the hard days. Shoutout to our Smutty Book Club: Jeni, Jen, Lexa, Amy, Erin, and Emily. Your check-ins throughout this process have only strengthened our resolve to finish this book. We love being a part of this unhinged group of hot human beings.

To our amazing friends: Janna, Kelli, Darek, Drew, and Angie, thank you for all the times we were able to replenish our creative well just by being around you.

Shoutout to the Portland Romance Writers group, it's been so much fun getting to know so many of you. The resources and community you have provided has been unparalleled. We're looking forward to more writing retreats and get-togethers.

Thank you to our local romance bookstores, The Romance Era and Grand Gesture Books for merely existing. Your support of local authors is vital and much appreciated.

We are so grateful for every ARC reader that has reviewed our book. We honestly never saw this thing reaching the hands of more than our friends, so the fact that you have taken the time to read and review makes you rockstars.

And to you, our reader. We would like to thank you for taking a chance on two new indie authors. We're so happy you came to camp with us and we can't wait to see you again!

Ellie would like to thank:

Lacey— my one-woman writer's group! It kills me that we spent years chasing the same passion without truly talking about it the way we do now. I love that this has brought us closer together. Thank you for being my sounding board every write night for the past two years. You are brilliant and strong, and I am grateful for the privilege of getting to watch your stories unfold. I love you with my whole heart, and I'm ready to keep doing this forever with you.

To my family for always being there and loving me even when I disappear for weeks on end. Kelly, my belief that I could do this started with you. I still have the Post-Its saying "you're a writer" that you placed throughout the house (sometimes I still need reminding). Both Lacey and I are so grateful for your insight, especially since you were somehow able to give it immediately after becoming a new mom. Kristy, for offering to read this thing in two days during a tumultuous time in both of our lives. Thank you for being there when I was stressed and for helping me stay excited. Shayne, you always know how to bring my stress levels down, whether it's through food or hugs. I'm so happy to call you my family.

Mom & Dad, you raised me to love reading and have supported me through every endeavor. I have never questioned trying new things, and without your encouragement, I never would have started writing a book, let alone finished it. GGW, I love that writing is in my blood. I will always remember sleepovers with your amazing storytelling. Thank you for all the moments I could talk stories with you.

Josie, Violet, and Ben. You are all geniuses in your own way, and it's so inspiring to see you grow up. To Owen for the cuddles, charming smiles, and for forcing me to get out of the house and enjoy moments with you. I treasure every second of our time together. Sue, Bethany, Sarah. I can't express how much I love you for all the interest you've taken in my life and my work. You have been constant cheerleaders, and your hugs keep me going.

To Mr. Ellie Belmont. You have been witness to every frustration and mini-breakdown I've had and have always held my hand through it. Having my partner tell people that I'm a writer was one of the first things that made it feel like I could finish this. Thank you for the unwavering support and for giving up time with me so I could work. I love you so much.

Lacey would also like to thank:

Ellie Emdash Belmont. You are the graceful turtle to my barnacle. I'm happy every day writing with you, even when it doesn't seem like it. But that's the thing with chosen family, they're with you through the highs and the lows, and you're that for me. I always wanted a sister, and you have two, so surprise, now you have three. There's no one else I could ever work on a group project like this with. The way you approach writing emboldens me to become a better writer. I love you.

Big thanks to my dad. You were with me every step of the way through this thing, and I'm so grateful for you. You have always found the fun in situations, and have been a huge inspiration to me and how I approach every day. Love you so much! For Cherie and Eric, thank you for the unending support. Your love of life and family is inspiring and so beautiful. And for the rest of my wonderful and caring family, I couldn't ask for more. Let's keep playing games, and being silly, always.

And speaking of being silly I have the best friends. For the Avery Group, love your shenanigans. Jennifer, Cori, Jessica, and Michelle, you brighten my world and I can't wait to go wine tasting with you again soon! And to the Glide crew, love y'all. Thanks for all the fun and letting me talk your ears off. Also, thanks to my coworkers for cheering me on through this endeavor and encouraging me. Here we go! Having you all in my corner means the world to me.

Sending virtual high fives to the authortube community, especially to Heart Breathings and the Write Now communities. While we might not meet in real life, that doesn't diminish the encouragement, testimonials, and advice that got me through writing challenges and work each day.

Finally, I want to acknowledge Mr. Lacey Cole. You are an amazing cat dad and partner. Your willingness to make me coffee and smoothies when I'm lost in worlds (and/or have come down with a terrible case of catlap) has been everything. Thanks for quit-

ting World of Warcraft with me. Without that monumental decision, I wouldn't be where I am today. Your patience and support
got me from my first 50k challenge to where I am now—releasing
my first book. Thanks for taking this chance with me. And for
giving the best hugs humanly possible.

About the authors

Writing duo Lacey Cole and Ellie Belmont met working at a video store, and have been best friends ever since their first friend date, where they danced around an empty theater while watching Step Up. They live with their partners in the Pacific Northwest and this is their debut novel.

linktr.ee/ellieandlacey